ADVANCE PRAISE

Dark Shadows Hover is the extraordinarily moving saga of one young man's unending bravery in the face of years of constant danger. Author Jordan Steven Sher masterfully weaves this chronicle of adversity, heartbreak and ultimately, triumph. Although Sher terms his work biographical fiction, this novel adheres quite closely to fact after remarkable fact: When World War II began, Moris Albahari was a young Sephardic Jew growing up in a small town in Bosnia. At the age of eleven, Albahari miraculously escaped a Croatian death-camp train. He survived a winter wandering alone in the frozen forests of Yugoslavia, then years as a teenaged courier and photographer with partisan guerrillas fighting against Nazis, Mussolini's Italians and Croatian fascists. Albahari is testament to the fact that the war produced not only unspeakable horror, but also remarkable heroism, even among those barely in their teens. However, Sher crafts this epic in a way to show that individuals like Albahari weren't one-dimensional superman caricatures, but real flesh-and-blood humans, displaying fear and vulnerability, as well as steely resolve and unwavering acts of self-sacrifice.
–Matt Miller, retired foreign correspondent

The Holocaust: as Jews, we inherently *"Remember the six million"* who perished at the hands of the Nazi regime. But what of the individual narratives behind this vast tragedy? It is a rarity to encounter a Holocaust story that embodies equal measures of sorrow and triumph, yet Jordan

Steven Sher has gifted readers exactly this. *Dark Shadows Hover* is a fictionalized account of a Yugoslavian Jewish boy thrust into manhood when his only chance of survival is to join Josip Broz Tito's Partisan resistance. Students of history will find an exceptional guide to understanding both the Holocaust and Yugoslavia's role in World War II. Readers of every stripe will learn about a little-known hero, a boy clinging to his "lucky marble" as tightly as his Jewish faith. Sher provides a rich portrait of Moris Albahari, a humanist and activist who remained loyal to his Bosnian homeland and its diminished Jewish community until his recent death. **–Dina Greenberg, author *Nermina's Chance***

Sher's work of accessible biographical fiction deftly blends historical context and the close imaginings of an extraordinary life to captivate us with Moris Albahari's story. Based on personal interviews conducted by Sher and those conducted by the Shoah Foundation, Albahari's private writings, and historical research on wartime Yugoslavia, Sher draws us into the capricious landscape of the Ustasha state. Sher traces the wider progression of events through Albahari's story, letting us into the everyday moments of the lesser-known experience in Yugoslavia, enriched by the Ladino/Sephardic Jewish world that served as Sher's point of entry. This is the kind of book that will reach the inner world of readers and expand their ability to imagine the life struggles and achievements of another person in their deeply uncertain place and time. It is also suitable for young adult readers, who may wish to savor Albahari's favorite raspberry cookies and remember his life and legacy. **–Rebekah Klein-Pejsova, Associate Professor of History, Co-director, Human Rights Program Purdue University**

Sometimes the essence of a period of history, or the truth about a person's life, can be reached more effectively through a well-crafted piece of fiction than through dry non-fiction. In *Dark Shadows Hover,* author Jordan Steven Sher has accomplished this admirably. Filling out what we know about the life of Moric Albahari with historically plausible vignettes, Mr. Sher has created a nuanced and moving illustration of the dramatic early part of Albahari's life. In a thoughtfully developed story, the author has depicted the personalities of the beloved Moric Albahari and his comrades in a rich and believable way. Sher has succeeded in representing the dangers of war and the spirit of liberation that shaped Albahari's formative years. –**Peter Lippman, author** ***Surviving the Peace: The Struggle for Postwar Recovery in Bosnia-Herzegovina***

I first met Morris Albahari in the fall of 2008 when visiting the synagogue/Jewish Community Center in Sarajevo. He served unofficially as its ambassador greeting all visitors and worshippers. His stories recounting the history of Bosnia's Jews, and his life during and after World War II were mesmerizing. In Jordan Steven Sher's book, you feel as if you are right there hiding in the hills with Moris and the partisan fighters. You'll follow him through desperate and dangerous times and rejoice in his survival. This is a heartwarming story that will be enjoyed by all. –**Phillip Weiner, former prosecutor, war crimes tribunal at the Hague on Yugoslavia during the war in the 1990s, former judge, international War Crimes Court, Sarajevo, Bosnia**

An enthralling historical fiction that reimagines the world of a young Sephardic Bosnian boy who navigates life prior to, during, and following the Holocaust. Based on the life of Moris Albahari, this powerful narrative weaves a tapestry of adventure, filled with separation, loss, friendship, hope, and the arduous task of rebuilding amidst the ruins of war. Sher carefully reconstructs this journey of survival, exploring Sephardic Jewish life in Bosnia and unveiling a lesser-known chapter in the history of WWII. – **Bryan Kirschen, co-producer, "Saved by Language," Professor of Hispanic Linguistics, Binghamton University (NY)**

Jordan Steven Sher's biographical fiction *Dark Shadows Hover* is a superb book. Based on the true story of Sephardic Holocaust survivor and partisan fighter Moris Albahari, it brings to life the often-forgotten Sephardic and Balkan narratives of the Holocaust.

The book employs interviews with Moris Albahari's son Dado (whom I have the honor to know personally) and widow Ela, as well as extensive research on the war in Yugoslavia, to piece together the story of Moris's life and survival as a partisan between the ages of 12 and 16.

Sher's book, with a riveting and engaging plot, remains true to history. It provides a rare insight into the complexity of Balkan Jewish identity through its account of Moris's life as a teenage Sephardic Jew in the rapidly changing political landscape of 20th-century Bosnia – a life that was brutally upended by the Axis invasion of Yugoslavia. The narrative then shifts to the fight against the Nazis, Italians, Ustasha, and their fascist allies, and the movement borne out of that struggle to reclaim a new Yugoslavia.

The unfolding of this underrepresented Sephardic perspective of the War and the Holocaust is powerful because it is relatable, as it brings to life shared human experiences: coming of age, love, family, friendship, loss, healing, and the resilience of the soul.

The Nazis and their collaborators obliterated more than 100,000 Ladino/Judeo-Spanish speakers during the Holocaust in the Balkans. Famous historical Jewish communities of Thessaloniki, Sarajevo, and Belgrade are in essence no more. When Moris died in 2022, he was one of Bosnia's last Ladino speakers.

Dark Shadows Hover has the potential to raise awareness of the Ladino communities and their role in the global Jewish identity. This is illustrated, for example, by Moris's initially tense encounter with the Hispanic-American David Garinjo whose only shared language with him was Spanish. This allowed Moris to communicate to the downed American fighter pilot in Judeo-Spanish that, as a partisan fighter, he was an ally and wanted to help. **–Franz Afraim Katzir, Founding Director Sephardic Heritage International (SHIN DC)**

DARK SHADOWS HOVER

JORDAN STEVEN SHER

ISBN 9789493322929 (ebook)

ISBN 9789493322912 (paperback)

ISBN 9789493322936 (hardcover)

Publisher: Amsterdam Publishers, The Netherlands

info@amsterdampublishers.com

Dark Shadows Hover is part of the series *Holocaust Books for Young Adults*

Copyright © Jordan Steven Sher 2025

Cover image: Moris behind the camera, photo taken presumably in 1943 somewhere in the lull of the war in central or western Bosnia.

All Rights Reserved. No part of this publication may be reproduced or transmitted in any form or by any means, electronic or mechanical, including photocopy, recording or any other information storage and retrieval system, without prior permission in writing from the publisher.

CONTENTS

	Prologue	1
1.	My Father	5
2.	Drvar	8
3.	Clouds Gather	14
4.	The Nazis Arrive	19
5.	Judita's Nightmare	22
6.	His Store No More	26
7.	A Shroud of Evil	28
8.	The Collection Camp	32
9.	The Cellar	38
10.	Anywhere but Here	42
11.	The Escape	46
12.	Colonel Marchione	56
13.	A Wolf Meets its Liberators	63
14.	Moric's Jobs	79
15.	The Battle of Kozara Begins	89
16.	The Partisan Air force	103
17.	Breaking through the Ring	107
18.	Cake	116
19.	Machi's Birthday	124
20.	Remarkable Mika	128
21.	Saying Goodbye	132
22.	Mehmed	143
23.	Battle for the Wounded	149
24.	The Nurse	156
25.	Welcome to Ribnik	165
26.	Messages	178
27.	Pliva Lake	192
28.	Travnik	200
29.	Pictures	208
30.	What Djuro Said	211
31.	Alone	217
32.	Partisan Education	221
33.	Family Reunion	223
34.	Moving Forward	228
	Epilogue	234

Acknowledgments	241
Pronunciation of Names and Places	245
About the Author	247
Photos	249
Amsterdam Publishers Holocaust Library	255

In Memory of Moris Albahari

Moris Albahari (29 October 1929 - 22 October 2022)

PROLOGUE
THE HOLOCAUST IN THE FORMER YUGOSLAVIA

Moris Albahari is someone most readers have never heard of. As a child, he escaped transport to a Croatian death camp and joined the Partisan movement to free the former Yugoslavia from the tyranny of Nazi fascism.

The saga of Moris's journey as a Partisan and his experiences after the war are a tribute to his resilience and strength but also to the reality that war's trauma impacts its survivors, especially children.

Thanks to his survival, Moris went on to do great things as an adult. However, there was also a vulnerability, which his son, Dado, reveals in his epilogue.

Many of us understand the Holocaust as the most heinous example of hate in human history. Sadly, there are also many lesser-known instances of the same targeted hate by autocratic leaders against "others" to support the perpetration of genocide. These actions are aimed at gaining absolute power. Bosnia, Cambodia, Syria, Sudan, and many other examples throughout history provide evidence of this.

Genocides are often systematic, following predictable patterns that might take years to unfold, but if left unchecked, they will lead to the potential destruction of a group.

Gregory Stanton, president of Genocide Watch, developed "The Ten Stages of Genocide" that outlines the pattern genocides can follow. I encourage you to read this resource to gain further insight.

It's worth studying the systematic nature of Germany's genocide, which resulted in the murder of six million Jews and five million other victims. Understanding this helps us grasp an event so massive and incomprehensible in its destruction of the human soul.

This quote by Primo Levi, who survived the Nazi concentration camps, is best suited for what I can only feebly attempt to describe:

"Perhaps one cannot, what is more one must not, understand what happened, because to understand [the Holocaust] is almost to justify...no normal human being will ever be able to identify with Hitler, Himmler, Goebbels, Eichmann, and endless others. This dismays us, and at the same time gives us a sense of relief, because perhaps it is desirable that their words (and also, unfortunately, their deeds) cannot be comprehensible to us. They are non-human words and deeds, really counter-human..." –Primo Levi, *If This is a Man - The Truce*

It is important to understand the trajectory of destructive forces, and it is also critical to learn how they are defeated.

Recently, the Partisan movement in Yugoslavia during World War II has been demonized by revisionist circles. Additionally, there has been an ultranationalist revival, especially in the Balkans through glorification of the Ustasha, the Croatian fascist and ultranationalist organization. It's concerning how vulnerable humans can be to the manipulation of truth, making targeted groups the scapegoats for economic, social, and political problems.

The Ustasha, led by Ante Pavelic, was essentially a terrorist group that came to power as an ally of the Nazis. They changed the name of the Kingdom of Yugoslavia to the Independent State of Croatia (NDH) (1941-1945), which controlled all of Croatia and parts of what was territorially – though at that time not officially – recognized as Bosnia and Herzegovina. With the support of many in the Catholic Church, the Ustasha murdered an estimated 340,000 ethnic Serbs, 30,000 Jews, and 25,000 Romani in villages, towns, cities, and concentration camps that rivaled any established by Germany, the largest of which being Jasenovac. The brutality of the Ustasha knew no rival, and those not horrifically killed within their camps were victims of intense violence or were sent to Nazi concentration camps.

On April 6, 1941, Germany moved into Yugoslavia after conquering Austria, Poland, Denmark, Norway, Belgium, the Netherlands, Luxembourg, and France. Four days later, they installed the Ustasha as their puppet government, and seven days after that, Yugoslavia officially surrendered.

The resistance movement in Yugoslavia was simply known as the Partisans. It stemmed from a communist ideology aimed at liberating all people from the Axis powers. Led by Josip Broz Tito, the liberation army grew from a guerrilla movement into a substantial fighting force that eventually won the backing of the United States, Great Britain, and its allies. The Partisans drew their fighters from many fronts, including former soldiers from Serbia, Croatia, Montenegro, and Bosnia, as well as ordinary citizens and those who were volunteers in the earlier-fought Spanish Civil War.

Though greatly outnumbered, the resistance managed to overcome Germany's superior manpower and weaponry, leading to Germany's surrender to the Allies in May 1945.

The Partisans not only fought against the Germans and their collaborators, but also faced opposition from the Chetniks. The Chetniks were royalist Serbs who wanted to establish an ethnically pure Orthodox Christian nation, similar to the Ustasha's desire to create a state for Catholic Croatians. Tito's Partisans waged war on multiple fronts, with their primary and most significant battle being against the German military.

To defeat the Partisan army, Germany fought "Seven Offensives." These included the Battles of Mount Kozara, Neretva, and Sutjeska. There was also smaller, but no less intense fighting for control of strategic points. Tito had to be captured or murdered in the hills around Drvar in Yugoslavia.

Despite the many losses on both sides, the Partisans were driven forward by the communist ideology of equality in their fight for liberation. This was not the communism of China or the Soviet Union. Tito's forces included people of all ethnicities and religions with fascism as their common enemy. This is not to idealize the movement; it had its share of callousness. However, for the purposes of this book, you will learn about some of the significant battles between the Partisans and the fascists, in which Moris Albahari participated.

The moniker of communism, promoted by revisionists, diminishes the impact of the World War II movement in Yugoslavia today. Tito was president of Yugoslavia from 1945 until his death in 1980. Though he led the Communist Party, he was not beholden to the communist leaders in the Soviet Union, and brought his country more in line with social democracy. This is not to minimize the heinous murder and imprisonment of the fascists who had opposed Tito. But the association of Yugoslavia with communism challenges the stereotype upheld by revisionist rhetoric, which continues to paint the movement in a dark, Stalinist light. Far from perfect, of course, communism fueled a more equitable course for Yugoslavs until the early 1990s, when the war in Bosnia and Herzegovina was sparked by the genocidal aspirations of ultranationalists who sought to revive their centuries-old dream of creating a "Greater Serbia."

This book is based on Moris Albahari's early life in World War II. At the age of 12, he was fighting with the Partisans in Bosnia. Moris died in October 2022 at the age of 93.

I had the privilege of speaking several times with Moris's son, David (Dado), who lives in Croatia, and Moris's wife, Ela, who lives in Bosnia, both of whom were learning more about Moris's early years as we all took a deeper look into his life.

There are many ordinary people who become heroic in deed and action. Many of those stories will never be told. Moris's story is an opportunity to learn about one such hero.

To aid in pronunciation of names and places, a list at the end of the book is provided

1 MY FATHER

Visiting his mother only a few weeks after his father's death, Dado Albahari walked through the streets of his childhood in Sarajevo. He passed the old synagogue, once the center of the city's Sephardic community. He recalled what his father, Moris, had told him when he was old enough to understand: "We Sephardic Jews have been in Bosnia for over 400 years. Your ancestors took a roundabout way to get here from Spain in the 15th century, and I know it wasn't easy for them. In a sense, it was another exodus for us Jews. This time, it wasn't out of Egypt because we were enslaved, but because of persecution from the Inquisition. As a people, we've encountered a great deal of strife over the centuries, and that hasn't let up. Despite this, we must always keep our rituals and practices at the core of our lives."

Moris, who had changed his name from Moric at the end of World War II, had many lessons to share with Dado.

Dado paused for a moment as he combed his fingers through his wavy salt and pepper hair. He stared at what was once called Il Kal Grande; a place where Sephardic Jews had worshipped. It was considered one of the most beautiful synagogues in Europe until the Nazis destroyed it. Now it housed the Jewish Museum of Bosnia and Herzegovina.

The Sarajevo Synagogue was the only one remaining in the city, serving both Sephardic and Ashkenazi Jews. It became the center of Moris's religious life after the war. Dado recalled that his father spent a lot of time there attending services and gathering with friends. Recently, he learned that his father helped to renovate it in 1946 upon his return from fighting the fascists.

Dado stopped at a bench in the garden across from the synagogue to look out onto the river Miljacka, trying to picture himself playing there as a boy. This river bore witness to the death and destruction perpetrated by ultranationalist Serb militias during the Bosnian War of the early 1990s, another conflict he and his family had survived. At that time, Dado was in his late-twenties. During that time, he was wounded in the foot by a bullet from a militia rifle, and upon his parents' insistence, he left the country until the end of the war.

As Dado gazed out at the river and watched a flock of geese flying in formation through the cloudless sky, he thought about his father. *It's time that I reflect on what my father meant to me, but also on the now small Sephardic community here. It's imperative to know more before my mother passes away. Her family experienced tremendous loss in the Holocaust, too. One thing is for sure, my father strove for peace among all peoples, something Bosnians lost in the last war, and something that was etched into his life's philosophy after the Nazis nearly destroyed all of European Jewry.*

Sure, Dado and his father had their differences, and Dado was still trying to make sense of them, especially his father's insistence on doing things his way. But he knew his father's experience surviving World War II as a child impacted his worldview, particularly how he wanted to raise his only child. Yet, despite the early horrors he and his family endured during the Holocaust, his father had a zest for life.

As Dado wrapped his head around this thought, he gained some understanding of the differences between them. Moris had been trying to protect his son from the pain he endured as a boy. It was very difficult for him to talk about his life from 1941 through the end of the war. When Dado asked him, his father would only say: "You don't want to know."

Dado did want to know. He wanted to piece together what made his father tick – what made him so respected, not only in the Jewish community of Sarajevo, but in Bosnia and Herzegovina, as well as internationally.

He saw his father's numerous accomplishments, like helping to build and design Bosnia's first international airport. He knew that his father had been interacting with dignitaries from around the world, including the Pope, during his working years. Those years marked the growth of Sarajevo, during which he played a role in hosting the city's 1984 Winter Olympics.

But what had shaped him? What molded Moris Albahari into who he was personally and professionally?

Dado was determined to delve into Moris's and the Albahari family's history, starting from the early days when Moris grew up in Drvar, a small city in northwestern Bosnia that was at the epicenter of the fight against the Ustasha and the Nazis.

Dado's need to uncover his father's early life fueled his search. It was that search for truth that could connect the dots between what shaped Moris Albahari's life, and his own.

2 DRVAR

After moving with his wife, Luna, and their children to Drvar, David Albahari opened a dry goods store. He was a gregarious, slender man of short stature, with a big heart.

It was 1930, less than a year since Moric was born. As their fourth child, and the only boy, Moric took on a special place in the family. Not that his sisters, Flora, Rahela, and Judita weren't cherished, but a newborn boy was a special cause for celebration.

The Albaharis lived in what is now known as Bosnia and Herzegovina (BiH). At the time, the Kingdom of Yugoslavia subsumed Bosnia and Herzegovina and other territories that were not officially recognize until after World War II, when the Yugoslav Federation united the republics of BiH, Serbia, Croatia, Slovenia, Montenegro, and Macedonia.

The Albaharis had been living in the city of Sanski Most with its large Jewish population and synagogue. The shop David and his brother Jakob ran did not do well. David moved 12 kilometers away to Lusci Palanka to try and build his business, and Jakob and his wife moved to Sarajevo. When David's second business wasn't successful, he found another building in Drvar where the wood industry was thriving. Fortunately, customers flocked to his new store.

By 1941, the girls had already finished high school in Banja Luka, as no such school existed in Drvar. They lived with their aunt and uncle who relocated again to open a new store. Living in the city of Banja Luka meant receiving a Jewish education with the local synagogue's Jewish Activity Center. David and Luna wanted their children to celebrate the Jewish holidays, even though they were the only Jewish family in Drvar. They would dress up, go to their old synagogue in Sanski Most, and follow the traditions their faith had practiced for thousands of years. They were deeply rooted in the rituals of the Sephardic Jews that had fled Spain and Portugal during the Inquisitions which began in the 15th century and that saw Jews tortured and murdered following hateful accusations concocted by Spain's Catholic Church. The ancestral Albahari family fled, and eventually found their way to Bosnia.

The wandering Jews developed a language called Ladino that was a mixture of Spanish, Hebrew, Arabic, Turkish, Greek, Aramaic, Italian, and French. It was also referred to as Judeo-Spanish. Just as Yiddish was the language of Ashkenazi Jews from Eastern Europe, Ladino was the language of the Sephardim. This was the primary language spoken in the Albahari home.

With the winter chill surrendering to the first days of spring in 1941, 11-year-old Moric raced through the front door and into his bedroom.

He was a slight boy, shorter than most of his classmates, with wisps of sandy-brown hair flying in every direction. Moric rarely deviated from his uniform: light-brown cotton pants or shorts, a long-sleeve button-down shirt, always beige, and a dark green wool sweater in the winter. His coat was a hand-me-down from one of his cousins. Once, when he was growing faster than his clothing could keep up, he had to wear his sister Rahela's pink coat to school. The teasing at school prompted his mother to borrow more suitable clothes from a cousin.

David and Luna were proud of their house. Though not much bigger or different than the others in town, the single-level wood-framed home contained three bedrooms, a kitchen, and a room where the family could gather to play Croatian card games, read, or talk. The large windows allowed for a good deal of light, creating a warmth that added to the joy of its inhabitants.

The attic, mostly used for storage, was also a place where Moric played with marbles or looked at the few magazines featuring military planes that his father had given him.

Moric dropped his rucksack full of books on the bed, running past his mother on his way out.

"Slow down," Luna said. With her dark, braided hair and warm brown eyes, she had a large presence in their nuclear and extended families.

"I can't. I'm riding bicycles with Milan. He's outside waiting for me," Moric replied.

"I made some cookies. Invite your friend in. They're still warm. Dusan just brought over milk from his farm."

"Yes, mamma. I'll get Milan."

"And what about your studies? When will that get done?"

Moric yelled back to her as he left the house to get his friend. "I'll get my homework done before dinner."

After wolfing down their snack, the boys shoved back their chairs and headed out to their bicycles. Meanwhile, Luna told them to stay close to home.

It was often this way with Moric. He was a very bright boy, and the teachers said as much. All of the Albahari children were good students; Moric just had a bit more restless energy than his sisters.

He cherished his bicycle, which he rode relentlessly throughout the town and beyond. He would pretend that he was a pilot flying one of the fighter planes he occasionally saw in newsreels at the movie house in Sanski Most. He would imitate the sound of the engine as it took off and soared into the vast blue sky. He vowed that maybe, just maybe, he would be a pilot someday.

Moric and Milan were off on another adventure. They would both pretend they were pilots, although Milan had never been to a movie house to see one on the screen. So, Moric described what it was like and showed him photographs he had found in his magazines.

Luna and David were well aware of the dark shadows that the Nazis were casting over Europe. They tried to protect Moric from this, but the topic invariably came up when one of their three daughters came home from Banja Luka. Even more troubling, the Ustasha, a fascist and cruel ultranationalist movement originating in the late 1920s, was increasingly making its presence known.

Hitler's army had taken control of several European countries on his quest to dominate the continent. There were obvious signs that the Kingdom of Yugoslavia would be involved. The Ustasha had earned Hitler's confidence, and prepared to align itself with the German dictator's plans.

News was spreading that Jews were the primary targets of the Nazis, and the Ustasha's racial policies were gradually being implemented by the government.

David and Luna's dry goods store was doing well. David was a very sociable man who was respected in Drvar and was amicable with many people in town. Antisemitism was virtually non-existent. Yet, there was a nagging feeling among those living in Drvar and all of Bosanska Krajina, a subregion in western Bosnia, that the Ustasha were trouble.

Petar Adamovic, who owned the butcher shop across the street from Albahari Dry Goods, stopped in after closing his shop early. Petar was also someone who paid attention to the darkness that was engulfing Europe.

"Hi Petar. Good to see you. What can I help you with?" David asked.

Petar, a stout man with muscular arms from cutting and pounding meat, moved forward to the register. "I'd like a large bag of rice. And please bring an equal-sized bag of flour. Vesna is running out."

"Of course. Anything else?"

"No, thank you. Well, yes, there is something else."

David rung up the items on the cash register and took Petar's dinars.

Petar leaned forward, lowered his voice and said, "There are dark forces in Drvar, as we both know. Someone wrote very disturbing things about us Serbs on the side of that abandoned warehouse near my shop."

"We saw that. It gave us chills, frankly," David replied, as he gave Petar his change.

"With all that's happened in so many countries in Europe, we wonder when it's our turn."

"I have some cousins in France that I've not been able to get a hold of. The Nazis set up the Vichy government there, and I'm afraid for Jews. And the Ustasha—"

At that moment, the door was roughly pushed open. Petar turned around and noticed two men in black shirts with guns holstered at their sides walking in. There was an air of arrogance around them. It was nothing that they said, in fact, other than "good afternoon" they said nothing at all. Their steely eyes swept around the shelves. The older of the two stared just a bit too long at David before they left.

David and Petar remained silent until the men were a safe distance from the store.

"Do you know who they are?" David asked.

"No, but I didn't like what I saw. Lately, the Ustasha have been making their presence known in Drvar. I wonder why they're coming into stores. Yesterday the same thing happened in my shop. It's been rumored that Hitler is ready to strike a deal with his Ustasha twin, Pavelic."

When the door opened again the men stopped talking.

"Hello, Mrs. Sofic. What can I get you today?"

"Hello David, hello Petar. I just need some jarred beets today."

"Of course."

David put the jar into a paper sack and handed it to Mrs. Sofic.

"Can I pay you next week when my husband gets his dinars?"

"Your word is always good with me. Pay me next time."

As the door closed, the men remained silent for another moment. They exhaled simultaneously, avoiding eye contact to prevent attracting unwanted attention if someone were to peer into the window.

"My neighbor is friends with a high-ranking soldier in the Yugoslav army. He says that our military is preparing for an invasion by Germany," Petar said.

"We need to be vigilant. I fear that we are in for some desperate times," David replied.

"Vesna and I are feeling somewhat helpless, too. Our children have heard unkind things about us from some of the Catholic students, and the teachers do nothing to stop them. Has Moric been telling you about any anti-Jewish problems he's seen at school?"

"Not yet, but we've sent our two older daughters to relatives' homes for safety."

"Well, let's be wary. I'm not sure what we can do?"

"We'll need to make sure our children are safe. There's a foul stench brewing these days. And that stench is getting very close."

The conversation came to an end. Petar said goodbye, gently closing the door behind him.

David hung up his apron and walked over to the door, deciding to close up his shop. Pausing for a moment, he looked around at the shelves stocked with all sorts of dry goods, jarred fruits and vegetables. It wasn't a big shop, but it had a life of its own, and David had given it that life. Of course, not without the help of his wife, whom he loved dearly.

She was strong, and he had relied on her confidence to help carry them through the difficult times they had faced before moving to Drvar.

He needed to talk to Luna about what was suddenly crystalizing before his eyes. His mind flashed to their four children. *The children,* he thought, *we must make sure the children are safe.*

3 CLOUDS GATHER

Moric rode his bicycle just outside Albahari Dry Goods and stopped. Through the front door he could see two men in black shirts with his father and Mr. Adamovic. He wondered what Mr. Adamovic was doing there at this time of day. He peered across the road and noticed that his butcher shop had a "Closed" sign on the front door. Even though Moric was only 11, he sensed that something was not right. He walked his bicycle over to the produce store to avoid being seen from his father's place. He stared across the way, watching as the black-shirted men left. A queasy feeling formed in the pit of his stomach.

He had been hearing rumors at school of Hitler, of the Ustasha, and of the hate that was being spread around Europe. But it didn't affect him; his life was good. He was just a young boy enjoying school, friends, and his beloved family. He always felt unencumbered joy with them, especially during the Jewish holidays.

When the two men were a safe distance from the shop, Moric walked his bicycle over to his father, who was about to turn over the "Closed" sign.

"Hi Papa."

"Oh, hi Moric, what are you doing here? I was just about to close up the store a bit early."

"Mamma wants you to bring her some jarred tomatoes."

"Of course. I'll put some in a sack, and we can walk home together. What a day. Not a cloud in the sky, and the breeze is mild. Good day for a bicycle ride."

Moric saw that his father was hoping to distract him. David was jovial, maintaining his usual light-heartedness. Moric enjoyed his father's upbeat personality, which made Moric feel that all days were beautiful, even in the worst of storms. Still, Moric wondered what could have caused his father to leave the store early. It must have been those men.

He wasn't sure how to bring up what he had witnessed. He didn't know what to make of it. As they strode along the sidewalk, his father casually asked about school and sports.

The boy blurted out, "Papa, what were those men doing in your shop?"

"Oh, you saw them."

"Yes, and they looked pretty angry."

"Well, I'm not sure why they were there. They were not customers looking to buy. I've never seen them before. And neither had Mr. Adamovic. But don't worry, they're gone, so I think we're alright."

Moric wanted to be reassured; his father had a way of doing that. Everybody loved him. He was the one who people often went to for advice or just to chat.

To Moric, David was invincible. He was a World War I veteran who had carried a wounded soldier many kilometers to get treatment for his injuries. Because he was Jewish, his heroism went unrecognized by the military. However, the soldier who survived gave him an expensive "Doxa" watch after the war that he still owned. Moric eagerly awaited hearing his father's war stories. David often said that war was not to be taken lightly.

In the Austro-Hungarian army, he had to fight against his two brothers because they lived in Serbia, while David lived in what was still the Austro-Hungarian Empire. He told Moric that the human toll of war was tremendous, but that hateful people insist on violence as the answer to their problems, often convincing others in their country that this was the only course of action to take to protect themselves. It's what is referred to as propaganda – to persuade citizens of their country's righteous path, even if it meant losing their lives and slaughtering enemy citizens. Propaganda was a word that Moric had trouble pronouncing or fully comprehending.

Thinking about the black-shirted men, Hitler's invasion of many European countries, and the increasing presence of the Ustasha in Drvar, Moric was more distracted these days. Sometimes his teachers would call on him in class and he didn't hear them until they assertively reminded him that he "needed to get his head out of the clouds."

When he and his father entered their house, Luna was surprised to see her husband and asked why he was home early. David said he would discuss it later.

As she cooked dinner, Luna added the jarred tomatoes to the stew. The aroma of the simmering lamb and vegetables immediately caused Moric's stomach to growl. He wandered over to the stove, dipped the wooden spoon into the stew, and came out with a hefty, scrumptious helping. His mother gently chided him, telling him to get away and rinse off the spoon.

At the dinner table it was just the four of them: his parents, Judita and Moric. A few weeks before, David and Luna had sent Flora to live with Uncle Jakob and Aunt Rena in Hrvacani, and Rahela to Kladanj with Aunt Serina. They told the remaining siblings that this was only precautionary.

Judita had completed high school and returned to their home in Drvar. Recently, she had been experiencing acute pain in her abdomen. The doctor suspected that she would need to have her appendix removed. Her mother placed a warm, damp towel on her belly when the pain flared up, combined with a local tea that resembled chamomile. It was a minor and temporary solution.

As Judita cleared the table, Moric went back to his room to study. He closed the door, but put his ear against it, a practice that he had adopted recently.

He pulled a marble out of his pocket and began to roll it in the palm of his hand. Its smooth, glass surface held an image of the earth inside, with swirls of blue and brown and white. His grandfather had given it to him when he was sick with a high fever. Moric placed it under his pillow and the next day the fever subsided. Ever since, he considered it to be his lucky charm.

On another night, after he crawled into his bed, a vicious storm rolled in. Black and violet clouds threatened to rip up Drvar, or at least, that was what frightened him. He had laid in bed twirling the marble; he couldn't sleep with the sounds of an approaching storm barreling down toward them. The wind howled, the thunder roared, and blinding lightning was quick to follow. But within five minutes, the storm was over. He knew it was his marble that stopped the torrent.

While the dishes were being washed, there was a momentary pause as David leaned in to whisper to Luna and Judita, "Today I was visited by black-shirted Ustasha. What we've feared for the past few years is upon us. Petar was in the store when they came. He said a different set of men were in his store yesterday acting the same way. They came in, looked around, and said almost nothing. One of them glared at me before they left. It sent chills down my spine."

"That's horrible, Papa," Judita said as she unconsciously twirled a strand of her jet back curls.

"Moric saw those men in the store today," David said.

"What? How?" Luna replied.

"Well, he arrived to get the jarred tomatoes when they were there. After they left, he came over and met me as I was about to put up the "Closed" sign and exit out the back."

"We can't protect him forever," Luna bemoaned, "although I wish we could."

"What did you tell him, Papa?"

"That he shouldn't worry; that they were Ustasha but hadn't done any harm to the store; and that I was tired and ready to go home."

"I guess that's the truth, but this evil is closer to us than ever before," Luna said.

"Let's make sure that we have clothes, food, and good, sturdy shoes if we need to make a quick escape."

Silence fell once again, interrupted only by the clattering of dishes being put away in the cabinet.

Judita rubbed her abdomen in a futile gesture to bring relief to the ever-expanding pain.

Seeing Judita wince, Luna brought over a warm towel.

"My poor daughter, you have a doctor's appointment in two days. If you have to go to the hospital, Papa will take you to Virovitica. Your cousin, Rahela, will meet you both. You can stay with her if you need to after you're discharged. Papa will be back as soon as you're ready to leave the hospital. I'll run the store while he's with you until you're ready to travel."

"That's fine, Mamma. Let's see what the doctor says."

Soon, Moric could see that the lights in the kitchen were off from under his door. He laid down in his bed and pulled the covers up to his chin. Visions of the black-shirted men swarmed his thoughts, joined by pictures of Nazis he had seen in the local paper. He worried that if Judita had to go she could be yanked from her hospital bed by the Nazis and thrown into a hole with other Jewish patients. He promptly cut off the evil ideas swirling in his head. He squeezed his marble and placed it under his pillow, hoping it carried the magic that he and his family needed.

4 THE NAZIS ARRIVE

It had been two days since Judita went to the hospital in Virovitica. Luna was anxiously churning the soup as it simmered on the stove. David had left the store early again, and although he said that the Ustasha had not visited him since that one time, there were hardly any customers. There was an ominous air permeating Drvar and all the Krajina, and he felt that his place was at home with his family.

Moric came home from school and immediately went to his room, not looking up or greeting his parents.

"David, what do you think is going on with Moric? I don't like what I just saw, him running right by us without saying hello."

"Let me go in there and talk to him."

David knocked on the door to his son's room. "May I come in?"

"Yes, Papa," Moric said with little enthusiasm as he lifted his head from the pillow he had buried it under.

"Are you alright?"

Moric hesitated. He didn't want to worry his parents any more than they already were. But he knew he couldn't just keep it in. With tears welling up, he said, "Today I was thrown out of school and told that I shouldn't come back anymore. After leaving, the students pushed me and Vladimir. They cursed and spat at me shouting 'you *čifuti*, you hanged our Jesus.' Why do the children hate me all of a sudden? Who was Jesus... who hanged him?"

David thought about what to say. It was only a matter of time before the invasion. He and Luna had been talking about where to go. The problem was that Judita was in a hospital in Virovitica and they hadn't heard a word from her, her cousin, or the medical team in charge of her care. This was cause for great alarm. And now, his son was confronted with the same hate that had been spreading throughout Europe.

David inhaled deeply. "My son, don't be afraid. From today you won't go to school anymore."

The boy fixed his gaze on his father, processing what he had just heard.

"Do you remember Judita told us about what happened during the last year of her studies? Because she is Jewish, they didn't want her back. It seems that it's happening all over the Kingdom now. You'll stay home until it feels safe to go again."

Moric got off of his bed and buried himself in his father's chest. David held him tightly as he gazed out of the window, contemplating when they would need to escape before that choice was no longer theirs to make.

There was still no word from Judita. She had been in hospital for three days and the surgery had surely taken place. Luna whittled away at her fingernails which had dried blood pooled around her cuticles. Moric played in his room and did some math that his mother had cobbled together to ensure that he didn't fall too far behind. David went into the shop as he did every day, but the atmosphere in Drvar had changed dramatically.

It was early in the afternoon when David came home. "Germany has invaded us. It seems apparent that our forces are no match." Sweat dripped from his face as he spoke, "The Ustasha have taken over Drvar. I came home to figure out what to do, but I'm afraid I have no answer. Petar heard on his radio that the Germans invaded from all directions. We're surrounded. It's only a matter of time before we surrender."

"Oh, dear God! And we don't know where Judita is."

Moric came out from his bedroom and heard his mother's voice crack at the mention of his sister.

"Where is she, Mamma? If the Germans are everywhere, they'll be in Virovitica, too, right?"

"Yes, Moric, all of our Kingdom will be taken over," Luna replied.

"What will happen to Judita?"

Neither Luna nor David could answer without showing their panic.

"She's a smart and brave girl," David said. "Cousin Rahela said she'd take care of her and bring her back to our house if I wasn't able to get to the hospital. She'll be alright."

Moric was young and could easily be convinced of things. He wanted to believe his father, but the situation in the Krajina and Drvar wasn't something he could understand. He nodded and slowly retreated to his room. He picked up the math homework his mother had devised and set to work, not wanting to let the outside world intrude on his task, even if it was math.

5 JUDITA'S NIGHTMARE

Three days before the German invasion, Judita underwent surgery. The surgeon told her that if she didn't have the procedure right then, the Germans would forbid it altogether because she was a Jew.

On the day that German soldiers entered the hospital, Judita was still recovering from acute pain. A soldier glared at her with his steely blue eyes as she lay in bed. The nurse disappeared into the entryway as the soldier crossed the threshold, his rifle at his side. "Let me see her chart," he ordered.

A nun, having heard the soldier's request, entered the room and said, "I'm afraid that with all the confusion, some of our patients' records were destroyed, mistaken for trash."

The soldier fixed a hard gaze on the nun. "Get this one out of this hospital. Now!"

The nun helped Judita up. Touching the silver-plated cross hanging from her neck to her habit, the nun placed Judita's few items of clothing into a small bag. Then she guided her through the long hallway, holding Judita up as she tried to regain her balance. "I'm sorry, dear. I'm so, so sorry."

As she left the hospital, Judita, still in her patient's gown, shaded her eyes against the bright glare blinding her. Several other patients were walking or crawling aimlessly on the sidewalk. Judita gently rubbed her wound, but the pain didn't subside. She had to stop numerous times, doubling over.

She noticed a group of teenage boys wearing caps with the letter "U" sewn into them for Ustasha. Their rifles were slung over their shoulders. She recognized some of them, but they paid no attention to her.

She continued down the street, heading towards a good friend from school's house as the hot sun beat down on the cobblestones. She knocked weakly on the door. When the mother finally answered, Judita noticed her eyes flicking between her and the street, as if anticipating unwanted guests. She beckoned Judita inside, "You can stay with us for one night only."

The message to Judita was clear: if anyone was caught helping a Jew, they risked their lives.

The family gave her a bit of food, after which they sent her to lie on an old couch in an unused room. Her friend made no attempt to visit with her.

That night, Judita's wound throbbed bitterly. Restless, her eyes flew open at every sound. Tossing and turning, her mind racing, she decided to leave early the next day.

Judita realized that she had to go to a Jewish home. A few blocks away was another friend from school. This time, the family was more welcoming, telling her to stay until she was feeling better before going back to her parents' home.

Still, there was a palpable fear that the Germans would make their way up the stairs of the apartment building and arrest them, or worse. They looked out the window, watching the horror below them. They saw German soldiers taking rifles from Yugoslav soldiers and smashing them in the street while they lay face-down awaiting their fate.

Judita and the family pulled away from the window when they heard shots ringing, while locals were ordered to drag away the dead. They were scenes that Judita could not shake from her head. It was clear that the evil that had befallen many other countries had found them.

Despite the kindness of her friend's family, she needed to find her cousin, Rahela. Yet, it was too dangerous since the road to Slatina, Rahela's village, was cut off by the Germans. In a few days, however, they moved to other parts of the Krajina.

Fortunately, Rahela decided to come to Virovitica when she received a message about her cousin's location from the mother of Judita's friend. By that time, Judita was in less pain after being tenderly cared for.

Rahela knocked on the door. The mother answered with Judita by her side.

"Judita! Are you alright?" her cousin asked as the two hugged.

"Yes, I had to leave the hospital while in a great deal of pain. But I've been well taken care of here. I really want to get back to Drvar to be with my parents and brother."

Judita gathered the few clothes she had, including what her friend had given to her.

"We'll have to get to the train station, and hope that the Germans don't discover that we're Jews," Rahela said.

Judita thanked the family for their kindness and said goodbye.

Rahela thought it best to go to her parents' house first before going to Drvar. To get there would mean crossing the Sava River on a ferry and then taking a train to the village. They hurried through the town to reach the ferry landing, avoiding the main road and slipping into cobblestone alleyways. Unimpeded, the first leg of their journey to cross the river was successful.

When they finally arrived at the train station, it appeared to be swarming with German soldiers.

The girls tried to act as naturally as possible. Judita wiped the perspiration off her neck and nose with the palm of her hand. One of the soldiers approached them as they waited for the train. He hinted that he wouldn't mind taking Judita to Germany with him to be his wife. Rahela turned to her cousin and spoke in Ladino, instructing her to cough a lot. "I'm afraid she's very sick. I need to take her to my home to see if we can get her better. I'm not so confident though. It may be tuberculosis," she said in the rudimentary German that she'd learned in school.

With that, the soldier quickly retreated.

Once on the train they heard the locals praise of their saviors, Hitler and Pavelic, who would free them from the "pathetic grip of the Serb, Jewish, and Gypsy vermin."

When the girls arrived in Slatina, Uncle Jakob and Aunt Rena swung open the door to embrace them. The girls were famished and devoured the food that had been prepared for them meal.

Judita recounted the problems she had in the hospital and being thrown out by the German soldiers. Exhaustion quickly overtook her and soon all she could think about was sleep.

The next day, more invigorated, she told Rahela and her parents that she was going to Drvar. It seemed that the Germans had not yet occupied the area and she felt strong enough to find her way home.

Withstanding their protests, she hugged them and left.

She knew the area well and used less-traveled routes. Fortunately, Judita made it home without incident.

Seeing Judita walk through the front door, Luna and David leapt to their feet and smothered their daughter with hugs and kisses. Moric came running out of his room and gave his sister a big bear hug.

"Oh, Judita, we've been beside ourselves with worry. With the soldiers in the Krajina, we didn't know what to do," Luna said.

"What happened to you? My God, we were crippled with fear. We couldn't get a message to Jakob or Rena," added David.

"I'm home now. I'm healing and much better. It wasn't easy, I can tell you that," Judita replied.

Luna sat them down over cups of hot tea and home-made cake, and made Judita recount all that had happened to her. Even Moric, typically talkative, sat with his mouth gaping and his eyes almost unblinking. When she finished, Judita retired to her bedroom where she threw herself onto her bed.

Staring at the ceiling, she couldn't believe what she had just survived. Her thoughts drifted into dark territory, contemplating what could have happened to her if she had fallen into German hands. Shaking away these thoughts, she closed her eyes. When she woke up, it was to the sounds of her mother preparing the morning coffee.

6 HIS STORE NO MORE

After the Germans defeating the Kingdom of Yugoslavia in 11 days, it became evident to all that their Ustasha allies were poised to mercilessly target those they deemed their enemies. Though some brave Catholics tried to assist the victims of Ustasha cruelty, those who were caught suffered greatly.

Although it took only four days for the Ustasha to take control of a large swath of the Kingdom, it was in the following month of the takeover that they changed the name of their conquered land to the "Independent State of Croatia," or NDH.

With German and Ustasha soldiers in the Krajina, the predominantly Serb Drvar was effectively under lockdown. Few dared to venture out, anticipating the worst.

David was in the dry goods store taking inventory. He had left the house before dawn to evade the watchful eyes of the Ustasha police. He was hoping to hide a select portion of his stock in a secret room below the store in case the world regained some sense of normalcy.

He was in the dimly lit shop when he heard voices near the front door. He quickly cut the light, but it was too late. Ustasha police were banging on the door, demanding that he open up. He had no choice.

"You, Jew, turn on that light and move to the counter. Don't talk. Say nothing."

David, a veteran of World War I, had braved many battles and seen many wounded and dead comrades. His military experience put him on high alert.

Clearly, this was different than the first big war. He didn't have a unit to fight alongside; he had no weapon; and he knew that the Germans and the Ustasha were completely in charge.

There were four black-shirted Ustasha who made sure to have their pistols in plain sight. David watched in silence as each one put bags of flour, rice, red beans, corn meal, as well as tins of fish, lentils, tomatoes, mushrooms, and cabbage into their canvas sacks.

The years of hard work put into turning the shop into a successful business were shattered in that moment. David had counted his blessings for turning around the failures in Sanski Most and Lusci Palanka, but with his once-thriving shop in Drvar, he succumbed to one hard fact: It was over now. More importantly, he wondered if his life would be spared and above all, he feared for his family's lives.

The police left several items on the shelves, and before exiting the lead officer spoke: "You'll continue selling these goods to the local population. We, of course, will be taking the profits. As a token of our gratitude," the man said with a smirk, "take this bag of wheat home to your family. We don't want you to starve. Then one of us would have to run the store. We'll be back to collect our money."

David stared after the men as they left the shop. Heart pounding, he straightened out the shelves and attended to a customer. He was too distracted to focus on his business. He hurriedly flicked off the lights and left through the back door. On his way home, David saw many bodies lying on the ground.

7 A SHROUD OF EVIL

David walked into his home to find his wife and two children sitting quietly around the kitchen table. Lunch had been served, but only Moric had eaten it. Judita stared at an untouched pile of scrambled eggs and hard-crusted bread.

Luna stood up and rushed to hug David. "What happened? We've seen armed Ustasha roaming about and heard gunshots. We were worried sick about you."

"Moric, can you please go into your room for a few minutes while we talk about grown-up things?" David asked.

Reluctantly, Moric did as he was told. He closed the bedroom door and pressed his ear against it.

"I'm afraid the shots you heard were the Ustasha executioners. Our soldiers' rifles were broken to pieces and thrown next to their bodies. I walked past citizens lying in their own blood."

Luna gasped while David continued, "And they visited the shop while I was trying to hide some of the merchandise."

Judita shook her head in disgust, "What did they want?"

"They took what they wanted for themselves but left some things on the shelves."

"Why would they do that?" Luna asked.

"They took my key and gave me the spare. They said they're the owners, while I'll only be selling their goods."

"This is terrible. They wiped away your years of hard work in an instant," Luna said.

"I was thankful they didn't shoot me. I'm sad about the store, but I'm afraid we have more important concerns. They've completely taken over Drvar."

The blood drained from Judita's face. Luna moved over to David and put her arm around his shoulder.

Meanwhile, Moric had heard it all. He lay on his bed and shut his eyes as images of dead soldiers swam through his mind. He pulled the pillow over his head hoping to block out the scene, but it was impossible.

He remembered photographs from the military magazines stored under his bed. He reached down and grabbed one. Moric stared at the British Royal Air Force pilots standing next to their Spitfire fighter planes, readying themselves for battle. He fantasized that he was one of them, soaring into the sky before diving down to unleash a round of bullets on the Ustasha.

Whatever conversation his parents and sister were having suddenly ceased. There were unfamiliar voices coming from the kitchen. Loud and angry voices.

He opened the door and stepped toward his sister, who was standing in the corner of the room.

"Who is this?" the Ustasha asked.

"Our son," Luna replied.

"Rather small. How old is he?"

"I'm 11," Moric said.

"Ah, an 11-year-old Jew. How sweet."

The man turned his gaze back to David and Luna. "My friend here is going to tour your home and see what appeals to him. You four can make yourselves comfortable around the table."

While his colleague roamed the house as the soldier who had spoken leaned against the kitchen doorway. He propped his rifle up against the wall next to him, as he smoked a cigarette. The other soldier returned from his search with many items including Luna's jewelry and Flora's treasured handmade clothing, given to her by her grandmother.

The smoking man told the family that he would be visiting again in the not-too-distant future.

After they were gone, David spoke, "I know that one. He's married to the Stankovic girl, they're a wealthy Serb family. I spoke with her father when I picked up supplies and he told me about his son-in-law. How could the girl's husband be a proud Ustasha? Will he threaten his in-laws like he threatened us? Will he do this to his wife?"

Fluctuating between rapid chatter and utter silence, a dark mood hung over the Albahari home. It had been almost two months since the Ustasha had taken over the store and robbed their house.

With great foresight, Luna had understood the danger early and was able to get a message to her older daughters to remain in the homes of their aunts and uncles where they might be safer.

The family rationed its food, doling out what they had in storage, staples of flour, salt, jarred vegetables, and potatoes. Otherwise, the local markets were mostly depleted and the new owners of Albahari Dry Goods kept a tight rein on merchandise.

While lying in their bedroom before going to sleep, David and Luna had a hushed conversation.

"There are rumors that the Ustasha have set up labor camps. If it's just for labor, maybe it won't be that bad," David said.

"I know. You've told us many times how you were in a camp in the first war and it wasn't so terrible. Maybe that's what they have in mind for us. But I don't trust them. Pavelic is a madman and he's allied with Hitler."

"I want to hope for the best in what's a very bad situation. Still, how can we feel secure with the Germans here in Yugoslavia," David said.

"It's been a number of weeks since they took over the store. There's nowhere to run; they control so many villages and the Nazis are an ever-present danger to anyone found trying to escape. We're trapped," Luna went on. "This existence, this day-to-day monotony, holding our breath for what comes next – it's maddening. And the children are in their rooms except for meals. I don't blame them. The fascists walk around Drvar like they own it. I guess they do, in a way. I don't sleep well, always waiting for them to come back and send us away."

"I toss all night too; and I worry a good deal about Moric. He's young, but he knows what's going on. I don't know that he understands the gravity of it, but he's quite aware of our circumstances."

Luna gently squeezed her husband's hand. They needed to try to get whatever sleep they could. She kissed him on the forehead and whispered goodnight.

They lapsed into another fretful night's sleep. Their eyes flew open at every sound, every creaking noise in the house, every hoot of an owl.

The somber aura that hung over everyone who lived in Drvar, the Krajina, and all of the Kingdom rained down upon the innocent people who were about to get swept up in the plans of the Axis.

8 THE COLLECTION CAMP

The thud of heavy knocking on the front door echoed throughout the house. Moric opened his bedroom door ever so slightly to watch his father answer it. The uniformed Ustasha police officer said they had one hour to pack their belongings and get ready for the 36 kilometer walk to the Bosanski Petrovac collection camp.

"But we have ten kilos of luggage each to carry," David said.

"That's not our problem. You better be ready to go when we come back."

David thought for a moment before he left the house. He passed the police who were standing in front of his yard glaring at him.

When David returned, he told his family that the police district commander said they could take a horse-drawn cart to Bosanski Petrovac.

Moric packed a medium-sized suitcase with clothing for all types of weather. He looked around his bedroom with the hope that he would return soon, so that he could unpack and get back to his "normal life."

He grabbed his favorite military magazine, some paper and pencils in case he wanted to draw, and a photograph of his father's parents that his mother had placed on his small chest of drawers a long time ago.

He stared at the picture and realized he had never looked at it closely. It was almost as if it was a part of the furniture. The old picture was taken in a field in front of what looked like a corral, maybe for horses, in the village of

Kladanj. Moric had never asked his father about his grandparents; they were gone before he was born. In the photo neither grandparent is smiling. They were dressed in fancy clothes with their hair coiffed. It seemed old-fashioned.

At that moment, he heard his mother call him. He stuffed the picture in his suitcase, zipped it up, and was about to leave when something caught his eye. It was the special marble that his other grandfather had given him. He picked it up and peered at its earthen colors as he put it into a pocket of his pants.

The family pulled their suitcases through town to the police station. The heat of the day made even this short walk tedious. Moric saw some of the students he knew from school playing in the street. None of them paid attention to him or his family. He guessed that they were happy that the only Jews in Drvar were leaving, though he still couldn't understand what it was that he had done to make them hate him.

Along the way, some of their neighbors kindly stepped outside and gave them food for the trip. Luna took the bags and hugged her friends as a tear slid along her cheek onto the dull gray street.

David, Luna, and Judita hoisted the suitcases onto the cart while Moric grabbed the bags of food.

Luna was the last to climb up. David held out his hand to help her, but she first looked back to see what she was leaving. Although the heat distorted her vision, she caught a glimpse of the store in the distance. She turned to take her husband's hand, sighing deeply as he pulled her up.

The two Ustasha who drove them talked incessantly about how they had finally taken care of the Jews, the Serbs, and the filthy Romani. And after that, the Muslims, even those who had helped them with this phase of the round-ups, would be the next ones to have their throats slit.

The four Albaharis sat in silence. The mid-July, heat weighed them down. Moric grabbed onto his mother's arm and buried his head into her chest as the cart dragged its passengers over the rough road.

The collection camp sat at the foot of Mount Ostrelj, giving it an imposing presence. On arrival, the Albaharis were informed that this was only a temporary collection camp.

They joined roughly 30 Jewish families, all together they consisted of about 150 people, mostly taken from the city of Bihac.

Judita spoke first, "We don't know any of these people. I asked a girl over there how long they'd been here and she told me since April. They don't look healthy. Papa, I remember your stories about labor camps, saying that they were not so bad, but I don't like what I see."

"I don't like this either," Luna said. "Sadly, we have no choice."

An armed guard came over to lead the family to their quarters. With no room available elsewhere, they were put into a small space originally intended to be used as a toilet. There was an outer hall with a wash basin, but otherwise, it was quite stark. The room contained simple wooden shelves for their clothing, a pan and a pot, some utensils (nothing sharp), and old, dusty blankets and pillows on the floor. A single light bulb hung from the ceiling. The room smelled of mold and rot.

Most of the other prisoners were living in the newly built, partially completed hospital wards on the grounds. Barbed wire surrounded the camp.

Moric sat on the floor while his mother did what she could to make the place livable. David and Judita had gone out into the yard to talk with some of the other prisoners.

Moric pulled out the magazine he had brought and stared at the front cover for several minutes. Luna looked up from cleaning and checked to make sure her son was alright, though she knew no one was. She wasn't sure what to say to pull him out of his shock. Physical closeness seemed to be the best option.

When she was done cleaning, Moric threw the magazine aside and broke the silence. "Mamma, how long do we have to be here?" he asked, choking back tears.

"I don't know, my sweet boy."

"I hate it. The people crying from that hospital scare me and I don't know how I'll be able to sleep with that noise, not being in my own bed. And that smell... I know that they can't help it because maybe they don't get to bathe much, but the smells of the others sting my nose. I want to go home!"

"We all do. This is a difficult situation. I've tried to make our little place more comfortable. That's all I can do. I know it's hard for you. Come here."

Luna held her son tightly. He swallowed the lump in his throat; he wanted his mother to see that he was a big boy. She rested her chin on top of his head.

When she released him, she said that it was alright to go play in the yard.

He slowly left the tight space and walked to the middle of the camp where some children were playing.

He found someone who appeared to be his age and said hello. The boy had dirt streaks on his face and two teeth missing. His ragged clothing bore the burden of the almost three months he had been there.

"My name is Moric and I'm from Drvar."

The boy looked at him, but said nothing.

"Can I sit here?" Moric asked.

The boy only nodded in response.

Luna watched as they sat in silence. A few minutes later, Moric came back.

"I hate it here," was all he said before lying down on some old towels that were to be his bed.

Luna felt helpless. For her and David, life now revolved around protecting the children from harm and shielding them from hate. These were the most difficult days of her life. The uncertainties of their situation made her shiver despite the heat.

The evenings were repetitive. What little food they had was cooked on an open fire in the middle of the yard. The women gathered around it with their metal plates and cooked potato slices. They made a kind of tasteless, thin bread and spread whatever softened or cut-up vegetable they had, usually beets. Hunger was a constant and the substantial lack of food became an ever-present problem.

A sinewy, sunburnt teenage boy named Moni, who had befriended Judita, was part of a small group that would sneak out under the barbed wire after the guards left. The boys went to a nearby village where they knocked on the windows of Serb families and were given food to bring back to the camp. Before the guards began their day at dawn, Moni and the others returned to share the food, mostly with the elderly and children.

"I guess he's your new boyfriend. Instead of flowers, he brings you cheese," Moric teased.

"Oh Moric, he's just a friend."

This made Moric laugh – a rare occurrence these days.

One evening, when they were alone, Luna spoke with Judita about the guards who had recently been coming around the prisoners' quarters in the mornings and afternoons.

"I know that you've been seeing what these guards are doing," Luna said.

"I'm scared. The women and girls come back with bruises on their faces and arms, and who knows where else. And they're silent. What can they do? Yesterday, a teenager named Leah took me aside with tears streaming down her face. She told me what they did to her. I was shaking almost as much as she was. I didn't know what to do for her. I don't know how to stop it if they come for me. There's a rumor about why Mrs. Levi hasn't returned to the camp. She is very beautiful and the guards have been awful to her. She and her husband have two young children. What I've been told is that she was killed after being..." Judita stopped mid-sentence.

"No need to say more my darling."

Luna held her daughter tightly and paused before speaking. She needed to protect her from the assaults that the others had been subjected to. *Those poor girls and women. How could this be happening?*

She went over to the flimsy shelf where they kept their clothing and picked out a couple of Judita's blouses and skirts. Tearing at the clothing, she grabbed dirt from the ground beneath her, and rubbed it into them.

"Every morning you'll put these clothes on. You can change them in the evening if you like, but put them back on the following day. I'll rub dirt onto your face and into your hair. We'll make you look unappealing to these monsters."

"Okay, Mamma. I hope this works."

"It's got to."

"I pray that we leave the camp very soon," Luna said.

"If this is just temporary, maybe it will be a relief to go to the next place. I overheard two women in the yard saying we may be sent elsewhere," Judita said.

"I've heard that, too. It's called Jasenovac. How can it be worse than this? Let's stay strong. We must survive."

At that moment Moric and David arrived. David had wrapped his arm around his son's shoulder.

"Moric just heard another boy say that we're going to be killed here. He wants reassurance from all of us that this is not true. I told him that as his parents, we won't let that happen."

Luna and Judita tried to calm the young boy, but the fragility of their lives in the camp made that a difficult task. As his tears subsided, Moric noticed Judita's torn clothing strewn on the tattered wood-framed chair nearby. He didn't want to know why they were there.

Luna hugged him as she whispered that he was safe from harm. "We hear lots of things, but they're not necessarily true. Your father and I haven't heard any of that being said by the adults. Please don't worry."

"Okay, Mamma. I won't listen to that boy anymore." Moric wanted to believe his mother. He decided not to tell her about the nightmare that woke him up very early in the morning. He didn't want to be reminded of it; he hoped it would never return.

9 THE CELLAR

Gunfire and the roar of cannons could be heard coming from the mountain town of Ostrelj. It was known that guerillas, fighting for the liberation of Yugoslavia, had taken the town from the Ustasha.

At night, the rebels sent the camp's prisoners signals through lighted torches. The prisoners could sense that something was going to happen, especially because the guards were fidgeting more than usual, yelling orders at the prisoners in even harsher tones.

Walking together around the camp, Moric paused and looked at his sister, "Where does Papa go at night?"

"He's made friends with some of the others here, so I think he's just visiting with them," said Judita, averting her gaze.

"Papa has made friends here?"

"Yes, he has. You know him, he had many friends in Drvar."

"I guess."

Moric didn't believe Judita, but he didn't want to press her. If he was being honest, he wasn't sure what to ask, even though it was clear to him that his father was engaged in more than socializing. He dropped the subject.

Judita did not want to alarm her baby brother. She knew that their father was meeting with others to plan an escape. If the rebels attacked, the hope was that they would overtake the camp and the prisoners would be freed. She dared not tell her brother. The planning was done in secret and needed to remain as inconspicuous as possible.

It was early the next morning, just as the sun was rising, when the gunfire began.

"What's going on?" Moric yelled.

"I'm not sure," David replied.

Just then, guards raced into their quarters and ordered them to descend into the cellar.

Moric grabbed his mother's hand and followed as all of the prisoners were shoved through the door, they stumbled down splintered wooden stairs, and into the small room which the soldiers locked behind them.

He was shaking as his mother tried to soothe him. Judita put her arms around her brother, while David spoke with some of the other men and women about an escape plan.

Sounds of shouting and bullets made their way down to the cellar.

"How will they know we're here?" one woman yelled.

"They may not," another replied.

"But if they don't know we're here, how can we possibly be saved?" This response sent a chill through the damp, musty room.

Moric tried to stiffen his body to control the trembling. It was dark and his mind went blank, unable to discern the conversations around him. He squeezed his mother's hand tighter. In his other hand, he held his lucky marble.

One of the teenage boys stretched up to look out a small window.

"The guerillas are retreating. The Ustasha have many soldiers who've joined the guards firing at them."

Some guards were outside the door, yelling that they had better shut up or they would be shot. "All of you!"

The Albahari family clung together. The older men prayed while the young cried.

When the heavy cellar door creaked open, the prisoners stopped their whispers and shielded their eyes from the blinding sunlight.

"All you Jews climb the stairs and go outside – heads bowed!" the guards commanded.

Some of the Ustasha were wounded or killed. Orders were given for the stronger male prisoners to carry the dead outside the camp gate while everyone else returned to their quarters.

"Papa, isn't that Mr. Turnsek, our neighbor from Drvar?" Moric asked. "He's bleeding."

He was the man who brought two chickens to Luna the day before, demanding that she make soup for him and his family.

"Fix him!" one of the guards yelled at Luna as he and another soldier carried Turnsek outside the Albahari's quarters.

"I've seen you tend to the wounds of your Jewish friends. Do the same for Turnsek."

"I'll try," Luna said, "but his stomach wounds are bad. I'm not a surgeon, all I can do is clean it out and bandage it."

"Fix him," the guard growled.

When Luna had made the man's chicken soup the evening before, the aroma had drifted throughout the camp from the fire pit. She had put it in a storage closet near their quarters believing she would give it to him the next day. Now, she was tending to what might be mortal wounds for the same man.

When the guard returned to get his comrade, he was met with the news that Turnsek was dead. Luna avoided his gaze as she braced for punishment. The guard called for David and another man to drag the dead soldier away. As they picked up the body, David looked back at Luna and then at the guard; his eyes spoke of fear for his wife's safety.

When he returned from the grim task, he found his family pacing inside.

"Did he hurt you?" David asked.

"He just walked away. I thought he would take his anger out on me, but he left without saying a word."

David hugged his wife and silently thanked God.

The family was exhausted from the events of the day. Although she was hungry, Judita told her mother that she wouldn't eat the soup that the murderer, Turnsek, had made Luna cook for him.

"We cannot," Luna agreed, "He was a vile man and anything associated with him is cursed."

"I'm sorry, Moric," she added, "I know that you wanted it."

"No, Mamma. I don't want it either. I'm sorry he died, but he was a very mean man."

"It's best if we just throw it away. We have some potatoes and carrots that I hid while making the soup," she replied.

"Let's all take a deep breath, and thank God that we're still alive," David said, as his wife began to prepare their meager meal for the evening.

10 ANYWHERE BUT HERE

Three days later, Moric was playing with a friend when they both froze at the sight of several armed Ustasha guards aiming their rifles at them. Time seemed to stop for everyone in the camp.

"You boys move over to that wall, and all you children, report to the yard. Everyone reports to the yard. Now!" they yelled.

The Albaharis gasped when they came out of their room and saw Moric and his friend lined up on one side of the yard. They approached the center of the camp, where the leading guard ordered the women to form a second side and the men a third. Judita was told to join the children.

Guns were trained at all three groups. In addition, there were two rifles lying on the ground in the middle of the yard.

One of the guards pulled out a small camera and pointed it toward the children. The other guards lowered their rifles. "You children, you must dance and sing."

The children were muttering to each other. The rest of the prisoners stared unblinkingly, some with their hands cupped over their mouths.

"No talking!" a guard shouted.

"The *kolo*. Now dance!"

The children did as they were told and took each other's hands, hesitating as they slowly formed a circle. Someone turned on music from a phonograph over the loudspeaker and the children began to move in unison. The tension between the prisoners rose as they sped up their movement to the rhythm of a traditional South Slav folk dance. The camera clicked harshly in the background.

With the spectacle in full gear, an older man in a medal-laden Ustasha miliary uniform strode into the camp. Colonel Adamec, the local commander in Drvar, put up his hand and ordered them to stop.

"Colonel," the leading guard started, "we want the Red Cross to know that these children are treated well and are enjoying their stay with us."

"That's fine," Adamec responded, surveying the men. "You send your pictures. But while I'm in charge, there will be no more threats against any of these people."

"Yes, Colonel. Thank you. We weren't going to hurt them. We're done here. All of you go back to your quarters."

As soon as they entered their shabby living space, their silence broke.

"Moric and Judita, are you alright?" Luna asked.

"Yes," they answered.

"That was very strange and frightening, indeed," David said, "but Adamec may have saved our lives."

"I know," Luna replied, as she wrapped her arms around her children.

"Why are they sending the pictures to the Red Cross?" Moric asked.

"Because they want to show them that everything is fine. They want to fool them," Judita answered.

"Well, the Red Cross should come here and ask us if they want to know the truth," he responded.

"You're right, my wise son," Luna said. "Let's eat a little something."

"How about that wonderful stuffed cabbage you make? Or rich lentil soup, so we can pretend it's Rosh Hashanah," David teased.

"Or real chicken soup that's for us and not the Ustasha," Moric said with a chuckle.

They laughed in relief as they settled down for a cup of stale bread soaked in watered down milk.

Life after Adamec's intervention was more tolerable. The guards eased up on their harsh and threatening behavior. Some of the prisoners were allowed to work in Petrovac, including women who worked as seamstresses and men who assisted with tasks at various companies. The mood was more relaxed, although it didn't lessen their yearning for freedom.

There was more communication allowed between families inside of the camp and their friends or relatives on the outside. David sent a letter to his sister Serina to see if her husband, a prominent Muslim in a town near Bosanski Petrovac, could get documents for them to leave the camp.

Their only response was a small package of food with no indication of anything else forthcoming.

Requests for help from the other families were either met with explanations that nothing could be done or were left unanswered entirely.

"I still hate it here," Moric said to his sister. "Why will no one help us?"

"I wish I knew. I think they're all afraid of the Nazis and the Ustasha."

"I don't care where we go. I just want to leave. It's been two months and even though they no longer treat us like animals, it's still bad."

"You're right, Moric. It's not good, but we have no choice. Maybe the freedom fighters in the mountains will save us. If they do come here, I want to join them and fight for our liberation. Don't tell Mamma and Papa; I know what they'll say."

"I won't. I wonder what Flora and Rahela are doing. I hope they're alright."

"Me too. I wouldn't be surprised if they're fighting with the guerillas."

"If this is still going on when we get out, maybe I'll join them too."

"I like how you say, 'when we get out.' You sound like Papa."

"All those war stories he's told me are hard to forget. I'd like to be a good soldier like him someday."

"You're a little young for that, but I'm sure you'd make a good soldier," Judita concluded.

Though it was difficult for young Moric to grasp time and space like adults, he was right to feel trapped in the camp. Two months felt like an eternity for everyone. For the children it had no end.

A sense of despair hovered over the prisoners like a thick, gray cloud. Though rumors were float around about an impending move out of the camp, it was not until October that something happened.

11 THE ESCAPE

It was late October and the mountain chill had arrived. The leaves of the deciduous trees were beginning to exchange their golds, reds, and oranges for brown. Moric had just turned 12 which was, understandably, barely acknowledged by his family.

The fire in the center of the camp which remained lit when it wasn't raining, became a gathering place for families to keep warm. The families only returned to their own quarters when the guards ordered them to get ready for bed. Like all the other families, the Albaharis bundled up under layers of old clothing and jackets to ward off the lowering temperatures.

Moric had developed a cold and cough. His mother was routinely boiling water for tea, which might only consist of grasses or herbs that Moni brought them from his clandestine food runs into the nearby town.

Moric was feeling a little better when Judita came inside their tiny hovel.

"I just learned that we're leaving this place. Thank God. Anywhere else will be better," she said.

"Where did you hear that?" David asked.

"One of the guards in the hospital was informing the families there. He said the trucks would be here in four days to take us to Donje Bravsko where we'll wait for a train from Drvar to Prijedor. Then we'll take a train to Jasenovac."

"I can't wait to get out of here," Moric said. "I'm so tired of being here. I hope it's better at Jasenovac."

"Don't worry about our next stop Moric, we'll be fine. At least we're going to Prijedor first, which was always a nice place for us," Luna said.

"Mamma, we used to go to Prijedor to visit relatives or see some friends. This won't be a holiday," Judita bemoaned.

"Of course, I know that, but it's knowing that we're leaving here that gives me some hope," Luna replied.

"In the meantime, let's try to stay warm at night, eat what food we can, and make sure Moric's cold goes away," David said.

Throughout the camp, there was a growing anticipation about leaving punctuated by hushed conversations. A group of young people discussed escaping when the trucks arrived. They nixed the idea knowing that they would be mowed down by machine gun fire once they hit the plains.

Another group, made up of prominent citizens from Bihac, got permission from Colonel Adamec to meet with Mayor Gutic of Banja Luka to see if they could convince him to facilitate their release. The mayor, an arrogant man and an ardent fascist, dismissed them almost as soon as the meeting began.

The trucks rolled in as planned. The large, canvas-covered vehicles rumbled into the camp and parked outside the gates in the early morning.

Everyone was already packed and they lined up next to their quarters or just outside the hospital doors awaiting orders to board.

The chatter was muted by the anticipation of the unknown. Nonetheless, the chirping of the birds and the blue skies lightened the mood.

When the camp guards gave the order, the older men, with their prayer shawls around their shoulders and their belongings wrapped up in sheets, began to make their way toward the gates. The others, most of whom were dirty from the lack of soap and shampoo, lugged their suitcases along the dirt yard. The guards yelled at them to keep moving forward.

As they all walked out of the camp gate, some thanking God, most just generally thankful, the able-bodied tried to aid those who physically couldn't enter the trucks.

"Stop!" yelled a guard outside the gate. "Old people and children go to the trucks behind me. The rest of you get into the trucks to my right."

Moric and Judita kissed their parents goodbye and went with the other children. The siblings were directed to different vehicles while their parents entered a third. The prisoners were silent, grimaces etched in many of their faces.

As the trucks rolled out, Judita, who was perched at the rear of the bay, could see Moric's truck behind her. She wondered how he was doing. She was hoping that being so young was an advantage. Perhaps he wasn't so aware of what was happening. But with Moric it was sometimes hard to tell. He had been known to surprise her and their parents with his mature insights.

Luna wrung her hands, thinking about her children on different trucks. She looked at David. He was usually the one trying to calm others, but on this ride he was quiet. She moved closer to him, slipping her arm through his. Lost in thought, he didn't seem to notice.

The trucks jostled their gaunt passengers rumbling toward Donje Bravsko, rattling their gaunt bodies as they drove over the rutted roads. When they finally came to a stop close to the train station, the prisoners were let out. Each child and parent reunited in an embrace.

Shots rang out.

The prisoners turned to face the hills as the bullets whistled high above their heads. They were frozen in place, like animals trapped against a rock wall in the woods. Did those shots come from the freedom fighters in the hills who might be trying to rescue them, or were they from the fascist soldiers?

They heard boots clapping against the dirt road, racing toward Donje Bravsko. Black-uniformed Ustasha emptied out of the cargo holds of military trucks just behind them; their bayoneted guns pointing outward. There had to be at least 100 Ustasha soldiers.

"Is this the end for us?" David said to no one in particular.

The soldiers ran past them, followed by the gasps of prisoners. There was a barrage of bullets and screams emanating from the small Serbian village just over the hill before them. It was not until two hours had passed that the screams dissolved into a deathly silence.

The Ustasha marched a few of the blood-stained resistance fighters toward the Jewish prisoners. The soldiers' bayonets were covered in the blood of villagers and resistance fighters alike. The air had a sickeningly sweet iron smell. The Ustasha lined up fighters and gouged their bellies in a gruesome act of terror. Many of the Jews retched.

Then, inexplicably, the Ustasha turned, ran past the Jews, jumped back into their trucks and left.

"My God," Luna shrieked. "What have they done to the villagers and these poor young people?"

There was no time to think or respond. Some of the Jews called out as they saw the train from Drvar arriving at the station. With what they had just witnessed, even the transport train seemed to be a better option than the carnage around them. Everyone grabbed their belongings and headed toward the station, most moving robotically, steering themselves toward the screeching of the train's wheels. Luna held Moric close to her as tears streamed down his face. Judita held onto her father.

As they climbed up a hill and onto the station platform, they were met by more Ustasha prodding them along with rifle butts and threats.

Moric, his parents, sister, and many others were shoved in a cattle car by the soldiers. There were several wagons, each containing some 75 people. As the doors were shut with a loud bang, darkness quickly enveloped the unwilling passengers, occluding the midday haze.

There was barely room to stand, let alone sit. Some of the captives were crying, others were angry, while a few older men were praying. The car still reeked of cows, and a small, open window on the rear upper wall provided the only light. Once the doors were bolted shut, the train slowly lurched forward.

People attempted to jockey over to what little oxygen circulated near the window, but there was no room to move. And, with nothing but a small bucket, those who were able to, maneuvered to its location and release their bowels and bladders into it. Those who couldn't, had no choice but to do so where they stood.

The stench made Moric dizzy. It was silent except for the gentle weeping of the children and the moaning of the sick. Mothers tried to soothe their young despite their own deep-seated fear. In a few minutes, the combination of the bloodshed, lack of air, and the stench of the enclosed space caused the tightly packed human cargo to panic.

"It's hard to breathe," Moric said.

"Take my hand," David responded.

It was he who then spoke above the din, "Listen, please! Everyone please let me talk!"

A hush gradually took hold in the wagon.

"We're going to Prijedor. It shouldn't be that long until we get there. There's only the small window, so we need to try to preserve what little air is in here."

"We haven't eaten or drunk anything all day and many of us have to relieve ourselves," a man responded. "What we just witnessed back there was meant for us to see!"

Others shouted in agreement.

"I understand. But we're locked in this cattle car and there's nothing we can do. Hopefully, we'll be in Prijedor soon. Let's try to remain calm."

Moni spoke up. "I'll put the little ones on my shoulders so they can be by the window."

The adults began passing the small children his way. Together, David and Moni had managed to quell some of the anxiety.

The train slowly made its way along the narrow-gauged tracks, slower than one would have expected. It took ten hours to arrive in Prijedor.

An older man, who had stopped praying hours before, died along the way. The stench from his corpse and the bodily waste was overwhelming. At the station, an Ustasha soldier opened the wagon doors only a few feet to let in fresh air.

"You Jews stink," he said. "Anyone dead in there, pull them over to the door and throw them onto the platform. We'll take some volunteers to put them in the truck."

Some of the prisoners moaned, some vomited, some whispered to others about the conditions they were in. But the cool air seemed to help.

There were requests for food and water. The Ustasha soldiers were silent in the face of their pleas. Then, groups of Serb villagers came close to the platform.

"We heard they were coming. We've brought food."

The Ustasha were in no mood to be generous. They allowed some of the Serb villagers to give food, but not others. The Albaharis were not so fortunate. They recognized some of the people who were willing to help, but were denied by the Ustasha. The villagers were hurriedly sent away.

"All of you, stay where you are. You'll remain here until the tracks are repaired."

The announcement caused a stir among the prisoners. Had the tracks been bombed?

A miracle, Luna thought.

Over the few days that the train remained immobile, the Ustasha got drunk. The prisoners silently opened the wagon doors wide enough to allow a few at a time to make their way out and walk around Prijedor, trying to find food, or to relieve themselves. But it was not safe to try to run. Where would they go?

The prisoners were called outside of the train car as the guards counted them. A number of new Ustasha had arrived. With the tracks repaired, it was time for their transport to Jasenovac.

Moric waited on the narrow wooden platform with his parents and Judita. Mostly, he remained silent. He couldn't keep his thoughts from wandering into the darkest of places. His family stayed physically close to him, hoping to stave off his trembling, which only stopped periodically.

The Ustasha soldiers yelled at the several hundred prisoners, ordering them up the platform to re-enter the foul-smelling cars.

Despite the October evening chill, sweat beaded on Moric's forehead and chin. Wiping it off proved pointless. He gritted his teeth expectantly. He heard angry dogs barking nearby and he imaged their sharp fangs gnawing at him. He remembered being bitten by a dog near his aunt's house when he was much younger. He never quite got over it and a fear of dogs still lingered.

The commotion of the other captives and captors surrounded Moric, but he couldn't make out what anyone was saying. He tried to shut his eyes and bury his head alternately into his mother's or father's shoulder, but this, too, didn't stop the unfolding nightmare. His mother was trying to whisper soothingly into his ear, but his thoughts were too jumbled to comprehend her words. Her touch alone had only a minimal calming effect. Behind him he heard a soldier yell, "bring the boy to me, I want to give him a sandwich and some water."

Moric and his parents whirled around, recognizing the man's voice. It was his music teacher wearing the black uniform of the Ustasha.

"Mr. Lipovac!" Moric shouted as he was yanked by another soldier.

With the boy next to him, Mr. Lipovac kneeled and said, "Moric. Don't talk. Follow me."

They walked to a vacant area of the station. There was a steady drip of rainwater from the corner of the roof.

"Take this sandwich and canteen. And this." Mr. Lipovac handed him a short iron bar.

"Hide it in your pant leg. After the wagon door is shut, tell your father to use it to remove a floorboard, and then you lower down, lie on the tracks, and wait for the train to leave. Also tell your father that if there's a ruckus and others want to leave with you, it'll attract unwanted attention. Do you hear me?"

"Yes, Mr. Lipovac."

"You must stay on the tracks. If you run, they'll shoot you. It'll be safe after the train leaves and is out of sight. I'll meet you right here. You have to do this if you want to live. Go to your parents now."

Moric turned around and walked slowly back to where his family was. He wondered what had just happened. Was that really Mr. Lipovac trying to save him from being killed? Or was his mind playing tricks on him because of his exhaustion?

Luna grabbed hold of his shoulder and pulled him close without saying a word. Moric briefly swiveled his head around to look at his music teacher, but he was already gone.

The captives were loaded into the cattle car. Moric squeezed in with his family, unsure of what to make of his interaction with his former teacher. He felt the iron bar beneath his pant leg. It was real – of that much he was certain.

As the light faded from the small window at the rear of the wagon, the latch of the door slamming shut echoed against the walls.

Moric removed the iron bar and handed it to his father. "Mr. Lipovac gave it to me," he said.

David's mouth was agape.

Moric repeated what Mr. Lipovac told him.

Tears formed in the boy's eyes as the gravity of what was happening to him began to sink in. Mr. Lipovac's warning ringing in his ears. "I don't want to leave you," Moric said.

"He wants to save your life. We know you're frightened but you need to do this. We'll see you soon. I promise," David said.

"But Mr. Lipovac told me that..."

"There, there," Luna said. "You need to leave now before the train does."

Luna and Judita held back tears as they hugged Moric.

He looked at each of his family members as if to burn the shape of them into his memory. They were much thinner and paler than when they lived in Drvar, before all this horror invaded their lives. Their clothing was tattered and dirty, but underneath it all, they were the people he loved more than anyone else. They were trying to be strong for him by not crying, but his own tears welled up; the lump in his throat prevented him from speaking.

When there were no longer sounds of Ustasha on the platform, David placed one end of the bar into a small opening between the wooden boards and began to pry them away from the nails that held them in place. He removed a splintered board and handed it to Judita.

"Moric," his father whispered, "remember what Mr. Lipovac told you. Stay flat on the tracks until the train pulls away and is completely out of sight. Remain still. Look around to make sure no one but Mr. Lipovac is on the platform before you get up."

"I know, Papa," Moric softly said through his tears. "But I don't want to leave without you, Mamma, and Judita."

Luna put her arms around her son one last time and kissed him on top of his head. "You must be brave. Mr. Lipovac said he'll help you. You'll be alright. We'll see you soon," she said without conviction.

Before his father helped lower him down to the tracks, he kissed his son on the cheek and stared into his face, misty-eyed, as he released him.

Moric lay face down onto the wooden planks. The air felt good, but a mixture of human waste, worn metal, oil, and smoke clung to his nostrils and made his stomach turn.

It felt like he had been lying on the tracks for hours, but it was less than 30 minutes when the train began to move. The squeaking of the wheels hurt his ears, but he dared not raise his hands to cover them. He was aware of the enormity of the beast rolling above him; he shut his eyes as tight as he could.

The sound of the train faded as it rumbled down the tracks. Moric could see almost nothing in the pitch black. His hearing slowly returned as he lifted his head up to see if his music teacher was on the platform.

"Moric, come here," he heard from the darkness.

He stood up and brushed his clothing. He tore off the yellow Star of David that his mother had been forced to sew into his jacket at the collection camp, and tossed it on the tracks. He moved toward the platform and grabbed onto Mr. Lipovac's outstretched hand.

"You did well. Brave lad. Come with me."

The two hurriedly walked behind the station toward a green military truck with an Italian flag seated atop the mirror on the passenger side.

"Moric, this is Colonel Lino Marchione," he said first in Serbo-Croatian, and then in Italian to the soldier.

"Go with him."

"Ciao Moric." Marchione gestured for the boy to climb up onto the back of the open truck.

Moric warily looked over at Mr. Lipovac and gave a weak wave. Another tear rolled down the boy's cheek. He looked around the back bay and saw boxes of guns, ammunition, and other equipment sticking out from underneath a canvas tarp. Marchione leaned his head into the truck and said in Italian, *"Vai al muro di fondo e nasconditi sotto il telo,"* while gesturing to the tarp.

Moric understood. Raised in a Sephardic family that spoke Ladino, and with his mother occasionally speaking Italian, his reflexive response of *"Sì signore, farò come dici,"* caused the officer to do a double-take. But there was no time for conversation. Marchione fastened the heavy tarp and hopped into the cabin.

Moric felt the engine from under the covering and was jostled as the truck pulled away toward an unknown that he couldn't imagine.

Lying on his back underneath the covering, Moric burst into tears. *What am I doing here? Where are they taking my mother, and father, and Judita? Where am I going?*

The truck stopped, interrupting his anguish. He wiped his tears on his grimy sleeve and waited.

The truck's engine was silent. Moric heard footsteps from all around the trunk before the tarp was lifted.

"Moric," Marchione said, "we're in Drvar. Please come with me."

12 COLONEL MARCHIONE

Though they were part of the Axis powers aligned with Hitler, Italy was not as cruel as the Ustasha and the Nazis. For the most part, the Italians believed that benevolent control, unless they were challenged by anti-fascists, was the best route with the Yugoslavs.

The Germans gave Italy swaths of territory after the conquest of Yugoslavia, including Drvar.

Once the only Jewish family, the Albaharis, were arrested by the Ustasha, the town was completely inhabited by Orthodox-Christian Serbs. Moric's extended family lived throughout the Krajina in Western Yugoslavia; a "free territory" because it was controlled by Italians. He remembered his aunts, uncles, and cousins at their last High Holiday celebration. He recalled his father leading them in prayer before their big meal. The laughter and banter of those times seemed to be a childhood fantasy now.

Colonel Marchione spoke to him softly in Italian. "Moric, I'm taking you to the Vojovic family. I'm pretty sure you don't know them. They've agreed to take you in. But you have to change your name. It's too dangerous to keep the name of Moric Albahari. If the Ustasha find out, they'll send you to a concentration camp."

Though he was being gentle in his instructions, the sound of the words "concentration camp" sent a shiver down his spine. He tried to focus on what the Colonel was telling him. He had escaped the train. His parents told him to be brave even if he didn't feel that way. He reminded himself that they wanted him to show courage and to survive; he prayed that they would see each other again someday.

Moric absently pulled at his left hand, biting his lip. He needed to come up with a new name on the spot. He thought of people he knew before the invasion of his city. He landed on Milan after his friend and Adamovic, after the butcher and his father's good friend.

"Milan Adamovic," he told Marchione.

"Milan. That's a good name. It should protect you for a little while anyway."

Marchione knocked on the door of the Vojovic home. Mrs. Vojovic answered it immediately, expecting her new guest.

"*Questo è Milan.*"

Mrs. Vojovic had a broad smile on her round face as she asked them both to come in.

"*No grazie*," the Colonel said. "*Devo andarmene per tornare ai miei doveri.*"

Moric translated for the family, emphasizing Marchione's need to return to his duties.

Marchione turned to Moric and told him to meet him at the bakery around the corner the following morning. Then, he tipped his cap and walked back to the truck.

"Milan, come in, come in. Let me introduce you to my son," Mrs. Vojovic said.

Moric met her teenage son, Branko, who led him to the bedroom he would be staying in. He told Moric that it had been his older sister's room until she was married two years before.

Mrs. Vojovic gave him a towel and showed him to the bathroom. Branko gave him some old clothes and a night shirt that he guessed would fit.

Moric sat in hot water of the bath and soaped himself up. The water turned black.

He hadn't realized how much dirt had caked to his skin and clothing over the past months. It was normal for the prisoners in the camp to smell and to be infested with lice, so except for the constant itching, it went mostly unnoticed. And in the train car, though the filth was overwhelming, there was no way to think of anything but survival.

He wanted to stay in the tub and never leave, but soon Mrs. Vojovic knocked on the door to tell him that she had prepared food.

He toweled himself dry, still itching from the lice and dirt that was only partially lifted from his skin, and put on Branko's clothing.

Moric felt grateful for the refuge Marchione provided, but the recent journey, including his time at the camp, made it difficult to think straight. He was consumed by constant fear for his family, especially his parents. Amidst all that had transpired, he hadn't thought about his two older sisters, Flora and Rahela, until now. *Where were they? Were they even alive?*

"Milan, please come out here for warm milk and a piece of cake I baked earlier."

This snapped Moric to attention. He sat silently at the table and wolfed down the treat, asking for seconds. It reminded him of home.

Mr. Vojovic had just returned and he pleasantly greeted their guest, telling him he could stay as long as necessary. He excused himself to do some household repairs before dinner.

Mrs. Vojovic and Branko recognized Moric's need to eat and sleep.

"Milan," Mrs. Vojovic said, "as my husband told you, there's no need to leave unless it becomes necessary to do so. Stay here as long as that is."

Moric nodded as he bid the family goodnight. However, the woman's words were a bit unsettling. Did she know something that he didn't?

It was a fitful night's sleep. He had a nightmare that the train his family was on crashed, sending body parts flying everywhere. He woke up drenched in sweat.

The next morning, he dressed, put on the coat Branko gave him, and walked over to the café to meet Colonel Marchione. He entered the building full of jovial, espresso-drinking Italian soldiers who were laughing and shouting good-natured insults at one another.

Colonel Marchione waved him over to his table. "Milan. Ciao. Come on over here so I can introduce you."

Moric hesitated. It took him a second to realize that Milan was him.

"Boys, this is Milan. Treat him well. He'll be coming here every morning to have breakfast with us. Right?"

Moric nodded.

One of the soldiers put his arm around Moric and said, "Giovannotto, you're always welcome to eat with us. Here, take this *pagnotto*. It's still warm."

Moric put a piece of the hard-crusted bread into his mouth where it practically melted. It sent his senses whirling. He hadn't had such a treat in months.

After eating and drinking espresso and water, Moric thanked Marchione.

The Colonel escorted him out of the café and asked Moric to accompany him down the street. "Tell me about this Ladino language?"

Moric smiled at the idea that a colonel wanted to know about him. He was even a bit flattered. "My family has spoken Ladino for centuries since leaving Spain. My father says that we Sephardic Jews developed the language from Spanish, Turkish, Arabic, Italian, and Hebrew. He says this helped us survive our exodus."

"*Molto interessante* [very interesting], Mor... Milan," Marchione said while patting Moric on the back. "Maybe someday you can teach me how to speak Ladino."

"Sure, I'd be happy to. I'll go back to the Vojovic house now. Thank you for helping me and for the good breakfast."

"You come back here every day. My men will take care of you."

Moric waved goodbye. This was the first time he'd felt some level of contentment in a while. He wished his family knew that he was alright.

The next day, as he walked away from another breakfast of *pagnotto* and coffee, he saw someone from school. He tried to avoid him, turning the corner to take a different route. Too late. The boy was quickly closing in.

He hadn't seen Danilo since school. Though he didn't know him well, he always found him to be pleasant enough. Danilo didn't mix much with other students. Some of them were cruel to him; they teased him because he was heavy and sweat through his clothes even in the winter. Moric never participated in the bullying but he never stood up for him either.

"Moric," the boy yelled. "Moric, stop!"

Moric had no choice but to comply and turned around. Danilo was thinner than he remembered. Likely, he figured, food was not so easy to get these days.

"Danilo. Hi. How are you?"

"I'm fine. Didn't you hear me calling you?"

"Oh, no. Not really."

"Glad to see you. I heard that you and your family were taken away."

Moric wanted to run. He didn't want to be reminded of what had happened to him and his family and he was unsure how Danilo felt about Jews. "Yes. Danilo, please listen. For my own protection my name is now Milan. Milan Adamovic. It's the only way I can make sure that I'm not picked up by the Ustasha. I know that the Italians are in control of Drvar, but that doesn't mean that I'm completely safe."

He hoped that Danilo was sympathetic. After all, he was not one of the students who had mocked him when he was told to leave his school for "hanging Jesus."

"Of course, Moric, I mean Milan. Your secret's safe with me."

Danilo hesitated before speaking. "I'm sorry you have to go through this. My older brother was murdered a few months ago when the Ustasha dragged him out of our house in the dark, yelling he was a Partisan. Of course, we didn't believe them. My brother was not a Partisan. They left his bloody body at our doorstep. It's horrible what the Nazis and Ustasha are doing to all of us. The Italians are not like them. At least we hope that's the case."

"His name was Boba, right? I'm sorry to hear about that. He seemed like a good guy. As for me, I don't know where my parents and sisters are, or anyone in my family. For now, an Italian officer found a home for me to stay in."

Moric didn't want to continue the conversation. He didn't want Danilo to press him on whose home it was, or to suggest they see each other again. He abruptly waved at Danilo saying goodbye.

Danilo raised his voice as Moric made his exit. "Let me know if I can help you?"

"Thanks, I will," Moric replied, without turning around. He wondered if he'd said too much. He'd have to move as stealthily as possible around Drvar. He didn't want to be confronted with a similar situation, especially by someone not as understanding as Danilo. In the off chance that Danilo revealed his true identity, the consequences could be grave.

A few days later, in the café, Moric overheard the Italian soldiers talking about the murders of thousands of Serbs after uprisings against the Ustasha in the Krajina, but also the retaliatory murders of Ustasha by Tito's Partisan fighters. The Italians talked about the stupidity of the Ustasha and how they were only going to rile up the locals. This is why, they said, they took control of the region: they wished to quell any more violence against the Serbs.

The fighting in the former Kingdom of Yugoslavia was complex due to the many of groups involved. The soldiers talked about the Chetniks, Serb royalists, who were fighting with Tito's rebels and the Ustasha. However, the Chetniks were challenging the Partisans for dominance. The Partisans found themselves organizing resistance against the Ustasha and the Nazis. The concern was that their fight might include the Chetniks at some point. Despite the Italians' best efforts to bring order to the tense situation, the fighting was beginning to take its toll on their enforced stability. At the same time, the Nazis were moving troops and weapons into the area with the aim of overtaking the Partisans' national liberation movement as it formed in earnest.

Moric's head was spinning. He could barely grasp what they were talking about but he got the gist of it. As confusing as it was, one thing was certain, the fighting had become a complicated mess.

For almost two months, Moric enjoyed the protection of the Italians and the safety that the Vojovic family provided him. He didn't reveal very much about himself, but they didn't ask.

One morning, he was in the café when Colonel Marchione asked him to step outside. "Milan, it's too dangerous here for you. The Germans are moving in and around Drvar to fight the Partisans in the mountains. The Partisans are gaining strength, which is what's worrying the Germans. For your own sake, you need to leave. We can't protect you any longer."

Moric felt like he had been punched in the stomach. Although life was far from ideal in Drvar, especially because he had no word about his family, he had developed a routine. He had hoped that by staying in his village, his parents would find him if they were alive. He didn't want to leave, but he knew that Marchione was not asking for his opinion.

Moric went back to the Vojovic home. It was winter and he knew that he would need whatever warm items Branko had given him. Mrs. Vojovic handed him a blanket she had knitted which he stuffed into a rucksack that Branko gave him, along with some water and food. He gave the family warm hugs, knowing that he had to escape immediately.

As he left he heard artillery fire echoing through the nearby Klekovaca Mountain. In that moment, Moric found his feet leading him toward a mountain called Kozara.

13 A WOLF MEETS ITS LIBERATORS

Moric was lost. Not directionally – he and his father used to hike over Kozara Mountain, just the two of them, when they visited family and friends in Prijedor – but emotionally, he was screaming. He had only minimal amounts of food and water, which he knew would run out of soon. His blanket was barely enough protection against the cold of the mountain, particularly at night. And worst of all, he was alone. *Where are my parents? Where are those who can help me now? How will I survive out here?*

He reminded himself that his parents had begged him to be brave. He could easily collapse against a tree, cry, and give up. But something inside of him wouldn't allow that. What if his parents and sisters were alive? Maybe they would be reunited.

The vastness of the mountain overwhelmed him; he had never been alone on one before. The silent presence of the tress, their density and height, along with the echo of his footsteps on the hard winter ground, made him feel vulnerable, especially at night.

On his third day on the mountain, he ran out of water and had only one slice of stale bread left. He pulled out the binoculars that Colonel Marchione had given him and walked as close as he could to a village to determine who was in control.

He trained his binoculars along the buildings and saw the Partisans' tricolor flag – blue, white, and red with a large red five-pointed star in the middle – waving in the cold breeze. He pulled his woolen cap close to his eyebrows and went into the village with his rucksack strapped across his shoulders. He knocked on doors begging for food and water. As soon as he got what he had come for, he slipped through the dead gardens of the locals and returned to the forest.

It was crucial to keep moving as if his life depended on it – which it did. His concern was that he would get caught by Ustasha or Germans who, at any moment, could attack villages under Partisan control. He mostly foraged for winter fruit and grasses, finding an occasional plum, apple, or wild chicory. He lived like a wolf; alone, taking shelter where he could, and finding whatever food the forest offered.

Sitting on a rock next to a thicket of barren bushes, he chewed on an apple until he reached its core. He was about to throw it away when he noticed a deer staring at him just a few meters away. Its soft brown eyes and tan fur mesmerized him. He said hello to the deer, who appeared to nod in response. *The two of us alone*, he thought. *Are you as hungry as I am?*

He gently tossed the apple core close to the deer. It stepped back at first, but then cautiously moved toward the fruit and gobbled it up. It then turned and walked away. Moric stared at it until it disappeared from sight. He reached into his rucksack and found a pear. He ate it, hoping the deer would return so that he could share its core. When the animal did not, he ate the core himself.

He was now in a routine of taking shelter in any protective, hidden natural space he could find, often within hollowed out trees and between thickets.

His days were spent finding friendly villages to get food, or eating what he could find in the forest.

He longed for human contact. He wanted his mother to put her arms around him and his father to let him bury his head in his chest. Instead, he wrapped his own arms around his body and pretended.

At night, he made sure to put on as many clothes as he could to keep the cold out, including a knitted hat and gloves from Mrs. Vojovic. He wrapped his blanket around himself and often woke up with snow dusted atop his makeshift cover. He knew he would need to ask for more clothes in the villages.

He heard the howl of a lone wolf some nights. True, it frightened him, but the wolves never appeared – only in his nightmares. In those dreams, the animal approached him sniffing out of curiosity more than hunger. Moric would ask the wolf if it knew where his family was. Invariably, the wolf shook its head and wandered off. He would wake up confused and a bit frightened, but he reminded himself that he was like that wolf – uncertain, tenuous, and searching.

When thirsty, he found a stream, often frozen. He would crack the layer of ice with a rock and dip his canteen into it, drawing out its life-sustaining water.

One afternoon, he came across a dead German soldier lying face down with a bullet hole through the back of his helmet. Despite the chill, the odor of the decaying man turned his stomach. As he walked away, suppressing his nausea, he stopped in his tracks. *If I'm going to survive, I'll need his coat to keep me warm at night.* He whirled around and without another thought, leaned down and started pulling off the coat. He was surprised, having never touched a dead body before, by how heavy it was. He ignored the thoughts flooding through him and brushed the ice off, shaking the coat to relieve it of its stiffness. He put the garment on to see how it fit. It was oversized, but it would keep him warm at night. He slipped it through the straps of his rucksack for easy carrying, and to let the odor dissipate. Fortunately for him, the layers of the man's uniform and the cold temperatures had kept the smell at bay.

That night, he assembled his layers around himself to keep warm. Along with his usual sweaters, pants, hat, gloves, and blanket, he now had the dead soldier's coat. The newfound warmth, combined with the total exhaustion of his mind and body, quickly sent him to sleep.

One of the dreams that had been haunting him almost nightly returned. In it, his mother's voice was calling to him from somewhere in the woods. There's a mist that obscures his ability to see her. The stillness is almost overwhelming. Moric is unable to move, feeling planted into the earth beneath him. She tells him to come home since his favorite stew is simmering on the stove. She's sorry if he's angry at her for telling him to leave the train, but it's what she and his father thought was best. At the end of the dream, her voice fades away and he hears her crying faintly, almost whimpering as she repeats, "Come home, come home, I love you."

Moric woke up in a cold sweat. It was silent except for the deep call of the Eurasian eagle-owl hooting in the distance. The moon was low and the stars remained in their familiar nightly alignment. And then the doubts returned. *How long can I live like this? Should I just give myself up to the Ustasha and hope they'll send me to a labor camp? Except, are they truly labor camps? I heard from people in the villages that they are death camps. I don't want to think that my family was sent to Jasenovac if it's a death camp. I have to keep moving. I want to be with my family again. I'm just a lone wolf. Remember Moric, wolves can survive in the harshest conditions.*

Moric was starving. For the past two days he had been eating grasses and berries that he had saved. Now, those were gone too.

The German army had occupied the few villages he could find. As hungry as he was, he couldn't be seen by them so he had been moving around, trying to locate a friendly village under Partisan control, or at least one that hadn't been marauded by the invaders.

Moric rose from under his coverings and packed them up into his rucksack. The morning was clear and still, not as cold as it had been in previous days. He headed down from where he had been sleeping, hoping to find something to eat.

He pulled a few strands of chicory along the way to get some nourishment, albeit limited, before he lost all his strength. With its bitter taste, he chewed it only as much as he needed to get it down. If he never had another piece of this, he told himself, he would be very happy indeed. But this was not the time to fantasize. He needed any source of food that he could find.

He came to a spot along a ridge just above a small enclave of smoldering houses. He pulled out his binoculars. There was no movement of any kind, just charred buildings. He moved closer.

The Germans' calling card was to capture and kill the village inhabitants or send them to labor camps, leaving behind the charred remains of their homes.

He moved closer still. One of the small, wooden houses was only partially destroyed. He slowly walked toward it, his head turning left and right to ensure that he was alone. The smell of smoke still hovered, though it was clear that it had been days since the attack.

He entered the house. Much of the furniture was ash apart from a small, partially burned cabinet. He looked around the two-room building and saw a broken family photograph on the floor, also spared from the fire. Two older peasants, a man and a woman, stared sadly back at him.

He turned toward the cabinet. Opening it, he saw the shelves were empty. Someone had found this house before he did. Then something caught his eye in another corner of the room. Next to an iron pot belly stove was a round loaf of bread. He picked it up and noted that half of it was blackened. Strangely, the other half was just hard, being days old.

Moric inspected it further. There was no mold because of the frigid temperatures, but it was hard as rock. He tucked the bread under his arm and left the house. Peering around the small enclave, his mind flashed to the terror that these poor people had faced. He turned away from the disturbing sight of the half-burned village and headed up the hill to ensure that he was safe before eating.

When he was at a distance from the houses, he pulled out his canteen and dripped water on the bread to soften it. When it was pliable enough to tear, he ripped it into edible pieces, fighting the desire to stuff too much in his mouth at once. At least now he felt full, even though he knew that there was little sustenance in flour, water, and yeast.

It had taken longer than he planned to execute this mission, as he called these forays to find food. He walked for a few more kilometers before finding suitable shelter to rest.

Moric lost track of time. How long had it been since he left Drvar for Kozara? Weeks? A couple of months? He had to continue until he found real protection from a friendly villager. That was the only plan he had, but the Germans and Ustasha made even that notion a long shot.

The sun was beginning to head west, so he knew it was early afternoon. Still, he needed to pause for a break after the accomplishment of finding something edible. He would lay down, only for a few minutes to rest, he thought.

However, he fell asleep. As his eyes began to open, he jumped up, startled, as five men surrounded him. He quickly noted that they were armed with rifles, though none were pointed at him. Their clothing had no particular markings, which added to his fright. He had heard that bandits sometimes wandered the mountainside, although he had never encountered any.

"Easy boy," said one man, who told Moric that his name was Milja and introduced himself as a patrol leader for the Partisans.

"We're not here to hurt you. What's your name?"

"Um, Milan. Milan Adamovic."

"Milan Adamovic, where are you from and what are you doing out here?"

Moric gathered his composure as best as he could, but he was shaking inside his coat. "It's a long story, but I'm from Drvar."

Moric wasn't ready to trust these men. He hadn't communicated with people since he left Drvar, except when he begged for food. He had to make up something that sounded plausible. "My parents hid me in our attic when the Ustasha came to take us away."

"How did you get way out here?"

"I got a ride from Italian soldiers. I told them that I had family in Prijedor. But there were so many Ustasha in that area, I wasn't sure what else to do except to come up here. I don't know how long I've been out here."

"Well, Milan Adamovic, we're fighting for the liberation of our country. If you want to survive, you should come with us."

Moric hesitated. He knew he couldn't survive for much longer living like this. This was the life of an animal, a wolf. But even wolves starve to death if they don't eat.

"Yes, I want to. I've been finding food out here and sneaking into villages to beg. I don't want to do that anymore."

"How old are you?" asked Milja.

"Twelve."

"How does a 12-year-old do what you've been doing? Brave! I am sure your survival skills will be valuable to us and our cause. And we'll make sure you're okay. Get up, pack your rucksack, and let's go."

Moric was at the same time relieved and skeptical. He had known of the Partisans ever since his time in the camp, but he had never actually met one. The image of the slaughter outside the train station was the only picture of the liberation movement he had. He wondered what Milja meant about his survival skills being valuable to them.

The five men and Moric hiked six kilometers along a crude path toward their unit's camp. They didn't ask more questions, only if he wanted some food, which he very much did. After arriving at the camp, they took him to their commander.

The Commander was a square-jawed, no-nonsense anti-fascist Croatian named Luka Juric. Other than a terse welcome Juric said almost nothing. He told Milja to take care of the boy.

Milja was an easygoing man with a more friendly demeanor. He introduced Moric to a young woman named Mika.

She was older than Moric, he guessed by three or four years. She was dressed in a thick wool sweater, olive-green pants, boots, and a cap adorned with a red star. Under her short blond hair, her striking blue eyes caught Moric by surprise.

He had turned 12 a few months earlier, and with it came a vague sense of his own yearnings. Not that he had ever had a girlfriend, nor did he want one. But he was an adolescent, which came with its own set of contradictions.

Mika stirred a pot of soup on an open fire. The aroma wafted upward. Moric had long ago become acquainted with the grumbling in his stomach. He hadn't eaten anything substantial in several days, or rather, in several weeks. Mika found a metal bowl, rinsed it along with a spoon using the water she had been boiling, and ladled a sizeable portion of the broth before handing it to Moric.

"Thank you," he weakly said.

Mika nodded and watched him down the soup greedily. "Would you like some more?"

"If you don't mind, yes please."

"When you're finished, go over to the tarp strung up on the branches. Peja will instruct you on what we do here. We are dedicated to our revolution. You'll find your place, you'll see. Welcome Milan."

Moric finished his soup, thanked Mika, and followed her to meet Peja. As she handed him off to the patrol leader, she flashed a broad, warm smile.

Peja's baritone voice opposed his slender build. He was not a tall man. His clean-shaven face was that of a teenager, although his brown eyes told a different story. "Milan, good to meet you. I trust Mika's soup was satisfactory."

"It was delicious. I was very hungry."

"Good. For now, just make yourself comfortable. Feel free to wander around the camp. Tomorrow you and I will meet, so that I can tell you about our movement. We'll turn in early tonight. Here are some blankets to lay on the ground under the tarp. It's not the most comfortable, but you'll get used to it eventually."

Moric thanked him and brought his rucksack and the blankets over to the spot where Peja had pointed.

He didn't feel like moving about the camp. It was enough to take in what was happening in that moment. Though he still felt alone, at least he had a place with people that seemed to welcome him. Peja, Mika, and the rest of the patrol treated him kindly; it made him feel somewhat safe.

As he lay on the blankets under the tarp, he set his rucksack close by. Despite some lumps underneath the blankets, he felt warm, and sleep quickly overwhelmed him.

When he awoke the next morning, he felt disoriented at first. Looking across the way, he saw Peja was attending to some chores. Moric remembered what happened to him the day before. He stood up, stretched, and went into the woods to relieve himself. He walked over to Peja, who had a cup of hot tea and some bread with a sweet, fruit preserve ready for him. "Good morning. What do you think of our hotel? Comfortable bed, don't you think?"

Moric smiled. He liked this man. "I don't remember falling asleep or dreaming. I guess I was tired."

"You slept for a long time. You needed it, I'm sure. I'm told that you're only 12 years old. We have some younger people in our brigade, but you may be one of the youngest. Still, everyone here does important things for the cause. We've already thought of some ways you'll be able to help us. Don't worry, you won't be throwing bombs or shooting guns. In the meantime, let me tell you about us. I know you just woke up, so sit over here and eat your breakfast. If you want more tea and bread, let me know."

Moric sat down. The hot tea warmed him, and the bread and jam, though not like his mother's, was delicious. He was not sure what Peja was going to tell him, or if he would even understand, but it was important for him to show that he was paying attention.

"I want to welcome you to our little collective. We are fighters, but we're also brothers and sisters in a struggle for what's right. We've had some encounters with the enemy in Drvar and other parts of the Krajina, as I'm sure you know."

"Yes, I know. I left Drvar, but I heard about the uprising there, and the Partisans helping the local people. The Partisans are heroes, you know. Oh, I guess you would know..." Moric said with a slight tinge of red on his cheeks.

Peja smiled. "That's good to hear. How did you survive in the mountains?"

Moric repeated what he told the patrol that found him.

"Very resourceful. Well done. All of us here have stories of escape and battle. And it's only just begun. We're all part of the people's movement to fight the fascists who wish to destroy our country. Our liberation will require us to stand together to defeat the enemy, and begin a new chapter in Yugoslav history."

Moric found himself straining to absorb this new information. It was above his head, but he grasped some of it.

"We Partisans wish for all of us to coexist in peace and harmony. But you'll learn more about that. Unfortunately, that means fighting for what is right. Do you know much about war?"

"My father was in the last big war. He used to tell me stories about it. He said it was awful at times, although he never really told me about what made it awful. He did tell me that he had to fight against his brothers because they were in the enemy's army. He hated that."

"He's right. War is very difficult. It can be scary too. You're with us now. We'll take care of you as best as we can, but you'll see for yourself that it's not fun and games. For now, here's a bag with warmer pants, shirts, and sweaters, warm underclothes, your own bowl and utensils, and strong boots. And here's a sturdier rucksack than what you brought with you. Make sure the shoes fit you comfortably. Now, let me take you to the comrade who will be teaching you about our mission. He's also the one that you'll be getting to know quite well."

As they walked together, Peja proceeded to tell Moric how the Partisans set up camp when it's safe to do so. He informed him that most of the comrades buddy up, so they can help each other out, and carve out a place to hang a tarp, if need be, and to sleep.

Moric nodded; he was unsure of how to respond. His time in the mountains had exhausted him. But he was beginning to feel thankful that he was with the Partisans.

Peja stopped to introduce Moric to a boy only a couple of years older who extended his hand towards Moric.

Though they had never met before, a strange sense of familiarity emerged. Was it his unkempt hair, his tall, gangly body, or his wide grin that reminding him somewhat of a cousin in Prijedor, especially with those overly large teeth? Or maybe it was how the boy immediately, without hesitation, greeted him with a welcoming smile. Whatever it was, Moric felt at ease right away.

"Hi, I'm Djuro. Whom do I have the pleasure of 'rooming' with?"

"I'm Milan Adamovic."

"Nice to meet you, Milan. Peja asked me to begin your first lesson. Put your stuff down, and follow me."

Moric tossed the bag of clothes next to his rucksacks, the old one and the new. He and Djuro then made the rounds around the camp.

"Do you know what our liberation fight is about?"

"Not really, but I do know how cruel the Nazis and Ustasha are. They took away my family. Maybe to Jasenovac."

"The camps are not nice places. The Germans have their camps and the Ustasha have theirs. No one knows for sure, but they're probably not just to keep prisoners from joining our resistance."

Moric thought about his time in the collection camp. Gooseflesh rose up on his arms.

As they approached Mika, Moric looked away, a bit flustered.

"I see you've met Mika. She's an amazing revolutionary. She's been on raids. She handles herself quite well."

"You do too, Djuro. Neither of us had ever used guns before, but we've been trained well. It's not easy though. We just have to keep in mind why we're doing this, and what we're willing to die for," Mika responded.

Mika's comment sunk in quickly. *Raids? Guns? That they're willing to die?* It was all somewhat dizzying; nothing he'd ever fathomed would be a part of his life. His life was bicycles, his mother's delicious meals, school, sisters, his father's store, and family celebrations. Nothing could be further from his reality now. That these people were willing to die for a cause was an unimaginable concept for him to absorb. He had never contemplated his own death, even in the collection camp with its hovering threats. Yet, here were two people, not much older than him, speaking of their willingness to give up their lives in the name of freedom.

"I, um, um..." was his only response.

"Don't worry. It takes time to feel what we are feeling. Our people will be in trouble unless we fight for what is right. Hopefully, we'll all get through this to enjoy a new day. We believe we will," Mika said.

Before continuing with Djuro, Mika told him that she would be making more soup later and that he and Djuro should visit her to enjoy some.

"I'd like that, Mika," Moric said.

"We'll be seeing a lot of each other, I'm sure," she said as the two boys continued their walk around the camp.

Djuro talked about the mission of the Partisans. Sometimes Moric couldn't follow what he was saying. It was political talk, and Moric didn't understand it. But Djuro told him that the villages, towns, and cities in the Ustasha-run state were fair game for the Nazi allies. Slaughter and deportations were increasingly becoming the strategy of the fascists. The goal of the Partisans was to bring the people of Yugoslavia into their movement.

When they returned to where Moric had left his belongings, he sat down on a blanket. Though he wanted to lie down for a few minutes, he had a few questions for Djuro. "How did you become a Partisan?"

"It's not an easy story to tell, but I'm sure you have one too."

Moric nodded.

"I'm from Novi Grad. The Ustasha came to our village, killed some of the villagers, and took others away. My parents were taken to a camp, and that's the last I saw of them."

Djuro exhaled and paused for a moment.

"I escaped into a field outside of town. A farmer and his family took me in for a couple of days, but we knew it was only a matter of time before they'd come to his farm. I had heard that the Partisans were in the forests nearby. So I left the farm to find them. It wasn't too long when I did. They took me in as one of their own, and here I am."

Djuro seemed to tell his story with little emotion. It was almost as if this young teen was reciting an adventure, detached from feeling, but when he finished, he turned away to wipe something from his eyes.

"What about you, Milan? How did you end up in the mountains alone?"

Moric laid back and placed his hands behind his neck. He closed his eyes and told of his journey, being cognizant of protecting his Jewish identity. He spoke deliberately, trying not to give away the sadness he felt so acutely. He opened his eyes and turned towards Djuro. "Do you have any idea where your parents are?"

"Same as you, I think they're in Jasenovac, but I don't really know. My hope is that we defeat the fascists, and can then find our families."

The boys lapsed into a brief silence; Djuro told Moric to rest. There would be time to get to know each other and to learn more about the revolution.

"I'll be back later to continue our tour of the camp," Djuro said.

Moric was still too exhausted to do much more than sleep.

The sun was setting when he opened his eyes again. How long had he been sleeping? He looked around and saw the liberators, as Djuro had referred to them, cleaning their rifles, washing out their plates and utensils, or talking with one another.

He sat up for a few minutes and reflected on his and Djuro's stories. They were not dissimilar in intensity. He guessed that for many, that part was no different.

In the brief time he had been there, he learned that the Partisans were truly brothers and sisters in both a war against the fascists, and a struggle to enlist people from all walks of life to join their campaign to free their state from the shackles of tyranny. At least, some of this was sinking in.

Moric saw Djuro beckoning him to join him and Mika around the fire. Like some of the others they were eating potatoes. They used sticks to cook the potatoes over the flames; someone was also passing beets around.

Moric was still exhausted but made an effort to introduce himself to his comrades. He got up and went to where his two new comrades were rinsing off their metal plates.

"Hi, I guess I was very tired. I didn't expect to fall asleep like that," Moric said.

"That's to be expected. You've been through a lot. Believe me, when we can get a chance to sleep, or even just rest, we take advantage of it," Djuro responded.

"I was hoping for some of your soup like last night, Mika. It was so good," Moric said.

"Thank you. I only make that if we have enough vegetables and stock. It was your lucky day," she said with a laugh.

"Unfortunately, we move around a lot, so cooking isn't usually possible. Still, I appreciate the compliment."

"Here's something to eat," Djuro said.

Djuro handed Moric his stick and a potato. It was reminiscent of the mountain camping he had done with his father, although their mother gave them more than just a potato.

"When I was in the mountains, I'd see the Partisan flag in villages, those were the ones I'd go to for food. But there were other times that those same villages were no longer under Partisan control."

"That's right," said Mika, "since we don't have a large presence yet, we might have to retreat back into the mountains. That means we've had to give up villages to repel the enemy. If they can, villagers join us. Sometimes, we call in special units to take their old and sick to our medical bunkers for treatment, but there aren't many of those. And sometimes, they just don't want to come with us. I always feel sad for them because I know full well what the fascists will do."

Djuro continued. "Our battles are unpredictable. The enemy is starting to show up more and more. We're outnumbered, but our strength is hiding in the mountains getting ready to give them another surprise. They don't know these mountains like we do. That's how we'll win this war."

"I see," Moric responded, though he wasn't fully sure he did.

"You don't need to concern yourself with any of that right now," Mika said. "We're at the beginning of our liberation. You'll find your place here. Give it a little time. First things first, most of us take care of one another. Consider me and Djuro two of those who will make sure you're alright. How does that sound?"

"That sounds very good," he said.

It was time to turn in; Moric and Djuro bid Mika goodnight before heading to where they had left their gear.

They lay on top of their blankets underneath a tarp in case of rain. Before saying goodnight, Djuro reassured Moric that he and Mika would look out for him.

Moric liked the idea of Mika and Djuro keeping an eye on him. Still, he would show them that he could take care of himself. After all, he had survived some very hard times in recent months.

Before he fell asleep, he pictured Mika by the fire. She was very impressive; he had never met anyone like her.

The next morning, Moric woke up to dawn's arrival. He felt stronger. He got dressed and left a snoring Djuro. Walking by several Partisans who were just waking up, he greeted them but had one purpose in mind.

He found Mika cleaning her rifle underneath her tarp. "Good morning, Mika."

"Oh, good morning. I see that you also like to get up with the early morning song birds."

Moric smiled. He could tell that Mika was light-hearted and welcoming. He felt that from the first moment he met her, almost as if he had known her for some time. Having three older sisters made it easy to connect.

"So much to think about," Moric said.

"It can be a lot to take in, while worrying about what we've left behind."

It was as if she could read his mind.

"I remember when I first got here I felt the same way. You'll get used to it. We have an important mission. In fact, it's more than a mission. We're trying to save Yugoslavia from the path of self-destruction that the Ustasha want to lead us down. I've learned a lot about communism in a short time and it's a wonderful antidote to fascism."

"I see," said Moric, although he actually didn't.

"Where are you from?"

"Drvar." He proceeded to tell her about his escape.

"How about you?"

Mika stopped cleaning her gun. She set it on her lap, and looked at Moric. "My family lived in Bosanski Petrovac. The Ustasha ruled the place with an iron fist. My parents and two younger brothers were in their crosshairs. My father was a local politician who was too outspoken, I'm afraid. He was arrested and taken away. We never learned where they took him." Mika paused and looked at a bird flying overhead. "That bird... that's what I want – to be free."

Moric just listened.

"My mother moved us from our house to a farm that my uncle owned. The Ustasha found out where we were, and they sent their police to the house one night. My uncle tried to tell them only he and my aunt lived there; their daughter and son had moved out long ago. The police said they didn't care about that, they just wanted to know where the communist's family was. My uncle said he didn't know. So they beat him, and set the house on fire. When we all tried to escape..."

"You don't need to tell me more."

"I want to because I want you to know why I fight. And to know that this is why we all want to liberate our people from this evil."

Moric took a deep breath. He anticipated a tragic story, not unlike what he had witnessed before boarding the cattle car to Jasenovac.

"They shot my family. My poor mother and brothers. I ran into the woods, and I guess with all of the shooting they didn't see me flee. I couldn't look back until I stopped behind a berm a couple of kilometers from the farmhouse. I saw the glow of the fire and kept moving. It felt like I wasn't in my body. I just kept running up into the hills."

Mika finished by explaining how one of their unit's courier's, Stjepan, found her. "I believe you'll meet him soon. He's a hero to me. This's why I fight. I won't stop unless a bullet finds me."

Moric was in awe. He reiterated to himself that he had never met anyone, let alone a girl, with such strength. Hers was a sad story, as was Djuro's. He wasn't sure what to say to her, though, and said nothing.

"Please don't feel bad for me. Your story, Djuro's, and so many others are what this war in Europe has begun to take from us. Hitler, Pavelic, Mihailovic of the Chetniks, they're all the same. They won't stop unless we stop them."

"Thank you for telling me. I'm sorry."

Not wanting to disclose any more for both their sakes, Moric refrained from telling her that he and his family spent time in the collection camp near her village. He no longer wanted to be reminded of the pain they all felt.

Mika's eyes softened. Moric had only recently met her, but he could feel the warmth that radiated in her presence.

"Well, thank you. How about we go get some breakfast? I hear they're serving fresh biscuits, eggs, cakes, fruit juices, and all on porcelain China with fancy silverware."

"They are?"

"Of course not. We're lucky if we get some bread and jam," she chuckled. "It's certainly better than grasses from the mountains, wouldn't you agree?"

Moric laughed. Mika had a way of moving on from difficult topics by making jokes. He liked her; he liked her a lot.

14 MORIC'S JOBS

Moric tried to avoid Luka Juric. His leadership of some 800 fighters in the Proletarian Brigade was already becoming legendary. The man intimidated him. Moric recalled a time when one of his teachers had the same impact as Luka Juric, making him feel like he wanted to crawl under a desk and hide. Moric had always been an excellent student and a fast learner, but this was a very different education.

Mostly, Juric didn't bother with the younger people in his charge. He communicated with the leaders "on the ground" such as patrol leader Peja Jovic.

It was late spring and Moric had been at the camp for a few months. Though he had seen a few battles, he was kept safely behind the action.

A reorganization and expansion of the Partisan liberation army had recently taken place. The resistance movement had stressed that this was a battle for freedom, and the many thousands who witnessed the cruelty of the fascists joined the ranks of the Partisans. This warranted a more organized approach to military operations. Therefore, a much more professional army was developed with various levels of command, and a fledgling supreme headquarters emerging with Tito at the helm.

Women were now included in the fighting because they were also part of the collective will of the people. He could see his own sisters being a part of this; they were strong and independent. He prayed that they were alright.

Moric learned that the struggle for liberation included all ethnicities and religions because that represented a unified national movement of resistance. However, he remained guarded about revealing his religion. Even if his fellow Partisans were his comrades, some came from towns, villages, and cities that were hostile to Jews. That they sang songs of unity, had drills together, ate together, and reinforced the higher purpose of their movement, didn't ease his concerns.

Machi, as Moric was nicknamed because of his small size and agility like that of a wildcat, was summoned by Peja. He was told he would be a courier and messenger, within the camp and outside. He was chosen because he knew how to navigate the mountains. Being a wildcat was an asset in what would be challenging conditions. His other role, Peja told him, would be that of a photographer.

As soon as his new roles were clear to him, a trim man in his early thirties holding a camera and various pieces of equipment joined him. He introduced himself. "Hello, Machi. My name is Ivan. Pleased to meet you."

Ivan had large green eyes that Moric thought fitting for a photographer.

"This is yours," said Ivan. "It's a Kodak Retina model. It takes 35-millimeter film. You'll learn how to take pictures and develop them."

Moric took the camera and inspected it, though he wasn't sure what he was looking for. He had never owned a camera before, though he did admire photographs in military magazines. Once, he saw spectacular photographs in an American magazine called *Life*. He never imagined he would be taking pictures himself. He followed Ivan to a small box of supplies, tamping down his insecurities as best he could so that he could concentrate.

Ivan opened a box and pulled out a large piece of black cloth. "Let me begin here. You'll need to always protect the film from exposure because light will ruin it. First, you'll take this cloth and drape it over a branch or something to create a makeshift tent. Or, in a pinch, here's another piece of cloth to make an even smaller tent, just enough to drape over your hands and hang down to the ground. Not ideal, but it's big enough to stick your hands underneath. It's best to do this when the moon isn't out, so you've got the maximum darkness."

Moric felt like he was in school again receiving instruction on some project that he and his team of students were to work on. He recalled that his enthusiasm often seemed to trump that of the others, and invariably he'd take over. If any of the others followed his lead, all the better. If not, so be it. He was not one to complain, especially if he earned an excellent grade for his team, one that no one else would complain about either.

"The film must be removed from its canister in the dark. Then, it's wound into this small metal spool," Ivan said. He handed the spool to his student. "The spool keeps the film wound in a loose circle so that one piece of film doesn't touch another. This part also needs to be done in the dark."

Paying close attention, Moric paraphrased for Ivan what he had just learned. Ivan smiled broadly.

"Remember that you'll only have negatives that you can view. They'll be in reverse of how your subjects actually posed. That gets corrected when you develop proofs and then prints. That, my young friend, is done either in a photographic lab, like at most of our headquarters, or in a city which we control that has its own labs. Either I or someone else will show you how to do that when you're there. But mostly, you'll be carrying either the undeveloped film or negatives with you. Your work must be protected from dirt and dust in small sacks like those in this box. But most importantly, never let the enemy get a hold of them. If you're captured, destroy them any way you need to."

Moric felt a stirring in the pit of his stomach. Captured? Destroy them? He didn't want to think about this possibility. Being captured could mean imprisonment, torture, or worse he had heard.

He'd hoped Ivan didn't notice his slight, though brief trembling.

"Machi, I'll walk you through how to develop film into negatives when it gets dark. Also, you need to know that you and I are responsible for the safekeeping of the equipment and supplies. We must put our cameras, unused film, and any negatives into our rucksacks. If you have room, put the cloths and chemicals in your pack, as well. It's too cumbersome to carry a second rucksack. So do your best to pack everything in this one. Alternatively, you can put this box onto a horse cart. If we have to run from our position... well, just be sure everything is as it should be before that happens. Others are assigned to attach the horses to the carts and guide them to our next stop or keep it out of enemy hands, that is, if you decide to put our things onto a cart. Again, it's best if you can hold on to them. The pictures we photographers print are very important to our liberation. Have you seen any of them in the liberated villages you've been in?"

"I don't remember. Before I joined the resistance I'd sneak into places where I could get food. I was starving, so I didn't pay attention to anything else."

"I'm sure eating was more important than seeing photographs," Ivan said with a wry smile.

"We've only recently been taking pictures of our people and sending or bringing them to the peasants' villages so they can see what we're doing. Many are joining our cause just because of seeing them. We have a very important part to play. Do you understand?"

Moric nodded.

"It will take some time, but you'll become a fine photographer, I promise."

"Where did you get a Kodak?" Moric asked.

Ivan hesitated before he said, "One of our comrades took it from a dead German and gave it to me. The Retina was made in Germany. I'll be by your side for the next few days teaching you what I know. The most important thing for us is that you take photographs that show our resistance."

"Will you want pictures of our battles against the enemy?"

"Whatever you think will portray the message we want to convey. Our pictures should remind others that it's the people who are our strength. Sometimes you'll want to take our fighters when they leave for battle or when they return. We want to entice the population to join us. We're counting on everyone to be part of our future."

Moric and Ivan moved about the camp, finding opportunities to photograph the "heroes of the revolution." They would take shots of their comrades with their weapons next to them or in their hands, and candid ones of the camp's activities. The backdrop of the mountains glorified the struggle. Moric learned that photographs were important tools to motivate the rural people to join the struggle. It was important to counter the sophisticated propaganda machine of the Third Reich.

Ivan finished his intensive photography training in three days. Although he lost some sleep over whether he could succeed, Moric absorbed all the information and was ready to go on his own. Ivan asked him to find more suitable subjects within the camp and begin his photo documentation.

"Djuro, Mika, I'd like to use you as my first subjects."

"Sure," responded Djuro, "but I'll need to find my best suit and tie first...!"

"And I'll need to get the formal dress my mother sewed for me for my first communion, though it might be a bit small," Mika said.

"Okay, okay. I just feel that you two are my best friends here, and what better way to show how much I care than to immortalize you. I think that's how Ivan used that word – immortalize."

"Look at you, Machi, a true revolutionary. And after only a few months," Mika quipped.

"I want to help. I've seen what the fascists have done to people here. We've got to do whatever we can to defeat them. That much, I know," Moric replied.

"Okay. Where do you want us to pose?" Djuro asked.

"How about you get your rifles and sit by that tree? Rest the guns on your laps and look out at the cluster of tall beech trees. Don't forget to put your caps on."

The teenagers grabbed their gear and sat on the instructed spot. Moric noticed that their youthful faces were rugged from months of living outdoors in the mountains. He knew that each one had engaged in guerrilla attacks. He admired their dedication, but knew in his heart that despite being given a Carcano, the Italian-made short rifle, he could never use it to kill anyone. Peja told him that he was too young to be part of the fighting anyway.

He focused the lens of his camera on the two subjects and waited until they naturally peered across the hills of Kozara. He snapped pictures from different angles, trying to get ones that would depict the right spirit, the one that could convince villagers to join the movement. He then asked each of his friends to move away, so he could take individual shots. As he gazed at Mika, he came closer. He was, once again, in awe of her crystal-clear blue eyes. He captured them dazzling in an afternoon light that was just beginning to fade. She was his friend, he reminded himself. Nothing more.

The next night under a moonless sky, Moric went to work as he had been taught. He transferred the film into negatives which gave him a vague impression of what the photographs would look like.

This was his first solo effort and he wanted to impress Ivan. He meticulously moved through the steps and watched as the negatives miraculously came to life. He took his hand lens to view the details. He could almost feel the robustness of his friends, and the message he was asked to convey.

"Ivan," Moric called. "My first negatives."

Ivan asked Moric to sit with him on the rocks nearby. He borrowed the hand lens to carefully examine each one. Moric wasn't aware that he was holding his breath.

"Well, comrade, these are wonderful. Your teacher is proud. Feel free to show your subjects, and then give them back to me. I'll be sure these find their way to headquarters to be developed. They capture how our youth are part of our struggle."

"Thank you. I'll do that."

Moric wanted to keep them, to be the one who developed them into photographs. Proud of his accomplishment, he understood that there was a higher cause than for him to ogle over his work. Besides, they weren't a finished product yet.

He showed Djuro and Mika who wholeheartedly approved. They teased him about being a photographer for *Borba*, the banned communist newspaper that was making its comeback as the central paper that spread news about the glories of the Partisans.

Throughout the spring of 1942, various Partisan units managed to liberate several towns and cities, including Bosanski Petrovac, Drvar, Glamoć, and Prijedor, which brought great pride to the liberators.

They often talked about these victories, some of which Moric's brigade took part in. Djuro and Mika had been on a raid into Prijedor. They spoke of sneaking in under the cover of darkness, ambushing Ustasha soldiers, and leaving behind commanders and liberators to secure the village while encouraging locals to join the fight. Some of the soldiers from the unit hadn't returned. It made Moric uneasy, and in his nightmares he would see shadows appear in the amorphous forms of his dead comrades.

It was now Moric's time to begin his training as a courier. His teacher, Stjepan, came to see him during breakfast, and announced that they would start today. They packed some supplies and left the camp. Their goal was to reach other outposts within a 10-kilometer radius to deliver orders given by Luka Juric.

Moric noticed a long and narrow scar under his trainer's left eye. He wondered if this was a result of his courier duties, but he wasn't going to ask.

Stjepan had soft brown eyes that had seen things Moric felt shouldn't have resulted in such a jovial demeanor. But lately he had been thinking about how things don't always line up very clearly when it comes to war.

One overcast night, as they traversed the terrain, they found a hidden spot to settle. They ate over a small fire, deliberately keeping low to avoid detection by the enemy, as his trainer had instructed.

"Being a courier is not an easy job. If you're on your own, it can be lonely and maybe even scary. Sometimes you'll go with another comrade, but that depends on many circumstances. It's good that they call you Machi because you'll need to be like a wildcat, moving in between the shadows and the light."

Moric used to think of his short and slight stature as a liability. He had always wanted to be taller and bigger. Now he recognized that his size was a big advantage, and might actually save his life. He recalled how lithely he slipped onto the train tracks in his escape from the cattle car; it seemed like an eternity ago.

"Moric, I know couriers who've been caught. I can tell you that for them it's been, let's say, not good. I'll leave it at that. Best advice is: don't get caught. The woods will be your best friend. It's better to take the long way rather than take shortcuts. You'll be asked to deliver messages as fast as you can, and that's true. But if it seems too dangerous, then slow down."

Moric swallowed hard as he listened to Stjepan's guidance. He welcomed the confidence the Partisans had in him, but the danger that accompanied this assignment was unnerving. Being a courier was completely foreign to anything he had ever done. He should have been home in Drvar, with his family. Yet, he pushed that thought aside to avoid sinking into melancholy. He had no choice but to listen carefully to the man and execute his job with the utmost precision. His life depended on it. "I'll do my very best to serve my fellow comrades, and the mission of liberating our people," Moric said, hoping he at least sounded like a true Partisan.

They settled in and Stjepan began to tell his own story.

One thing Moric had learned from being with the Partisans was that it was important for them to tell their stories. They wore them like a badge of honor.

"I'm from Glamoč, a city of mostly Serbs. My family was one of the few Croatian families there. The Ustasha had a rather strong influence about a year ago, spreading their hate with posters, flyers, and intimidating visits to local stores and homes. My family was told to watch out for the Serbs and anyone else who wanted to take away 'our rightful place in the NDH.' They claimed that by allying with the Germans, Catholics would be well cared for. My father nodded and smiled. He and my mother mostly said nothing. My beautiful younger sister was there, hiding behind my mother. One of the black shirts kept looking over at her. She was the same age as you are now. He didn't say it out loud, but he let it be known that if my family didn't show loyalty to the greatness of our newly formed state, even Croatians could get hurt. I hope it's alright for me to tell you this."

"Of course," Moric said. "I've learned a lot from the stories from others."

"That's good to hear. So my parents got together our things, and the next day we all tried to flee to Zagreb, hoping to reach my cousin's house and then flee to a country in Europe that hadn't fallen to the Nazis. Of course, we knew this wouldn't be easy. The Ustasha were everywhere, collaborating with the Nazis. But my parents said we had to try."

Stjepan hesitated, but before Moric could ask a question, the man continued. "I turned 19 this past January. I have friends, Serbs, who encouraged me to join the Resistance. My parents were always preaching to me and my sister that this was too risky. The night before we left, my father came into my room. He said that it would be best for me to go to the mountains and find my place with the liberators. He wasn't sure they'd be able to find their way safely to Zagreb, and besides, then where would they go? I was worried about my family. Very worried. I didn't want to leave; but my father insisted. He hated the Ustasha for their alliance with the Nazis. He hated that fascism had risen to such heights in Europe, especially the

Kingdom of Yugoslavia. So before dawn the next morning, I took my rucksack, filled it with food, warm clothes, and set off for the mountains. I had a friend who told me that the units move around a lot, but that there were some encampments of liberators on the mountain. That's how I found myself here. It took me days to get here, avoiding patrols, but I made it."

Moric realized that everyone who joined the movement to free Yugoslavia suffered in their own way. He wanted to ask him how he had gotten the scar, but the man only spoken of his journey. There was no need to burden him with what was likely a painful memory.

"Do you know what happened to your parents and sister?" Moric asked.

"I'm afraid I don't. I worry about them constantly, and I don't know when or how I'll see them? My parents are clever. And they're Catholic, so they'll find a way, I hope."

"I hope so too. I worry about my parents, sisters, grandparents, and everyone else. I sometimes have nightmares about them," Moric responded in a soft voice.

"Where are you from?"

"Drvar. We had visitors like you did." Moric hesitated. He had managed to keep his Jewish identity a secret so far, and he wished to keep it that way. He told Stjepan what he had told the others about his escape. He felt a lump forming in his throat, but he tamped it down.

Stjepan handed Moric a piece of dried beef and a cold, roasted potato. Moric extended his metal plate and looked away from his trainer, so he wouldn't see his watery eyes.

When he looked back, Stjepan had stood up near the fire, staring at its flames. He doused it, so that there were no signs of them being there. "Machi, you must be prepared to see some horrible things. On my runs, I've seen villages smoldering from fires that the enemy set, and dead people strewn about, including babies. These images sometimes visit me in my sleep. I don't really know how anyone prepares for such things, but I don't want you to be surprised. Still, it's important that we never give up hope. I don't know when or if we'll ever see our families again, but I want to believe that we will. We have a long struggle and you and I have an important part to play. Let's get some rest before we make our last stop at the southwest camp. We can talk more tomorrow."

Moric said goodnight and lay down underneath the stars. It was a cool spring night on the mountain. He pulled his wool cap below his ears and tugged his blanket up high on his chest. Gazing at the stars, he wondered whether Stjepan was right that they had to maintain hope despite the terrible things that happen in war. Before he dozed off, he decided that he agreed with him. *Don't lose hope*, he told himself. *I must always have hope.*

Moric abruptly woke up to the sound of cracking branches. He listened carefully but figured he had just dreamed it. Glancing over at Stjepan, who was sound asleep, he took a couple of deep breaths to calm himself before closing his eyes again. He immediately drifted into a haunting dream – there was a baby, stripped naked, lying face down with blood dripping from its tiny head in front of his home in Drvar.

15   THE BATTLE OF KOZARA BEGINS

Moric returned from his courier duties feeling exhausted but satisfied that he had performed admirably. Stjepan had told him as much. He was met by Peja who also commended him. "You're ready to be on your own as a courier and a photographer. Both of your teachers gave you high marks."

Peja proceeded to spell out Moric's first solo mission. The Germans were preparing for an offensive to take back what the Partisans had gained in the Free Territory of Trieste. They were setting up plans to defend those gains, but the fascists had a lot of weapons and soldiers at their disposal.

What alarmed Moric, was Peja telling him to keep his rifle at hand should he need it. This was one task Moric was not ready to take on. Though there was no expectation that he would join in the fighting, he might not have a choice. Djuro trained him on how to load, shoot, and clean his rifle, and Moric was reasonably comfortable with his instructions. Still, to think that he might have to actually end a human life was something he couldn't reconcile.

Peja said, "There's one other thing that we're contending with in eastern Bosnia. Since March, Chetniks have destroyed villages and are killing anyone who is not Serb. They continue to believe that this is their moment in history to create a pure Serbian state. We must be ready for them, too. Fortunately, many of us Serbs are part of the people's liberation movement, and will not tolerate what the Chetniks stand for."

Moric had heard the same message from his comrades: be prepared for great battles on whichever front required it.

It was time to muster his courage, gather his belongings, and secure his camera and equipment. Moric assisted in loading supplies onto a horse-drawn cart. Later, Moric, Mika, and Djuro sat around the fire for the evening meal. They spoke quietly of victory; there was no other choice.

The mood was upbeat. Though Moric had heard the Partisans sing their songs of liberation, underscoring pride in their movement, he hadn't paid as close attention until this evening. He could sense that the impending battle would be dangerous – very dangerous.

Two comrades began singing. Then, not only did many of those sitting by the fire join in, but others from around the camp started singing as well. The sounds of a Partisan revolution song echoed in the hills nearby. Soon, even Moric sang:

> *One morning I woke up,*
> *oh goodbye beautiful, goodbye beautiful, goodbye beautiful, bye, bye, bye*
> *One morning I woke up*
> *and I found the invader.*
> *Oh Partisan, take me away,*
> *oh goodbye beautiful, goodbye beautiful, goodbye beautiful, bye, bye, bye*
> *oh Partisan, take me away*
> *Because I feel as if I'm going to die.*
> *And if I die a Partisan,*
> *oh goodbye beautiful, goodbye beautiful, goodbye beautiful, bye, bye, bye*
> *and if I die then you must bury me.*
> *Bury me up in the mountain,*
> *oh goodbye beautiful, goodbye beautiful, goodbye beautiful, bye, bye, bye*
> *bury me up in the mountain*
> *under the shade of a beautiful flower.*
> *And the people who pass by,*
> *oh goodbye beautiful, goodbye beautiful, goodbye beautiful, bye, bye, bye*
> *and the people who pass by,*
> *will tell me "What a beautiful flower."*
> *This is the flower of the Partisan,*
> *oh goodbye beautiful, goodbye beautiful, goodbye beautiful, bye, bye, bye*
> *this is the flower of the Partisan*
> *who died for freedom.*

When the song ended the fighters stood up. One of them yelled: "To our victory over the oppressors!" Cheers were heard before they dispersed to go to sleep.

The three friends walked to their respective sleeping spots. Moric was very quiet while the two others talked. They walked Mika to where she had placed her rucksack, and Djuro said goodnight. Moric was not tired. He told Djuro that he would see him shortly.

"Mika, can I talk with you about something?"

"Of course, what is it?"

Moric practically whispered, "I'm scared."

Mika put her arm around her young friend. "Deep down, we all are. We sing these songs and know that if we die, we die in the name of freedom. We die knowing that we've come closer to realizing a liberated Yugoslavia. But I can't think about what it means to actually die. These songs have been sung by revolutionaries in many wars, like the Spanish Civil War, where my uncle fought and died. It's not an easy thing that we're doing. It's very dangerous, but we must know what our greater purpose is. We want to live to see the day that our freedom is won. I wish I had more encouraging words, but sometimes we just have to push forward and have faith in ourselves and our cause."

"All of the people here say similar things. It's what I've been taught in the time I've been here. I believe in it, too, but I'm still scared," Moric said.

"All right, then let's be scared together. When we move out, stay near me. We'll make sure that Djuro is with us, too. He and I will be fighting and you'll need to stay back when we do. But when there is a pause, we'll try to get back to you."

Moric nodded. Mika gave him a hug as she said goodnight. It felt good, but it reminded him of his mother's hugs, his father's, and even his sister's reassuring warmth. He missed them.

As he lay down underneath the stars, he made sure that no one could see that he was holding back a flood of tears.

It was early June, 1942. Word had just been delivered that Prijedor and

Ljubinje had been taken back by German, Croatian Home Guard, and Ustasha regiments. On the mountain Partisan brigades were on high alert.

That afternoon, a group of ten villagers wandered into the Partisan camp. "They burned our village to the ground. They executed most of the men. We were lucky to escape, but we've lost everything," cried one of the peasant women.

The woman collapsed near Moric. She was wailing, making it hard to understand what she was saying. Mika went over to console her while other comrades went to attend to the others who had escaped.

"They lined up my husband against the wall with the other men and boys and shot them in cold blood. Then they dragged them all into the field. They kept saying that we were Partisans. My husband was a farmer; he had nothing to do with them. We were only married two months ago. Two months ago!"

Mika brought over some water for the woman. "How did you escape?" Mika asked.

The woman took in a deep breath before speaking, "In the chaos, while they were rounding everyone up, yelling that the rest of us were going to be sent to the camps, we snuck into the barn. When we heard the trucks move into the town square we raced out the back and up into the hills. We were so desperate and frightened, but Dejan, over there, said that he had seen your camp just yesterday while foraging for mushrooms. He led us here."

"The others, where are they now?"

"The Germans set our village on fire while the people watched. We could see the smoke and flames as we made our way up the mountain. I'm sure they're going to put them in the trucks and take them away."

Moric stared, eyes wide and fixed. He had seen a lot since being taken to the collection camp, but hearing this made a big impact. Djuro could see that his friend was shaken.

Luka Juric appeared, having heard that villagers were in their camp. He consoled them, which moved Moric; he hadn't witnessed such compassion from the Commander before. Juric turned to the nearby fighters. "We're called to arms against the enemy. Get yourselves ready for battle."

He beckoned his patrol leaders to join him, and they hurried back to his tent. In what seemed like only a moment, a group of 20 Partisans with Peja as the squad leader, made their way downhill through the brush less than a kilometer away. They sped toward the only road out of the village, and set a plan of ambush into motion.

Two fighters, one to feed the string of bullets and one to fire, sat behind four machine guns on a ridge overlooking the road. The rest had rifles and hand grenades. Two Partisans moved an empty horse cart onto the road as a blockade. In the distance the squad could see the line of several trucks heading toward the cart.

The noise of German engines grew louder while dust and dirt kicked up from the heavy tires sprayed in all directions. The line of vehicles wound its way toward the cart, with the German commander's jeep at the head of the snake. His jeep stopped at the decoy. The Partisans could see frightened villagers inside the trucks. The Commander got out and ordered several of his men to move the cart, swearing at the stupidity of peasants.

As they took hold of the front shaft of the cart, grenades exploded, killing the soldiers that were trying to move it. In the chaos, the Partisans started to fire at them. The Wehrmacht soldiers, the conscripted infantry of the German army, scrambled out of their trucks onto the road to take cover and fire in the direction of the Partisan machine gun nests. The Partisans continued to spray rounds at the Germans, killing several of them.

The captured villagers saw their chance and leapt from the trucks, escaping into the hills. The Germans were now also firing at the fleeing peasants, several of whom collapsed.

Some of the Partisan fighters sprinted toward the villagers to direct them, while the others continued to fire as they retreated.

The Germans, unfamiliar with the terrain, stayed down below, unsure of their next move. Meanwhile, the Commander kept yelling to attack.

The plan was for the Partisans to unite with the next line of fighters only 100 meters away. There, another set of machine gunners were ready to cut down the pursuing Germans. Some villagers joined them in their fight as much as they could.

Overhead, the Luftwaffe with its attacking Stuka bombers entered the fray. Simultaneously, the Wehrmacht soldiers retreated to let the planes do their work.

Moric's heart pounded as the fighter planes buzzed overhead, having never seen such a sight. The hair on his neck stood stiff and sweat dripped from his skin as the planes dove, spitting out a siren-like sound. At first, he just watched as the planes nosedived and soared upward just as quickly. He was fascinated and petrified at the same time.

Djuro yelled at Moric to keep moving. At the original site of the brigade's position, they grabbed their rucksacks, spun around, and joined the others heading up the mountain to a pre-designated location where they would rendezvous with the rest of their comrades. As they ran, those who were in charge of directing the horse-drawn carts carrying equipment and supplies through a clearing couldn't get the frightened animals to move. The roar of the planes made it impossible for the horses to follow the commands of their handlers. The horses were bucking and naying, trying to escape. Several Partisans released them as they attempted to scatter away from the danger. The carts were left in place with the hope of retrieving them at a later point. But many of the horses were slaughtered by the air assault.

"Take cover!" yelled one of the patrol leaders.

The planes were strafing the earth with buzz bombs, their explosions rocking the ground beneath Moric's feet. Despite this, the Partisans and villagers had to keep moving up the mountain to attempt to escape the onslaught.

Moric scrambled up the hill with the others. He had no time to think, only to make sure that his feet kept moving, even though they felt like jelly.

The boys hid behind a large rock so they could scan the area below. They saw at least 100 villagers climbing the hill toward them. Dressed in their local garb, it was an odd sight: a forest suddenly turned into a killing field with the villagers as vulnerable targets for planes. They could see some of them being swallowed up by dirt and rock as the explosions cut them down.

Moric could taste metal in his mouth, and the smell of burning flesh. He held back the retch that was building in his throat.

Peja rallied his fighters to gather the frantic villagers and make haste deeper into the forest.

The planes continued their relentless onslaught, circling the sky only to return and release more of their devastating payload.

"Take only what you can carry," was the order echoed by squad leaders.

Moric and Djuro did as they were told. But now, the planes were unleashing bullets from their turrets. With no options other than to find some semblance of safety from the German attack, a squad leader yelled for the boys to follow him, and his fighters as they headed straight for the protection of a thicket of massive evergreens.

In an instant, one of the leader's commands were cut off as he was hit by a torrent of bullets. Blood spewing from his body as he rolled backwards down the hill. Moric looked away. He had to get to the protection of the forest.

Villagers and Partisans gathered nearby, cutting and then pulling the low-lying brush over their heads. Within minutes, the attack subsided.

"The planes are leaving!" said one of the villagers.

Everyone could hear that what they said was true.

Peja yelled to everyone to get up and head further up the mountain. What seemed like hours to Moric, was only several minutes, but the carnage left in the wake of the German onslaught made him tremble.

The villagers were crying from their ordeal, especially those who had lost someone in the violence.

"Machi, are you alright?" Djuro asked.

"I think so."

Peja yelled, "They won't be gone for long. Let's help those who are wounded. If there are younger ones, go to them and help them out. I'll take a few volunteers to help the elders."

Moric went to a boy who was, perhaps, seven or eight years old. He was wincing in pain, limping. His tear-streaked cheeks cut through the dirt etched in his face.

"Let me help you. Take hold of my shoulder. As soon as we get further in I have a small kit with bandages."

The boy looked up warily, but he was willing to let Moric support him. When they got to a thick grove of trees, most of the villagers sat while the Partisans tended to the wounded. Some of the fighters were also injured and required medical attention. Some of their own were also missing.

The boy's parents were not among those who made it to the grove. He was calling for his mother, but only his older sister rushed over to him. She hugged and kissed him, thanking Moric for taking care of her baby brother. Moric thought about his own family. The girl took her brother and some alcohol, gauze, and a bandage to join other people from her village.

The pain of loss was evident in the tears shed and the prayers offered for those who had fallen in the attack.

Moric turned to Djuro and asked where Mika was.

"I don't know," was his answer.

The patrol leader, Milja, was tending to a slightly wounded comrade near the two friends.

"I'm afraid I saw her go down during the attack. I wanted to, but couldn't go back to help her. I'm so sorry."

Moric's thoughts were racing. Mika couldn't have been hit. She just couldn't have. He had to do something. Mika needed his help. He had to find her. "Djuro, I have to go back to find her."

"We don't know where she is?"

"I do," Milja said.

Moric gathered his rifle, as did Djuro.

"Machi, you stay here. We'll inform Peja about what we're doing, but you'll only hold us back. Please tend to the wounded as best you can," Milja said.

Moric began to protest, but he knew that Peja was right. He was not a warrior like they were. Teenagers like Djuro were, and certainly Milja was, but not him. True, he could navigate the mountain fairly well, but if there was a fight, he would be useless.

Djuro and Milja set off down the mountain.

Moric paced. *What if they can't find her? What if she's wounded or dead?* There was so much that had happened in this short period of time. Mika had told him that she was ready to die for the cause. He recalled her saying that only a bullet could stop her. He tried to go about helping people who needed it, but found it difficult to concentrate with Mika missing.

The minutes ticking by were agonizing. Moric finished bandaging an older woman with a wrist wound. Instead of moving on to someone else, he trotted several meters downhill to see if he could see them. With his binoculars, he scanned the terrain, but the dense brush made it hard to see.

Suddenly, he could see three figures making their way up the hill, partially obscured by the brush and large trees. It was them. As they came closer, he could see that Djuro was supporting Mika, while Milja was doing the same for a young peasant woman.

"Mika!" Moric yelled.

When the four of them made it to the rest, a nurse came running over to tend to the two young women.

"Both of you, please sit down over here."

The nurse examined her patients and applied isopropyl alcohol, iodine, and bandages. She declared that both would recover, but the dressing would need changing daily to prevent infection.

"I'll help you do that, Mika," Moric volunteered.

"Thank you."

Moric gently put his arm on Mika's shoulder. "What happened? I was worried that I'd never see you again?"

"I found Sofija down on the ground as I was heading up the hill with the rest of our comrades. I couldn't just leave her, so I picked her up. But a bomb from the planes exploded near us, and a piece of something, maybe a rock, found its way to my thigh. A flesh wound. It's nothing very complicated. Fortunately, Sofija wasn't hit again. We had to move. So we dragged ourselves up and, lumbering like turtles, made our way. The planes stopped flying over us. We would have made it here eventually, I suppose, but I'm glad Djuro and Milja found us. I was getting tired. Sofia is rather light, but she wasn't moving too well on her own. Anyway, you remember, I said until a bullet stops me, I'll fight for a free nation. I forgot that flying rocks might also get me," Mika said with a smile.

"Can you walk?" Djuro asked.

"Of course. It's just a nuisance, really."

Just then, Luka Juric asked everyone, including the villagers, to gather. "I'm sorry for those we have had to leave behind. Sadly, this is the cost we must pay. Be brave, all of you. We'll carry their memories with us as we go forward."

The Partisans spoke words of solidarity. The peasants were silent, staring at their wounded friends.

"We'll move up the hill another five kilometers. We'll dig trenches and set up for the enemy invasion. We also need to dig earth cabins along the mountainside, so whenever our comrades need a place to hide, we'll be able to add to the thousands our comrades have dug throughout the mountains. The Germans and their friends have been spotted massing along the mountain top. We'll need everyone to help carry the wounded. We leave no wounded behind, not even the most severely hurt," Juric proclaimed. "Now, let's move out."

Moric and another Partisan took each end of a stretcher to carry a comrade whose foot was severely damaged in the Luftwaffe attack. She'd been carried by villagers who found her as they were heading into the forest. Moric was instructed to soak iodine and alcohol in a rag and wrap it around the oozing wound. While he treated her, she muffled her pain through gritted teeth.

As they were all walking to their next destination, Moric noticed that various villagers were carrying rifles. The liberation army was growing.

After trenches were dug, the fighters set up their guns and got ready for an attack. The villagers and some Partisans stayed with the wounded about 100 meters behind. Moric had joined squad leader Drago, a stocky man known for his aggressive attitude, especially when drunk, who ordered his small group to have their guns drawn. They were equipped with either rifles or machine guns, and grenades. Drago told Moric that it was too dangerous for him to send messages to other squad leaders, but that he should be ready in case his services were required.

Moric looked around at his comrades. He was on high alert, knowing that they were about to be attacked and that he might be called upon as a courier.

Bullets began to whiz toward them. There was no time to be frightened.

German and the NDH's Croatian Home Guard were on the march, joined by armored vehicles that sent mortars in their direction. The fury of the incoming bombs, and the sounds of the explosions rocked the ground once again. In the trenches Drago told his fighters to wait for his order to fire. When several dozens of the enemy were only 50 meters away, Drago yelled the order. Immediately, attacking soldiers dropped to the ground. Drago's soldiers tossed their grenades, after which they appeared from the trenches and ran toward the enemy, firing away.

"Move forward! Charge!"

Moric remained in the trench, unsure of what to do next. He felt naked. A sinking feeling folded around him. He pulled out his rifle and waited. He looked to either side of the trench and noticed he was all alone. He stared ahead as comrades dropped to the ground, dead.

Just then, several other soldiers jumped into the trench, and fired away at the enemy. Milja was in charge of this squad. "Remain here," he ordered. "When the enemy leaks through our forward defenses, fire at them. Bombers, throw your grenades at any vehicles that head toward us. Let's hope nature stops them first," he said seeing that the dense brush and trees were impeding their forward progress.

It took over an hour of battle, before it finally stopped. Moric had remained in place, thankful that Milja's squad had joined him. He took inventory of his body to make sure he wasn't hit. A strange feeling of detachment came over him. He could have easily been killed. Killed. He let that thought sink in – but only for a moment. Staying with it would serve no purpose. He lifted himself out of the trench to join the others.

The enemy had retreated. Patrols of Partisans left their positions to scour the area for any remaining fascist soldiers. One squad discovered a ragtag dozen or so ill-equipped Croatian Home Guard soldiers. The Partisans took their weapons and marched them back to their camp, now established behind a ridge.

"Machi," Milja called, "go back to battalion headquarters and let them know we're coming with prisoners. They'll give you our next orders."

For Moric time had sped up. He needed to focus on the assignment he had just been given. Yet, his head spun after just witnessing a heated battle. Death surrounded him, and it was hard to internalize any of it. He tried to calm himself by taking deep breaths as Mika had taught him. It worked, though only marginally.

He picked up his rucksack which contained some food, water, binoculars, and his rifle. This was going to be his first big test as a courier on the battlefield. Headquarters was not very far, perhaps five kilometers away, but there were enemy soldiers on Mt. Kozara. Before leaving, he found Djuro.

"That was rough. How are you doing?" Moric asked.

"I'm good now. I couldn't think about anything but shooting the enemy. My mind went blank. It was me or them, that's all I knew."

"I'm still shaking, but I've been ordered to go to battalion headquarters to tell them to expect prisoners," Moric said.

"You can do it. I know you can since you know this mountain well. Just stay low if you hear anyone. Use your binoculars before you move anywhere. You got it?"

"I know. I'll see you tomorrow."

"Be safe, comrade."

Without hesitation, Moric took off using the map he had been given. He had read maps before, but he needed to orient himself. He saw that the sun was getting low, and he headed in its direction.

He had done some solo runs bringing orders and information to other units, but never during such a tense time. He had been to battalion headquarters once before, and this gave him a bit more confidence. He hoped that the enemy didn't know its location, hidden deep in the forest and covered in camouflage.

Moric was alert to any sound. He heard the evening birds chirp, the creeks gurgle, and the gentle wind whisk through the tall branches of the fir and oak groves.

Sitting on a downed tree trunk to rest and gather himself, he took out his canteen and sipped slowly. As he screwed the top back on, he heard something that stood out from the natural sounds he had been surrounded by. Voices. Croatian voices.

Moric dove into brush, praying that they would cover him. He wedged his slight frame deeper as he burrowed himself into the bushes.

He could hear what he guessed was a small patrol. Unable to see through the thick greenery, he raised his head slightly, and noticed four Croatian troops, perched about 50 meters away. One of them pulled out a flask. As they each took a swig, he realized that it didn't contain water. He could hear them praising the rakija, a fruit-infused brandy. The laughter got louder. They were bragging about killing villagers. One of them said he could top that – he had taken a teenage girl into a barn and had had his way with her before he slit her throat. They all laughed.

Moric saw no way out – nowhere to run if they saw him. He remained motionless, controlling his breath, fearing any sound could give him away. The sun was sinking rapidly as the soldiers grew drunker. Suddenly one of them stood up, announcing his need to relieve himself. He staggered over to where Moric was hiding, yelling: "I'll just find a nice bush and mark my territory."

His comrades laughed uncontrollably.

The man was coming closer. Moric made a slow move toward his rucksack. He opened it and felt for his rifle, quietly pulling it out. Was this the time he would have to use it? Could he use it?

In an instant the man tripped and fell to the ground. He uttered a string of curses while his friends laughed loudly, and said, "Don't piss in your pants, Marko. We don't have a change of clothes for you."

More laughter.

The man pulled himself up and peed right where Moric was. He turned around and walked back unsteadily.

"Give me one more sip. I deserve it for all the pain I feel."

After tipping back the flask, tapping the bottom to see if he could coax out any of the remaining brandy, he handed it back to one of the Croatians. "It's empty. Damn you."

"We need to get out of here anyway. It's getting dark and I don't want to run into those damn Partisans."

With that, the four lifted themselves up, grabbed their rifles and helmets, and reversed course, disappearing into the woods.

Moric took in a very deep breath and exhaled slowly. He knew it would be safest at battalion headquarters. He slipped the rucksack onto his back and straightened out his cap. Exiting the brush that saved his life, Moric looked around before resuming his mission. Within an hour, he arrived at headquarters.

As he walked into the camp the following day, Moric went directly to Luka Juric. He had completed the second part of his assignment, returning to his unit with new instructions.

"How did it go? Do you have our new orders?"

"Yes, Commander. Here they are."

Juric took the paper. His grim expression told the boy a lot. "Thank you, son."

Moric felt proud that Luka Duric appreciated his work; it eased his dislike of the brigade leader a notch.

After leaving Duric, Moric immediately went to find Djuro and Mika to recount what happened.

"Oh, God," Mika said.

"It was a close call. And when I returned with a message for Commander Juric, he just stared at it. He didn't look very happy."

Mika and Djuro briefly glanced at each other, and then turned back toward Moric.

"Well, good work. Go get some food, and meet us back here," Djuro said.

"I have a strong feeling we'll need to leave this place very soon," Moric said.

He grabbed water, bread, and apple jam, quickly ate, and went back to see Mika. He remembered what happened the night before and added it to the stock of wartime experiences that he was amassing daily.

"We were definitely worried about you last night," Mika said.

"I'm okay. I'm glad those soldiers were drunk, or it may have been a different story for me."

Mika put her hand on his shoulder and gave it a gentle squeeze.

She had a way of always making him feel cared for. Mika, once again, lifted up his spirits. He recognized that his feelings were stronger than just friendship, but he was much younger than her, and he knew there would never be any reciprocity on her part.

Moric found Djuro packing up. They greeted each other, relieved that the day's events were behind them.

No sooner had they finished gathering their things than the foreboding sounds of Luftwaffe planes could be heard closing in on their position, but the Partisans were embedded too deeply in the forest to be seen by the pilots and their gunners.

16 THE PARTISAN AIR FORCE

The journey to leave Mount Kozara was in front of them. Moric's unit was camped out in Lusci Palanka, a small town where his parents once lived. The lushness of the mountain, imbued with late spring freshness, seemed almost misplaced amidst the dangers surrounding their location.

It was silent for Moric and his comrades, with the Luftwaffe returning to its base from its search. So it was a surprise when overhead a small 1920s French-made Potez 25, formerly of the Yugoslav Air Force with red star emblazoned on each side, noisily touched down on an open field where Moric's unit was camped out.

A patrol of Partisans was dispatched to intercept whomever had piloted the aircraft, and bring him back to their encampment. The small patrol of six, led by Milja, quickly moved through the woods. Luka Juric peered at the activity below through his binoculars. He told his aid that the pilot had been taken and was headed up the hill with the patrol. Within minutes they arrived.

"Comrade," Milja said to Juric, "this is Franjo Kluz and his engineer, Andro Saric. Comrade Kluz and his engineer stole that old biplane at the Urije Airport and landed here knowing that we were in control of this area."

"Pleased to meet you, Commander. We've left the Ustasha in Banja Luka to join the Partisans. Our sympathies are shared by more than a few of us in the Ustasha government there, and are quietly making their presence known. I'm a pilot, so my presence might be a bit, well, let's say, noisier."

Juric grinned.

"Me and a few other Croatians who defected are the new Partisan Air force. Not much of a force, I must say. But others have created a bomb factory underground, and we're also dropping leaflets in villages on Kozara to encourage the people to join the fight."

"We've heard reports about that."

"I plan on dropping some bombs on the Germans and their friends here on the mountain. Of course, I'm outnumbered, but they don't know that, so I'll get my plane up and running again, and take to the sky. If it's alright with you, may I stay with your unit for a bit until I move on?"

"Of course," Juric said. "I'll see that you're welcomed by the others here." Juric shouted, seeing Machi stand nearby, "Help Comrade Kluz with his accommodations."

Moric was staring at the pilot and plane. He had never met a pilot or seen a plane this close before. He was excited.

"Machi!" Luka Juric yelled.

"Oh, sorry Commander. Coming right away." He couldn't believe it. Juric wanted him to set up the guests. He hardly felt capable of setting himself up, let alone a pilot and his engineer.

"Yes, Commander. Thank you. I'll take Comrade Kluz and engineer Saric to get some food and supplies."

Moric escorted the men to get what they needed. He had so many questions... *How had Kluz managed to get away from the Ustasha in Banja Luka, drop leaflets and bombs, and end up here? This was an incredibly brave man.*

Kluz was very easygoing. He instantly struck up a conversation with Moric as they walked. "You're young, my friend. I can't remember much when I was your age. I'm guessing you're about 12 or 13. I recall I was about that age when I wanted to be a pilot."

Moric started chatting incessantly. "Comrade, I want to be a pilot, too. My father used to give me military magazines, and I stared at the pictures of the pilots and their planes. I went to picture shows sometimes to watch the newsreels that showed air force planes. I just loved it! And–"

"Bravo. Maybe this is something you'll do when you're older?" Kluz interjected.

"What's it like? I mean, when you're up in the air?"

Kluz smiled. "I feel as birds must feel. Though I have to admit, my old French biplane is not much of a bird. The German Luftwaffe are like eagles compared to my little finch."

"Can I see your plane some time?"

"Sure thing. I'd be happy to show it to you. How about tomorrow before I make another leaflet run?"

"Yes. Thank you!"

Moric floated about the camp after his conversation with Kluz. Following the evening meal, he cleaned up and went to sleep early, knowing that Kluz would be heading out on his mission at sunrise.

That night, Moric dreamed he was flying a biplane with a flock of birds accompanying him. They were soaring high into the clouds, and then diving down, almost touching the farmlands that dotted the mountainside before rising again.

At dawn, he found Kluz already dressed in his pilot's gear, ready to walk over to the plane hidden in the nearby brush. Moric eagerly accompanied the pilot. He observed the movements of the men as they checked the plane for any damage, and then they hopped in and started the engine. The single propeller began to turn and then kicked into its high-speed rotation.

Moric could feel the wind generated by the spinning blades. As the plane started to move, Kluz turned his gaze to Moric and gave him a thumbs-up. The boy was grinning from ear to ear. He watched as the plane disappeared from view.

Kluz returned later that morning after a successful run. As the men entered the camp, Moric waved.

Kluz nodded his head, and went to Juric's tent to report his activity. All Moric could think about was seeing the plane again. This time, he wanted to ask Kluz questions about how it worked mechanically.

Later that day, Kluz agreed to show Moric the plane and teach him about it.

During Kluz's month-long stay in the camp, Moric's curiosity was piqued. Not only did he learn about the mechanics of the plane, but Kluz also shared stories of his recent exploits deceiving the Ustasha and carrying out missions over enemy territory. When he departed the camp, he sought out Moric to bid farewell. "My boy, I have no doubt that if you want to be a pilot, you will be someday. You're a quick learner. Your interest in how things work is rare, especially for someone your age. I was like that. I hope to see you in the Partisan Air Force, which will grow a hundredfold someday. I'll be looking for you."

Moric beamed, though he was sad to see the man go. He worried that the powerful Luftwaffe might not want to see Kluz in the sky, but he pushed that thought away and waved goodbye, knowing that his desire to be a pilot was now cemented.

While helping Kluz, Moric had stumbled upon an old, tattered notebook and ink pen in a pile of supplies. He decided to start recording some of his thoughts about his life with the Partisans. It would be a diary of sorts.

He sat under a large oak tree, filtered sun hitting the ground around him, as he reflected on where his life had taken him. He didn't intend to write long-winded entries; instead, he planned to write the gist of what intrigued or worried him.

He wasn't the best writer in school, but he remembered one of his teachers saying that writing could free the mind, and that students like him should have no problem putting words on paper. Though he hadn't paid much attention to that teacher before, at this moment the man's words resonated with him.

Pen to paper, he wrote some thoughts that popped into his head: *Birds fly, why can't I?* He smiled at this rhyme. *Can I, Moric, help to fight the fascists? I'm not that strong. I've never been very strong. But meeting some people here in my unit makes me feel a little safer. And meeting Franjo Kluz was something I'll never forget. I want to be a pilot like him and someday, I will be.*

Moric closed his notebook and found a secret lining in his rucksack. He tucked it inside and promised that he would write in it periodically to "free the mind." Before zipping up the lining, he saw something he had forgotten about. It was his grandfather's marble; the one that brought him good luck. He put his hand around the glass and said a little prayer to stay safe that he had learned in his Hebrew studies. Of course, he knew that a good luck marble and a Hebrew prayer were incongruous, but he wanted all the help he could get.

So much had happened to him in a short time. He zipped up the lining of his rucksack and stood. There was more than one way to free the mind, he thought. If he ever saw that teacher again, he would let him know.

17 BREAKING THROUGH THE RING

There was increasing evidence that the Germans were planning something. What that was, couldn't fully be anticipated. Battalion Headquarters' message to Luka Juric was that the enemy's goal was likely to encircle the Partisans around the mountain, and cut off any chance for the outnumbered liberators and civilians to escape. The enemy had more than 50,000 troops in their several regiments, armored vehicles, and tanks. However, the well-honed tactics of the Partisans attack – retreat into the mountains, move elsewhere, and attack again – often caught the invaders and their allies by surprise.

In less than three weeks, the Partisans, though inflicting many casualties on the enemy, suffered their own great losses. They had to find a way to break through the ring that the Germans were forming around them.

Moric was told he would remain at the rear of the newly designated First Shock Brigade that would attempt to bring themselves and thousands of civilians through the encirclement. The new brigade was going to head along the Sava River into the "Free Territory" of Bosnia, which was still controlled by the Partisans. The plan was to be set into motion at midnight.

On the day the brigade planned to escape over Mount Kozara, there was a lull in the invading forces' attacks. Moric, Mika, and Djuro made preparations.

Moric had a faraway look.

"You seem distracted today. Am I right?" Mika asked.

"Oh, it's nothing. I'm thinking about what an upside-down world we live in. My mother used to use that expression once in a while. It certainly fits now. I'm also a little tired."

"We can't be too tired, we have a dangerous trek tonight," Djuro said. "And we must keep trying to make the world right-side up."

"I know. But... well... I'm hoping that we get through. I'll be ready. It's just that I hate what's happening to the people of Yugoslavia."

"Exactly. That's why we're going to defeat the fascists," Djuro said.

"I don't know if I should think or even say this, but I will. Sometimes I wonder if I'll make it out, and if the two of you will make it out. So many of our comrades are gone already. I see them in my dreams sometimes. I see the wounded people here, and I know that they're feeling pain. It's hard to see."

"You care so much for such a young boy. I'll bet you've grown ten years since being with us. I know that's not a good thing for you, but we have to keep up our fight, and someday you'll see that it was worth it," Mika said.

"But when?"

"When we defeat the occupiers," she replied.

This time, Djuro put his arm around his friend. "I'm not that much older than you. I hate what's happening to our Yugoslavia, too. I never thought of myself doing this either, but here we are. I just don't think about anything other than what we have to do now. If I did, I would never stop worrying."

"I guess you're right. I'll do what I've been trying to do for the past months: what's asked of me. Forget about everything else. I'll try that, Djuro, I really will."

When Djuro removed his arm from Moric's shoulder, Mika put her arm around him and squeezed. "I'm happy that you tell us when you're not feeling right. It's important that you don't keep it inside. I learned that lesson not too long ago. It's too painful the other way."

Moric smiled at his friends, reassured by their words and warmth.

Moric pulled out his camera. This was a moment to be captured. Partisans were cleaning their guns, a few nurses and medics present were attending to the wounded, and civilians were huddling near each other.

There wasn't much food. It had to be rationed. Children and older people got theirs first. Adults, including those who were to lead the charge, went next, and all others went last.

Moric looked around at what the civilians were doing. Some were praying, some were consoling others, many were quietly talking about the difficult journey ahead.

With a backdrop of overcast, deep in the woods, the camera caught the expressions worn by its subjects: an older woman, peering upward with hands against her chest in prayer; a farmer, perhaps 30 years old, with creases in his forehead that made him look much older, staring into the distance; a mother cradling her infant son, trying to smile at the baby, dark circles under her eyes; another man in his early twenties, a peasant with a hardened look of determination, cleaning out a rifle.

Moric tried to ensure that his pictures captured the fortitude that kept those on "the side of right" from ever giving up. His mentor Ivan's words were etched in every click of his camera: "Let our people know what we fight for. Let them know we want them to join that fight."

He wandered around the camp snapping away. One thing in particular caught his eye. It was the boy he had bandaged earlier; the one whose sister had led him back to the fleeing villagers when the Stukas were unleashing their terror. His sister was not with him.

He didn't want to be intrusive, but he had a sinking feeling in the pit of his stomach. As he came closer, the boy looked up. Moric lowered the camera to his side.

One of the adults nearby beckoned Moric over to her. "You were the nice boy who helped Jakov. His leg is better now. You're so young yourself, but your actions were that of a grown man."

"Thank you," Moric said. "I'm glad Jakov is better. May I ask, where is his sister?"

"That's why I asked you to join me over here. She's dead."

Moric gasped. "My God."

"She was very brave, too. A few days ago, when we were all fleeing into the woods a bomb – I think it's called a mortar – exploded near her."

"Where was Jakov?"

"Fortunately, Jakov was with me because I told his sister, Jelena, I could take her brother for a while to give her a break."

"He would have been killed, too," Moric said. "My God!"

"I am so sad for this little boy. He lost his parents, and now his sister. I pray that we make it through. My husband and I will take him in. Our children are grown, although God knows where they are now."

"Maybe they're with the Partisans, too."

"I hope so. You're a wise young man. I wish this would end soon, so we could all be reunited, but I'm afraid it'll be a long time. By the way, my name is Radmila."

"I'm Milan, but they call me Machi."

"Ahh, like a wildcat.."

They both smiled.

"Why don't you go say hello to Jakov. I think he'd like that."

Moric thanked Radmila for telling him about Jakov and walked over to the young boy. He could see the redness in his eyes.

"Jakov, that's your name, right?"

"Yes," the boy said, eyes facing down as he scratched at the dirt with a small stick.

"How's your leg?"

"It still hurts sometimes, but it's getting better. I saw you talking to Radmila. Did she tell you about Jelena?"

"Yes, I'm sorry. Radmila is nice. She said she'll help you."

"I know. I want my sister and my parents. I want to go home."

"Me too, but we can't. I don't know where my parents and sisters are, just like you."

"You don't?"

"No. They're missing. Or maybe I'm missing. Sometimes I don't know what to think. You need to try to be strong. Your family would have wanted that. I know that mine would want that for me. Can you do that? Stay close to

Radmila and her husband. They'll take care of you. If you need me, I'll help you out, too."

"What's your name?"

"Milan. But you can call me Machi."

To Moric's surprise, Jakov stood and gave him a big hug.

Moric felt an emptiness that stabbed at his heart. He promised himself and his friends that he would only think of what he was doing at that moment, but Jakov touched him.

A steady rain had begun to fall as the light of day faded. It was time to get ready for the unknown.

It was very dark. The rain had only recently stopped, and the ground was still slick and muddy.

The Partisans had sent out numerous patrols to sabotage the enemy's equipment, laying mines near their encampments before scampering back to their own position. The plan was to divert the enemy away from the passage that several Partisan squads, along with thousands of civilians and an equal number of the wounded, were going to take. The First Shock Brigade broke off into several smaller units. Mika and Djuro were split up into different squads.

It was after midnight when the diversionary tactics began. Several units were on the opposite side, away from the Sava River escape route, to draw the fascist soldiers away from the Sava River escape route.

Moric, some of the other younger Partisans, the civilians, and the wounded, waited for the signal that the German and Croatian positions had been breached. They were joined by Partisan fighters waiting to lead the way out.

The sounds of the fighting pierced the damp, heavy air, while blasts from the German cannons lit up the sky as it rained death upon its targets. The smell of gunpowder and diesel fuel permeated their noses.

Moric's thoughts wandered to what it would feel like if, or rather when, he would be in the direct line of fire. His stomach's queasy response required him to refocus on the task at hand.

Sunrise was about five hours away when the Commander was alerted that the time had come to move.

All those who joined the exodus were instructed to remain as quiet as possible. The bulk of the fighting force remained behind, leaving last. The rest escorted the civilians as they pushed forward.

The air was damp and cool, causing Moric to shiver, though he wasn't sure if it was due to the temperature or his fear. He found Jakov, and the little boy took his hand, which Moric gently squeezed. Radmila was right behind them; her husband had joined the fight earlier.

Each grouping of civilians had ten Partisan fighters assigned to them. Moric was glad that Milja was in his group, bringing up the rear.

"Forward!" commanded Bogdan, a patrol leader at the head of his group.

Moric squeezed Jakov's hand a little tighter. That particular command, simple as it was, gave him a sense of foreboding. In fact, Djuro had told him that sometimes he would scream that command in his restless sleep.

He turned around to see Radmila right behind him, and Milja just behind her. They pushed up a dirt path and through overgrown bushes. Thus far, the escapees managed to avoid the enemies who were distracted by fighting to the east. Still, the explosions and gunshots whistling through the woods brought gasps from many of the civilians.

The group slowed down to cautiously skirt a deep, wide mud puddle. Moric tried to slow down Jakov, but the impatience of a seven-year-old is not always easy to manage. As he was about to tell the boy to slow down, their hands parted. Jakov immediately fell over an embankment next to their path and tumbled down the hill.

"Jakov!" Radmila yelled.

The Sava River was down below. Though the hill wasn't steep, the river's currents were strong. Moric's immediate reaction was to yell for help, but with explosions nearby, it was hard for anyone to hear. He headed through the bushes after him.

Radmila kept calling for the boy.

Moric ducked under tree branches, calling out for Jakov. He lost his footing and tumbled towards the river but latched his arms around a tree trunk before falling in. He steadied himself, looking up and down the river for

Jakov. Nothing. He got up and began to follow the direction of the river's flow.

Out of nowhere, Moric spotted Milja along the river's edge.

"Milja! Milja! Over here!"

Milja was soaking wet. Water was dripping from his clothing. He was carrying a crying Jakov, also drenched.

"Machi! Grab Jakov's hand."

Milja practically pushed the two boys up the hill. When they got back to their escape route, Radmila was only a few meters away, as was the rest of their group.

"Jakov!" Radmila yelled.

Bogdan grabbed the boys and pulled them up the last two meters. Radmila hugged Jakov and dug inside her rucksack, pulling out three small blankets to wrap around them, placing the last blanket around Milja, and kissing him on the forehead.

As they all turned to resume their escape, prayers of thanks quietly echoed along the line.

Moric walked behind Radmila and Jakov, just ahead of Milja. He briefly turned around and smiled at the man behind him to acknowledge the gratitude he felt. Milja gave him a wink and a thumbs-up.

Moric's thoughts turned to how he had just risked his own safety, maybe even his life, to help Jakov. He hadn't hesitated for a moment in going after him.

The groups of Partisans, civilians, and wounded who had gone out ahead of the diversionary maneuvers finally made it out, but thousands did not.

As his group joined with many others deep in the valley on the other side of the mountain, Moric decided that the exhaustion and strain of the previous night's escape were not something he wanted to capture with his camera. *Too many of our comrades were left behind and lost. Too many suffering civilians.* He had no desire to photograph anyone or anything in the wake of such destruction. He was grateful for those who were saved, but needed time, as did most everyone, to take stock of what they had just survived.

He sat with some comrades as they shared cold potatoes and old fruit. Most were silently chewing, eyes dulled by the expended energy.

Moric thought about what had happened with Jakov. *Poor Jakov has been through so much. I'm so glad Milja acted quickly. He proves again that ordinary people can be heroes. Where did I hear that? My father.*

Moric looked around for Mika and Djuro, but didn't see them. He was too tired to get up, and he also felt a pain in his lower right leg. Glancing down, he saw some blood had pooled at his calf. Pulling up his pant leg, he discovered a gash. In that moment of calm, however temporary, he realized that the emotional ride they had all taken had submerged any recognition of his own injury. Now he could feel the stinging sensation.

Radmila, who was giving Jakov the few morsels of food that were being passed around, noticed Moric grimacing. "Machi, may I see your leg?"

"Oh, it's nothing. I must have scratched it when I went down to find Jakov."

Radmila lifted his pant leg. "I don't think that's what it is. I'll go find someone to take a look."

Moric was in more pain than he'd revealed to Radmila. He welcomed her help, sucking in his breath with each throb, trying to be brave.

Radmila returned with one of the medics. Most of the medics were untrained, but it was their role to do what they could under the dire circumstances that the Partisans often found themselves in.

Pulling up Moric's pants exposed an oozing wound.

"It looks like a bullet grazed your leg. We don't want to see the wound get infected."

As he cleaned it out, Moris grit his teeth. The realization that he had been shot, mixed with the pain from the wound being cleaned, almost caused him to pass out. But when he saw looks of concern from Radmila and Jakov, he took stock of what they had all gone through, and thought about anything but his own fears.

The medic put iodine on the wound and wrapped a long bandage around his leg. He told Moric that he would check on him later.

Moric thanked the man and Radmila. He sat back taking in a deep breath. Radmila gave him his canteen for a drink of water.

As the stinging somewhat subsided, Mika and Djuro found him. Their faces were drawn from the escape, but their concern for their friend took precedence.

"We heard about your leg," Mika said. "But it looks like you'll be fine. We'll make sure you keep it clean. I told the medic that I had some supplies, so he can tend to others."

Moric felt whole again with his friends there. They all settled down for the night, though it would not be easy for anyone to rest, let alone sleep. He was turning 13 in a few months, but he was starting to feel like his childhood had never actually taken place.

18 CAKE

The Partisans entered towns and villages to recruit fighters and supporters for the liberation. It was mid-winter 1943 and Prijedor was back in their hands.

Moric's unit was in the nearby hills not too far from family friends who lived there. He wanted to go and see them if this it was at all possible. They were like an aunt and uncle to him. He hoped they hadn't been discovered by the Germans.

He told Peja that since Prijedor was now under Partisan control, he'd like to take the opportunity to visit his family. If they were not there, he assured him, he'd be back in no time.

"Stay alert. Things change quickly, as you know very well," Peja said.

"I'm Machi. I always look before I leap."

Peja's laugh was muted by concerns the veteran fighter had for his young comrade.

Moric knocked on the solid wooden door until Jovan opened it with a start. His shock quickly melted into a wide grin as he hugged the boy. "Magda, you'll never guess who's here?"

Magda joined the two of them as the door closed. "My God, Moric!"

Magda wrapped her arms around him. She was rather thin, his arms almost made it all the way around her.

"What are you doing here?"

"I've been with the Partisans since this past fall when they found me in the mountains. We're nearby, so I thought I'd come here to visit you."

Moric scanned the small, single level home. It was like he remembered cozy. When his family visited before the war, they were always greeted by the smell of stews, roasts, soups, and cakes that "Magda the Magician," as her family called her, had prepared before they even entered the home.

"Smells just like I remember. What cake are you baking now?" Moric asked.

"It's a cornmeal cake and it just came out of the oven. With less supplies available, I have to resort to simpler fare," Magda replied.

"But no less delicious," responded Jovan.

Moric proceeded to tell them about his life, including not knowing what happened to his parents and sisters.

"I'm so sorry. Your poor family. You poor boy," Magda said. "We don't know where some of our family is either. We know that some tried to escape, but to where, I have no idea. My guess is that they either joined the Partisans, like you did, or the Ustasha or Germans got them. For now, we feel safe."

"You have to be very careful," said Moric. "I hear the Nazis show up without much warning. What did you do when they attacked Prijedor before we drove them out?"

"We hid in our attic and they didn't find us. We stored some food up there, along with blankets and some other supplies. Now that the Partisans are in control, we can resume a somewhat easier existence. But we know that what you say is true."

Moric remembered that Jovan had injured himself a few years ago from a fall while trying to patch their roof. His broken leg went untreated for a long time, leaving him unable to move quickly.

"How's your leg, Jovan?"

"I'll put it to you this way, do you remember that American track star, Jesse Owens? The one who put Hitler in his place? Well, that's not me," he said with a hearty laugh.

"Enough of this talk, let me get you a big piece of cake while it's still warm. I have some fresh milk to go with it, a rare pleasure these days. Please sit down at the table and I'll cut you a slice. If I know you, I think one slice won't be enough, so you can start with two," a smiling Magda added. They never had any children themselves, but knew exactly what a child needed.

"Moric," Jovan asked, "where is your unit now?"

"Some are here in Prijedor, others are nearby in the hills. I told my patrol leader that I'd be coming here. I wasn't sure I'd find you, but seeing you and eating this delicious cake makes me glad I did."

"Thank you. There's plenty more for you. I'll even cut you a large piece to take before you leave," Magda said.

Moric bit into his second piece when Magda sprung from the table to the window. "Moric, you must be in a powerful army, there are tanks rolling through town. Look!"

Moric chewed as he walked over to look at what Magda was seeing. The roar of tank engines pierced the stucco walls of the small house, rattling the windows. "My God," he shouted, "those iron crosses on the tanks are German; that's the German army! You two need to hide. Put away the cake and plates. Don't leave anything to let them know you're here. Head up into the attic. I have to go. I'm sorry. Thank you. I'm glad I came here, but I have to leave before they find me. Please be safe." He headed toward the back door.

"But the Sana River is back there. It's freezing now. How can you get across?" Magda yelled.

"I'll swim if I have to."

"But Moric–"

"Magda, he has to flee. And we have to hide!" shouted Jovan.

Moric quickly left the house and slid down the hill that led to the river. The bridge he had crossed to get there was too far away and too risky. There was no time to think. The Germans were retaking Prijedor. He worried for his friends, but right now he had to swim across the narrow, rapidly moving water. He saw no other way. At least he would find warmth and dry clothes when he got to his unit.

He took off his boots and tied them to his belt so the current wouldn't carry them away. He put his wool cap inside the deep pocket of his jacket. As he jumped in, he didn't stop to think about how cold and difficult swimming across would be. It was 40 meters to the other side but this was better than being caught by the Germans.

The water was frigid. He kicked as hard as he could, steadily pulling his arms with each stroke. The torrent was choppy and waves were moving over his head, but he tried to ignore them. Normally a good river swimmer, his clothing made it hard to move. He held his breath as long as he could, so that he wouldn't swallow any water. When he had to exhale, he forced the air through mouth and nose. The temperature of the water froze him, but he just kept pumping his arms and legs toward the other shore.

Losing all sense of time, he finally pulled himself out. He quickly put on his soaked boots. His adrenaline carried him up the embankment toward where he had left his unit.

The ground was slippery with ice; he kept falling back before steadying his stride to go forward. When he reached the top there were no signs that anyone had ever been there. They must have seen the tanks, packed their gear, and fled.

Moric stood there breathless, scanning the terrain, he only saw trees and bushes. He hastily walked further up the mountain looking for any signs of his unit. Nothing. He was soaking wet and shivering now.

After 30 minutes, his search unrewarded, Moric desperately needed to find shelter. During the winter the sun sets early in the mountains.

He left the wooded area and stepped onto a plain. In the distance, he could still vaguely discern the contours of a house. It was probably the home of a farmer whose small plot of land and barn provided some meager form of livelihood. He hoped that whoever lived there was friendly.

Nearing the house with its peeling outer walls, he saw an old wooden cart at the barn door with a horse's harness on the ground next to it. He opened the door, but there was no sign of any livestock.

He walked to the front door of the house and knocked. He listened for any indication that someone might be inside, but it was silent. He jiggled the door handle and pushed the door forward, stepping inside. It was dark and chilly inside.

He could feel his body shiver, his clothing and boots were stiff with ice. He needed to warm up. Moric recalled his mother often telling him that he would catch a cold if he didn't dry off and change into warm clothes after coming in from the rain or snow. This situation was much more dire.

He looked around the small confines. It was sparsely furnished with oil lamps in a bedroom and kitchen. He bypassed those, spotting a wood-burning stove against the far wall opposite a torn couch, with a mottled throw rug in front of it. Next to the stove was a box of wooden matches. Split wood was piled behind the old stove. He found a container of oil inside a cupboard in the kitchen.

Placing the wood inside the stove, he doused a small piece of kindling with oil and lit it. A flicker became a flame, which lit the larger piece of wood above it. In a few minutes, Moric added another piece of wood. He placed his boots and wet clothes at the foot of the stove. The numbness in his fingers and toes were fading.

He was keenly aware that the smoke rising through the small pipe could attract unwanted visitors. However, he was too cold to not take the risk.

Naked, he found a small blanket, an Afghan, not unlike one that his mother had crocheted. This one was nothing like his old one. The colors were muted and it was covered with dust and dirt. No matter, he needed something to keep warm. He sat on the couch, blanket wrapped around him, and watched the fire in the stove through a small grill on the door. Hypnotized by the glow, he thought about Prijedor and what happened to his comrades. Where were they? He was back on a mountain – a lone wolf again, needing to find his pack. *Where are you Mamma and Papa, Mika and Djuro, Peja, anyone?*

There was a steady wind outside, and a draft came in from the leaky front window.

He thought he heard voices, but it was his imagination. He quietly sang a song that his mother used to sing to him when he was frightened.

Moric woke with a start the next morning, the sun barely visible over the edge of the mountain. The fire was out, replaced by the chill of winter.

He lifted himself up and moved toward the wood-burning stove to feel his clothing, which were still damp. He removed the Afghan and put the clothing back on.

Now, hunger had found him. He went to see if he could find any food. Nothing. *If only I had taken some of the cake that Magda had said she would give to me.* Then he remembered that it wouldn't have survived his plunge into the river.

In one corner of the ceiling, Moric noticed a spider with a fly in its web. *The spider has its breakfast, but I'm no spider.* He needed to find his unit, find safety, and find food.

Leaving the house with a cup and the blanket, Moric headed further into the woods. He needed to look for signs that his comrades were in the area. Typically, the brigade would scatter to make it harder for the enemy to find them if they were on the run. That his comrades were like ghosts, easily disappearing into the forest, would now be a disadvantage.

The cold pierced his clothing again. He was famished. He came across a stream and dipped his cup into the frigid water.

He slowly sipped the water. To his right, he saw winter berries dangling from a bush. Memories of his time after escaping Drvar were rekindled. He gobbled down the fruit and found some winter chicory, complete with its displeasing bitter taste. His shivering was becoming more pronounced. He pulled the Afghan around his shoulders; it didn't help him much. He wasn't feeling well at all.

Moric continued to wander around the mountainside for his unit or some of its members. The coughing began slowly and intermittently at first. By sunset, it was more constant. His head hurt and he could feel the heat of fever on his cheeks and forehead.

He needed to rest. But where?

About ten meters to his left, he saw what looked like a hollowed-out piece of earth covered by branches that had been laid on top just slightly askew.

Partisans dug earth camps throughout the forests for comrades needing shelter. He had helped to form one on Kozara not that long ago. Sticking his head in to get a better look, he noticed a metal box. It appeared to be unlocked. Moric went inside the dugout.

Opening the box, he found dried fruit and nuts. There was also a loaf of hard bread, but it looked like it had been placed there not too long ago, perhaps by his own unit. He couldn't believe his luck. Examining the food for any mold and seeing none he scarfed it down ravenously. There was also a canteen with water that he hoped was alright.

With a raging fever, Moric laid down on the pine needle bedding. He pulled the Afghan over himself. In an instant he was drawn into sleep. Nightmares flooded him, but when he awoke the next day he couldn't recall any of them. His body was sore, likely from the swim across the river and the fever. Still, he felt a little better. The cough and fever had both diminished.

He wasn't feeling well enough to search for his unit. He needed more time to regain his strength.

He rationed the food. Though sleep overtook him, it was regularly interrupted by the strong sound of wind outside. He thought about his life while alone in the earth camp. He didn't know how he would survive like this. Despite the pervasive fear associated with surviving a war, being with the Partisans provided a level of comfort from being part of a group with the same goal. His strong connection with Mika and Djuro was especially important. Alone, he was vulnerable to the enemy and the elements. He hoped he would better soon.

The next day the cough remained. He had to find his unit. He had run low on food and water, and remaining there was no longer a viable option.

He went outside to relieve himself, and returned to eat a few nuts. He was careful to leave some of the food for whoever might find their way to the same dugout.

Moric poured the canteen water into his cup, grabbed another piece of the fruit and headed out.

While walking, he gathered whatever food the forest could provide. He put them in the pockets of his large winter coat. To his surprise, his lucky marble was inside one of the pockets. He held it tightly for a few seconds as if to draw its magic into him, before continuing his trek.

The next two days and nights were similar to the others, except he was starting to feel better.

In the morning, Moric heard voices not far from the thicket of bushes he had bedded down in. He was cold and hungry and hoped that the enemy hadn't found him. Carefully peeking though some branches, he spotted a patrol not 30 meters away. He didn't recognize any of them, but their clothing told him they were Partisans.

"Hello," he yelled. "It's Machi, a comrade. Over here."

The patrol turned, and cautiously walked toward him, spreading out in a straight line. "Don't move. Raise your hands high so we can see them. We're coming over to you."

As they approached, one of them turned to the patrol leader, saying he knew of Machi, and that he was indeed one of them.

"Okay, Machi, you can put your hands down," the leader said. "What are you doing out here all alone?"

"It's a long story, but I'll tell you in a minute. Do you have any food? I'm starving."

They all laughed and each pulled out something for Moric to eat. "No manners, Machi. You must be really hungry," said one of them, while he stuffed their offerings in his mouth without hesitation.

As they walked, he told his comrades what had happened to him, and he thought about the marble in his pocket. He touched the side of the coat where it rested, patting it ever so gently before he asked for more food.

19 MACHI'S BIRTHDAY

It had been a couple of weeks since Moric had survived his ordeal in the woods. Reports had come in that the Germans slaughtered thousands of villagers, and sent nearly 25,000 to Jasenovac, which by now was known to be a death camp. Only 900 of the 3,500 Partisans survived the battle of Mount Kozara, but the legends of the fallen heroes were spreading.

It took several weeks and a string of victories before the First Proletariat Brigade reached the small city of Bosanski Novi, the last of the villages to be liberated from the German and Croatian forces.

Moric and Mika watched as Djuro trudged up a hill to view the city and catch a moment of solace.

"Come on slow poke. What are you, tired?" teased Mika.

As he sat down next to them, Djuro said, "Yes, as a matter of fact, I am. But sitting here with you two is about as close to peace as we've had in weeks."

The three friends sat silently, looking at the city below. Djuro broke the silence. "What should we do for your birthday party, Machi?"

"You remembered?"

"Of course. You make sure we don't forget," he teased.

Mika laughed. "I remember when I turned 13. Four years ago. How can I forget? What could possibly get in the way of me remembering such an auspicious milestone in my life?" With a smile she continued. "There was a huge celebration in the Krajina. The mayor of my village was there, and he presented me with a beautiful sash with the Kingdom's colors. When he put it on me, the villagers cheered and yelled their approval. A band played in the square to honor me."

"That's amazing," Moric said, facing her wide-eyed.

"And then I woke up!" teased Mika, as they all laughed.

"We'd better get back to camp. No time for planning Machi's big event. Sorry, no mayor and no band for you this year, my little wildcat," said Djuro.

They went back down the hill and joined the rest of the brigade, which had set up its camp outside the city. Sporadic fighting continued inside Bosanski Novi, but it was tame compared to what they had experienced before.

It didn't take long for Bosanski Novi to be totally in Partisan control.

Moric carried several rolls of undeveloped film. He had been tasked with carrying supplies as the brigade marched to its victories, leaving him with no time and space to develop them. Now, he finally had a brief window to attend to them.

Photography was his safe space, his sanctuary, even if it meant processing film outdoors. As the sun set, he removed the dark cloth from his rucksack. He dreamed of the day he could use the enlarger to see his negatives become proofs, and proofs become actual photographs. He removed the first roll of film and began the development process, continuing until all the rolls were negatives.

Viewing the negatives one by one revealed the genesis of each shot's story. It was like viewing history, recent, of course, but with a rich story.

Sadly, some of the comrades who were staring at him or posing bravely had given their lives.

Using the hand lens, Moric focused at one negative in particular. He had caught Mika looking away as the sun set after a grueling battle.

In the negative her face had a somewhat mysterious look. He couldn't make out minute details, but he could tell that she was drained. Moric badly wanted to make this into a photograph. Even in an exhausted state she was beautiful. There was no mystery in that.

Deep inside, he felt a strong bond with her that had begun from the first day they'd met. He wished he were older so his age wouldn't matter to her, maybe she'd like him in a different way. At least they were close friends.

As he completed the process, Ivan came over and asked how it went.

"I've developed three rolls and placed them in the sack."

"I figured as much. You were over here for a long time. You show great patience. I'm proud of you."

Moric was happy to hear the praise. He needed it at that moment. The violence and loss brought him down. Immersing himself in photographic work, even if just producing negatives, helped take his mind off the hell they experienced.

The next day Moric turned 13. *My parents would have had a family celebration with Mamma and my aunts making a delicious dinner.*

In Jewish tradition today was his bar mitzvah, a milestone to acknowledge a boy's entry into adulthood. In normal times, he would have read from the Torah at the synagogue in Sanski Most. This was always a day of pride. Yet today, he had simply turned another year older with no recognition of the significance it had in his life.

The evening meal, scant as it was with the usual potatoes and beets, was ready. He found Djuro sitting near the fire with some food. Djuro congratulated him. During this rare pause from the fighting, one of the fighters played the accordion while many got to their feet to dance to a traditional Yugoslavian folk song.

"Where's Mika?" Moric asked.

"She said she wasn't hungry. She grabbed a couple of roasted beets and went to lie down."

"Is she feeling alright?"

Just as he was about to delve further into the reason his friend was resting, Mika came from behind them and covered Moric's eyes. "Happy birthday!"

Moric broke free of her hands and turned around. She gave him a scarf that she had knitted for him. It was dark blue with a white stripe running down the middle.

"This is really nice. How'd you even find time to make it?"

"I have my ways," she responded.

Mika wrapped it around Moric's neck. She had brought a piece of a mirror that she kept in her rucksack. He stared at the reflection, barely recognizing the older version of himself.

"Thank you. It's... beautiful."

"Glad you like it. It'll keep you warm in the winter, which will be here before we know it."

"I have something for you too," Djuro said. He pulled out a leather case for Moric's camera.

"That's beautiful. Where'd you get that?"

"Not telling, but I'm glad you like it."

"I do. You two have made me very happy. I thought today would be just another day of liberation," he said wryly.

"Happy birthday," they each said, as they watched the festive mood engulf the fireside.

20 REMARKABLE MIKA

The city of Bihac was liberated in early November. Josip Broz Tito had relocated his Supreme Headquarters some 68 kilometers west of their camp. Consolidating many brigades in the vicinity, Tito oversaw a change that brought about an even greater sense of unity for the Partisans. The Partisans' fighting body was renamed the Yugoslav People's Army (YPA).

In addition, the anti-fascist Council of Peoples' Liberation of Yugoslavia convened that month in Bihac. This was the first session of the council with delegates from all regions of Yugoslavia, representing all nationalities and ethnicities.

Also in November 1942, orders came down for the First Proletariat Division, as it was now known, to move out from Bosanski Novi, and make the long trek westward. In the course of three weeks, it had destroyed numerous enemy garrisons and in January captured the towns of Teslic and Prnjavor.

Each victory etched its toll on Moric. The pattern was always the same: the Partisans would enter a town or village and find scenes that were almost apocalyptic – fire, smoke, dead mothers, fathers, children, and elders; smoldering homes and shops; dead animals; a village in ruins. Those who had survived were presumably sent to camps, where they would've surely died. The smell of death permeated Moric's sense of equilibrium. He tried to numb himself to the scenes before him, but his nightmares revealed the futility of his efforts. Yet, each day the numbness returned – a temporary protective mechanism.

As the Partisans achieved more victories and Tito prompted organizational changes, the Germans stepped up their attacks and destruction.

As the First Proletarian Division marched toward the Neretva River Valley spirits remained high. Climbing into the mountains proved treacherous due to the cold and snow, typical for February. However, this did not deter the hearty warriors. Final preparations were being made for their next assault before advancing to the Neretva Valley. The leaders of the Division headquarters decided that only certain brigades would battle the enemy.

Moric wrapped Mika's scarf tightly around his neck. His brigade was ordered to stand down, as only two smaller brigades were to move in on the targeted railway the next day. Another division would back them up.

Pulling out his camera, Moric thought this would be a good time to honor his comrades. Besides, he was cold and tired from the steady action they'd been engaged in, and walking around the camp would warm him up.

"Hey, Machi, come over here," said patrol leader Drago.

"What is it, comrade?" Moric asked. He smelled rakija, the fruit brandy, and cigarette smoke on the man's breath.

"I want to get a picture with Mika. You seem to have her ear," he sarcastically bemoaned amidst slurred speech. "I know you can get her to sit next to me."

Drago's entourage, which included some very gruff and drunk men, laughed. Moric realized why he had often avoided Drago.

"I don't know. I'm not even sure where she is," Moric responded.

"She's about 20 meters behind you."

Moric couldn't figure a way out of this. He had seen firsthand that Drago could be mean. He was respected as a fighter, so he had special privileges that he took advantage of.

Moric turned around to see Mika sitting with some friends on an embankment next to one of the many small fires in the camp. He walked over to her. "Mika, can I speak with you, please?"

She was the person closest to him since he joined the Partisans, and his guard was up over Drago's request.

Mika stood up. "What is it?"

"Drago saw me getting my camera ready, and he asked me to bring you over. He wants me to take pictures of the two of you. I'm sure he's drunk."

"Hmmm... I don't like him. He's someone I'd want on the battlefield with me, but off it, not so much. I don't want him to make trouble for you. Take me over to him."

Moric hesitated but did as Mika said.

They arrived back at the spot where Drago was sitting. He put the bottle of brandy near his feet. "My lovely Mika. So nice of you to join me. I was right that Machi has your ear. I think the boy likes you... a lot. But he's a boy. And I'm a man. Come sit next to me, so the boy can take our pictures."

Mika looked around at Drago's comrades before sitting next to him. Drago was acting with false bravado. The smell of alcohol and cigarette smoke hovered in the air. She sat on the ground next to him with half a meter of space between them. Drago reached out his arm and pulled her closer.

Moric flinched.

"Now that's better," Drago said.

Moric wanted to take the pictures quickly to free his friend. After he had taken five pictures, he thanked his subjects and was about to move on.

"Wait! I want more shots with your friend here." He put his arm around her shoulder and drew her closer.

"I don't need to be that close to you, comrade. And Machi has taken enough pictures of us."

"Not yet. Take more, Machi."

Moric wasn't sure what to do. Should he say he's out of film? Or that the cold froze up the lens?

As he was weighing his options, he saw something unexpected happen. Mika grabbed Drago's wrist, pulled it off her shoulder, and twisted it with force.

Drago yelped. "What are you doing?!"

"There's no need for more pictures. Time for Machi to move on to the rest of our comrades." She stood up and walked back to her friends.

Drago massaged his injured wrist. His friends teased their comrade who was not pleased with what had happened.

Moric felt relief, but he was also in awe of Mika. She was a teenager, but handled herself like an adult. He took several more photos around the camp, and then circled back to where she was sitting.

"That was quite something, Mika."

"I guess it was. I don't care who it is, they don't have a right to tell me what to do. I took some pictures with him, so he'd leave you and me alone. I've seen him look at me and I don't like it. I'm sorry you had to witness that."

"No, no. You amaze me. I just hope he doesn't bother you anymore."

"I hope so too. I'd rather not tell Juric what's going on, but if he does, I will. I know the Commander won't be pleased."

"I don't know if I'll develop those pictures. Maybe I'll just lose that roll of film."

"No, develop them. My look of disgust will definitely show. I know that this isn't what your photographs are supposed to display. Even if you send the pictures to headquarters, I can't see it being anything that they'd want."

"Probably not."

"I'm tired. I'm with one of the brigades that'll support taking over the rail station. This mission will require a fairly long trek, so it's time for me to get some sleep. You should go to sleep, too. Goodnight, my dear friend," she said as she gently touched his shoulder.

Moric reflected on how uncomfortable it had been to see Drago act that way. He felt so helpless. Mika, however, was such a powerful woman. This was part of what drew him to her. He felt safe near her. Her presence always warmed him, even on the coldest of nights.

21 SAYING GOODBYE

One of Tito's top priorities was to save the wounded. The battle for control of the city of Prozor involved a brigade deemed to be the "central column" of fighters. It was their job to clear out the Germans and establish a protective space for the wounded to escape.

All Partisan divisions in the area needed to coordinate attacks for maximum impact; they were heavily outnumbered by the Axis troops.

The First Proletarian Division sent two battalions to capture the Ivan Sedlo Pass and Rastelica Railway Station so they could gain control of the Sarajevo-Konjic rail line. The battalions would be fighting against the Ustasha Railroad Battalion and the Italian army. On February 17, the Pass was captured, and the next day the Italian forces were defeated by a surprise attack near Rastelica Railway Station. The Partisans were now in control of the Pass and the Railway Station.

Battalion Headquarters decided to leave very few troops to guard the pass. "There is no indication that the enemy is regrouping or sending in reinforcements from Sarajevo," they mistakenly informed the brigades. Troops were ordered to move on to the next rail station in Tarcin.

An additional surprise raid on Konjic, a town in Italian hands, was to be made by another two brigades attached to the First Proletarian Division. This was the fighting force Mika belonged to.

It was up to Moric to make contact with the Fifth Brigade of the Third

Division to deliver the message that all units were in place to support the attack. Djuro accompanied him on the mission.

Timing was imperative, as the two attacking battalions in Konjic required military muscle that could be provided by the Fifth Brigade. The two battalions set off for Konjic while the other battalions headed to Tarcin.

Moric and Djuro set off as couriers for this important mission. Although they packed lightly, they were dressed heavily. February was a cruel month of cold and wind. Their boots crunched the hardened snow and ice as they crisscrossed the valley and hills to connect with the Fifth Brigade.

A couple of hours into their mission, a cold and exhausted Djuro said, "If we want to survive this cold, we need to stay the night in some earth camp before we make contact with the Fifth Brigade."

"I agree," Moric replied. "The sun is setting and the icicles on my eye lashes are blocking my vision."

"Same here. It'll be so much harder to find safety when the sun is completely gone."

The two boys trudged up and down hills but remained in the woods to stay hidden from the roving eyes of fascist scouts. The wind picked up again and the snow thickened. Moric tightened his scarf, pulling it up over his chin and mouth. It was freezing.

"Djuro, where's your scarf? You're going to get frostbite."

"Unfortunately, it got torn by a branch earlier. It's still in my rucksack because I don't want to leave any trace of our presence in the woods."

"Is it of any use at all? It could at least cover part of your face?"

"No, it's useless. I'll try to cover my nose with my gloves, but I'm getting really cold. We need to find shelter soon."

Moric unwrapped his special scarf and handed it to his friend. "You take this for now. We'll share it. I don't want to have to cut off your nose because of frostbite…"

"Don't make me smile. I'm afraid I'll crack my lips wide open." Djuro took the scarf and wrapped it around his face. After some time, the warmth from his breath was slowly beginning to thaw his jaw, cheeks, and nose. "That feels better. Now let's find that earth camp. Quickly!"

They constantly slipped on the icy rocks, but miraculously, neither went down. The falling snow became more intense and further hampered their vision.

"This is getting serious," Djuro said. "We've got to find shelter."

Moric veered off to his right and Djuro followed his friend.

"Where are you going?" Djuro yelled through the sound of heavy snow-laden wind.

"I think I see our lodging for the night."

Moric moved swiftly with Djuro right behind him. They came upon a group of branches that seemed to crisscross randomly, but they gave a familiar signal to those who knew what to look for.

As they entered the small enclosure, Djuro lit a candle he had packed with his supplies. He waited for his eyes to adjust to the dimly lit hideout. He lit a torch that had been left for visitors. He placed it in a funnel carved into the dirt wall.

"And the Lord said, let there be light!" Moric boomed.

Djuro laughed. "Amen!" After a minute he asked, "How's your face?"

"Frozen. But here the wind can't touch us."

"Thanks for your scarf. It probably saved my skin from turning black from frostbite. You might have actually had to use your knife to remove my nose."

"Glad I didn't have to do that."

The boys took off their heavy coats and gloves. They left their hats on, pulling them over their ears, and set their boots aside to dry next to a small fire they'd lit in a pit in the center of the camp. Of course, they were wary of the smoke spiraling upward through a small hole in the ceiling, but with the weather and how deep they were in the woods, their fears were minimal. They pulled out some food they had taken from the camp a little raw meat and grasses. Food supplies hadn't reached their brigade in days, and lack of food was becoming a big problem.

Each of them opened their canteen and drank the frigid water, tapping their bottles repeatedly on the ground to dislodge the ice that had formed inside.

"We'll need to get an early start tomorrow. I'm hoping that the storm dies down, or we may not make it to our destination," Djuro said.

"I'm worried about that, too. What can we do if we're stalled because of the storm?"

"I don't know. We'll have to wait it out and try when we can. We have to keep the timing in mind to make sure we don't get to them before they move elsewhere."

"Let's make sure we get out of here as soon as the sun comes up."

Djuro took a bite of meat, chewing steadily to soften it.

"You've been with us for over a year; I've been with the battalion for about 18 months. Doesn't it seem like this is all we've been doing for our entire lives?"

"I'm having trouble remembering my life in Drvar. It seems such a long time ago. When I stop to think about it, I can't help but wonder where my parents and sisters are. I miss my old life."

"Me too. I can't believe that this is what we're doing. I used to like playing soccer on a field near my house. I wasn't very good. But it was always fun. Now, I'm playing with guns instead of soccer balls, and my life is always on the line."

A pregnant silence lingered between them.

"I guess we should try to sleep. We have a mission to complete and we'll need our rest," Djuro said. He got up to douse the torch and threw some more wood into the small fire.

Sleep was restless for the boys. The wind howled outside the dugout, and the branches that covered the opening rustled loudly.

For Moric, ghosts of the dead floated on the dirt wall with each shadow cast from the flickering flame before the usual nightmares visited him.

When daylight began to show through the branches, they woke up, confronted with the storm.

The wind continued to howl ferociously as the snow piled up outside the entrance of the earth camp. The conditions were too harsh to make any attempt to continue on their mission.

"Now what?" Moric asked.

"I don't quite know. We'll never make it in this storm. I think we just have to wait until it slows down and then move as fast as we can to deliver the message."

"You're right. But I'm worried that if we miss making contact, our own brigades won't be able to go ahead with their attack, or they'll go with no support."

"I know. They're counting on us."

Very few words passed between the two friends, each chewing their breakfast of stale bread and mashed beets.

Djuro got up to check for indications that the storm was passing. The wind wasn't as strong as before, but they didn't feel it was safe to leave the shelter until midday.

The snow at the entrance was deep. They pushed with their hands and feet until they dislodged the blockage. They had been given coordinates for the Fifth Brigade. The wind and snow had subsided, and the sun was peeking through the sharp-edged clouds. It was eerily quiet in the aftermath of the storm. It had left so much snow that their movement was slow and tedious.

After some climbing they reached a ridge where they could look down to make sure the brigade was there before descending to give the orders.

"They're gone," Djuro uttered.

Moric took the binoculars to see for himself. All he saw was the thick blanket of white from the storm and smoldering fire pits with the remnants of discarded food strewn about. Boot prints trampled the snow that was once their camp. Indeed, they were gone.

"This is not good," Moric said.

"That damn storm. It cost us hours. I just hope that our brigades didn't go ahead with the raid. We don't know how many enemy forces might be waiting for them."

"We need to get back as fast as we can to tell Juric," Moric said.

The two headed back to their camp. They didn't let their aching feet and growling stomachs slow them down. They only stopped for a few minutes to eat whatever they had left in their packs, and continued at a frantic pace, cutting deep tracks in the snow.

Entering the camp, they went directly to Juric's tent.

"Commander," Djuro said, "the Fifth Brigade wasn't where they'd been camping. There was no sign of them anywhere."

"Hmmm... This is not good. There was a big storm up on the mountain. I was concerned that this might slow your progress, and frankly, I was also concerned for your safety."

"We're fine. But we're worried that our comrades may not have the support they need if they went into battle," Moric said. "We just had no way of getting through until the storm slowed down."

"Thank you for trying. You should go now, get some food, and change into warm clothes. We're moving out soon."

The camp had a hollow feel to it. Certainly, there were still a number of soldiers there, but there was an uneasiness in the air. It became clear that the brigades out fighting would suffer heavy losses without the reinforcements.

Recognizing that there was no support for the brigades on their current missions, Tito cancelled further activity and ordered Juric to have his fighters return to their base.

Squad leader Bogdan, a hardened Spanish Civil War veteran, entered the camp with far fewer fighters than he had left with. He reported to Commander Juric, informing him of numerous casualties.

Moric was pacing, taking inventory of his photographic supplies and equipment for the third time. His mind kept wandering, and he would have to start his count over again.

Djuro tapped his friend on the shoulder. "Machi, we need to talk."

"Sure. Let me put this stuff in my rucksack."

They walked together, skirting the boundary of the camp, when Djuro stopped to face his friend. Softly, he said, "Mika's dead."

"What did you say?"

"She's dead. I just found out from Bogdan."

Moric froze. He shook his head and replied that this must be a mistake; Bogdan must be dazed and exhausted; he didn't know what he was saying.

Djuro grabbed hold of his friend's shoulders as if to shake him into the present. "No. I asked Bogdan several times if he was sure it was Mika. He kept telling me the same thing. Machi, it was her!"

Moric doubled over in anguish, bursting out in a torrent of tears. "NOOOOOOOO! NOOOOOOOO!" He pushed Djuro away and ran into the forest.

Djuro chased after him. He heard sobbing as he drew closer to Moric. Djuro put his arms around him and cried too. He wanted to be strong for Moric, so he tamped down the sharp pain of grief as best he could.

"My God. What happened?" Moric finally asked.

Bogdan hadn't been sure. He knew Mika was backing up the attacking company at Konjic, but there were only two companies that made it through. Very few of the fighters returned. Tito ordered the attacks on Konjic and Tarcin to cease, and the remaining soldiers went back to their camps.

"But it was too late," Bogdan said to Djuro.

They went ahead with the attack even though they hadn't heard from the Fifth Brigade. They believed they would show up, but they never did.

Moric threw his hands on the top of his head and walked aimlessly past some nearby trees. He couldn't feel the cold. He turned to face Djuro. "It was us. We killed Mika. We killed her!"

"We didn't kill her. We had no idea the storm would slow us down, or the Fifth would be gone. No idea."

"But because of us there was no support. Because of us, only two companies from her brigade made it into Konjic."

"It wasn't because of us. It was the Germans who killed her. Supreme Headquarters ordered the attack because they saw how well we were doing up until then. As soon as they realized that leaving Sedio Pass made us vulnerable, they ordered our fighters back. It was just too late – the fighting was already underway."

"Mika's gone, Djuro."

Moric went down on his knees on the frozen ground. He wiped his eyes with his sleeve and got up, walking further into the woods.

Djuro wanted to catch up to him, to soothe him. But he felt the same emptiness and understood that Moric needed to be alone. In his own way, Djuro needed that for himself.

Moric felt an emptiness deep inside his soul. He racked his brain, trying to determine what they should have done to prevent Mika's death. As he sat on a frigid rock, he felt inside his heavy coat pocket, almost out of habit. He touched the outline of the marble. He unzipped the pocket and took it out. Looking at it, seeing the roundness of it, the colors of the earth he had always liked, the special power that he wanted to believe it had.

He stood up. Pulling his arm back as far as he could, he threw the marble deep into the woods, watching it fly until it disappeared. He yelled into the dense cluster of trees and brush, not caring who heard. "I'm not a child! I don't believe in stupid magic anymore. If it was magic, Mika would still be alive. I hate this war. I hate it!" The sobs began again, but this time the intensity flared out quicker. He turned around and didn't see Djuro, or anyone for that matter.

He slowly made his way back to the camp where he found Djuro sitting by the fire. He sat down next to him. Neither said a word.

Moric got up and went over to where he had left his rucksack. Opening it up, he grabbed the negatives from the envelope marked "Mika," which he had secretly created for himself. He had anxiously awaited developing them.

He looked at each square piece of film and stared.

Mika. What happened to you? Why did you leave us? You were my best friend. I loved you.

Wiping away tears, he focused on Mika's face. He envisioned the strength of her character, the warmth of her smile, recalling how her gaze could shift from hard to soft in an instant. He looked at the film roll taken with Drago, he smiled at how she had repelled him before he jolted back to the realization of her death.

Djuro appeared at Moric's side just as he was placing the envelope into his pack. "We're moving out tomorrow to retake the Ivan Sedlo Pass. I thought that we could have a ceremony for Mika with her friends in attendance, too. I've spoken with Peja; he liked the idea. Nothing big. Just a way for us to say goodbye. One of our comrades used to be a lay person in the Catholic Church and he said he would say a little something. It won't be religious, but more like helping Mika return to wherever she is destined for."

Moric responded in a quiet, despondent voice. "When?"

"Tonight, after our meal. I've asked her friends, and Peja wants to attend. So does Bogdan. We're keeping it small and respectful."

Moric gave a slight nod.

Djuro left to inform a few more people about the service, but Moric called out to him before he got too far. "Djuro. Thank you."

"Of course. We're going to be lost without her."

That night, some 20 of Mika's friends and comrades walked into the woods next to camp. The solemn gathering consisted of praise for their brave friend and lots of tears. When it ended, Peja reminded the attendees that they needed to be ready to head to Sedio in the morning. He concluded by saying, "Let's take Mika's revolutionary spirit with us and be the liberators she'd want us to be."

Returning to the tarp that Djuro had fixed between some branches, Moric slipped under his blanket and put a hand inside his large coat pocket. He felt the bottle of plum-flavored rakija that one of his comrades had given him at the ceremony. Standing up, he walked to where the ceremony had taken place and sat on a rock. Untwisting the cap of the rakija, he took a long swig. It burned his throat, but the next sip was not so strong, and neither were the ones following. The numbing feeling it brought was soothing. Recapping it, he slipped the bottle back into his pocket and returned to lay down for the night.

When he woke up the next morning, his head ached, and the muddled, disturbing dreams were a blur.

The First Proletarian Division set up camp in the Sedio Pass. In a futile attempt to keep dry, Moric and Djuro placed their rucksacks on top of a wrinkled plastic cover to shield themselves from the persistent snow and rain mix that had been falling for the past two days. As he pulled his rain cape hood off, Moric checked and rechecked to ensure that the reels of film and negatives were safely covered with protective cloth.

The division erected a blockade to prevent enemy troops from seizing control of the crucial route. Luka Juric called for a meeting of all Partisan soldiers to be held after their meal. "We've had heavy losses in recent weeks. Our comrades will not have died in vain. We must protect our wounded, who are in the central hospital that we've relocated in Scit. But the German-Italian-Chetnik forces are mounting attacks that threaten the hospital. We have reports that the Chetniks have moved from Mostar to reinforce the eastern side just across the bridges over the Neretva. In their wake, they've killed thousands of villagers. The world is witnessing their brutality and beginning to recognize that they are not the legitimate voice of the people, as they have falsely claimed. The West is aligning with us. Their militaries will be on our soil soon. Our goal is to get the wounded across the Neretva and head into the mountains. We must continue to be strong for the people who we are fighting to liberate."

Juric's speech, though it softened the pain felt by his soldiers, didn't ease the heaviness that weighed Moric down.

The next day Moric woke up early. His sleep had been particularly troubled since Mika's death. He removed his blanket, exposing himself to the cold air. He grabbed the camera from his rucksack, put on his coat, hat, and gloves, and walked into the woods.

He saw deer munching on whatever winter greenery they could find. A young doe was part of the group. He brought the camera up to his eye, pointed, and took several pictures. The doe looked at him with mournful eyes. Continuing to wander further into the woods, he looked for more subjects to photograph.

Moric captured an outcropping of rock with icicles glistening over the edge. The morning sun passed through the crystalline ice revealing the full spectrum of colors. He marveled at their sharpness and clarity.

In this moment, Moric found himself observing these details in a way he had not experienced before. His life had been turned upside down ever since the Ustasha took over Drvar. Since then, most of what he had witnessed was measured in calculated survival risks. Nothing was as it should be. Being alone, observing the natural world, grounded him. It also made him feel incredibly small. Nature was perfect, he thought to himself. *Why are human beings so imperfect?*

He found more of natural wonders to photograph: the regal snow-capped mountains; tall fir trees with sun-dappled canopies; a cloud that passed overhead. This is a place of peace, of harmony, and of the divine beauty he had been taught God created on Earth.

As he walked back to the camp, he thought of Mika. He could almost feel her wrapping her arms around him. He paused. *I miss her so much.* A tear dripped onto the crunchy snow. *And I want to be with my family.*

22 MEHMED

Tito had taken over the reins of military planning for the Partisans in Neretva Valley. The central column brigades had successfully pushed the Axis forces out of Prozor and moved the hospital to safety – but that was changing. Alarming reports were coming into Supreme Headquarters that the hospital was about to come under a direct threat. The German-Italian-Chetnik alliance had amassed troops and artillery surrounding the Partisan brigades, and moved them into the valley.

Fighting was intense and casualties were high. But the attack by the Partisans on Gornji Vakuf was successful. The First Proletarian Brigade advanced to slow down the Germans heading to Jablanica along the Neretva River, which was of strategic importance for the liberators.

The role of couriers was never more important than in this battle to ensure that the wounded could be brought to safety.

Moric was called upon by his commander to deliver a message to the Commander of the Second Division. He was not as familiar with this part of Bosnia. This time, he was on his own. With the fighting going on in Gornji Vakuf, and Germans, Chetniks, Italians, and some Croatian troops in the area, his ability to move as stealthily as possible was imperative.

The night before he left, he ate his evening meal with Djuro, Bogdan, and Milja.

"Why are you so quiet, Machi?" Bogdan asked.

"Am I? I'm just thinking about what I need to bring with me to the Second Division Headquarters."

"Your gun, for one thing," Bogdan responded.

"I always have it. I just don't want to use it unless it's absolutely necessary."

"We're facing lots of Axis troops, artillery, and planes. You'll have to be smart about how you find the Second Division."

"Of course. Having one gun won't save me if I'm captured, so I'll be sure not to get caught," Moric responded with some irritation in his voice.

"Machi is one of our best couriers," Milja said. "He knows what to do."

"I'm not saying he doesn't. But please forgive me, he's not a fighter. I've never seen him use his gun. That will be a problem if he runs into trouble."

"Machi is right. His gun is no match for the entire Axis force out there," Djuro said, slightly annoyed with Bogdan himself.

Moric was not paying much attention to what was being said anymore. He was mentally preparing for what might be a difficult mission, and simultaneously trying to tune out the acute grief that had found him again.

"Machi, Machi!" Djuro said, raising his voice.

"Oh, yes. Djuro, what is it?"

"Are you sure you're ready for this?" he asked.

"I am."

Djuro wasn't convinced. He stood up, as did Milja and Bogdan, and wished Moric good luck before saying goodnight. "Let's get some sleep now. Don't let Bogdan put fear in you. You're good at what you do," Djuro said. He watched his friend walk away without saying a word.

They slipped beneath their tarp, which barely protected them from the freezing rain.

"What's wrong? You'll have to be ready to do this tomorrow. I wish I could go with you, but I'm needed here."

"I know that. I'm fine on my own."

"Then what's wrong? You weren't even paying attention to what Bogdan was saying to you."

"I heard him. I just need to go to sleep."

Djuro said no more.

Moric's body was turned away from Djuro. He listened to the sounds of artillery echoing in the mountains, and the voice in his head telling him that Djuro did not believe him.

The clouds kept the sun from showing itself the next morning, but at least the frozen rain had stopped.

Dampness cut through the camp like a knife. For the second week in row, no fire was lit to prevent the enemy from locating them.

Moric gathered his rucksack, food, and water, and walked over to Luka Juric's tent. His aide alerted the Commander of Moric's presence.

"Good morning, Commander," Moric said.

"Good morning, Comrade. You have a very important delivery today. They all are, but this one will determine our next tactical maneuver. The Commander of the Second Division is awaiting your arrival. His brigades are only eight kilometers away, but it may be difficult because of the weather, and the enemy forces gathering on all sides."

Moric took the envelope containing the Commander's order and put it into the secret compartment of his rucksack. After one of his first missions, Peja asked Mika to sew it into his pack. He peered into the compartment with a heavy heart.

"Go now, Comrade. Be safe and return to us soon."

Moric pulled his outer gear tighter around himself. He wrapped a scarf around his neck and covered his chin. His boots were a bit worn; in fact, they had begun to separate ever so slightly at the seams. He looked at his map for coordinates before he left the relative safety of camp.

Familiar with staying out of sight, Moric trekked deep into the woods. Though it might be more tedious, this was the only way to ensure safe delivery of his messages. The early morning clouds had disappeared, and the sun was filtering its rays through the dense trees, creating a maze of shadows and light.

Moric's mind kept wandering. Unrelated to the mission, memories were intruding upon what he was tasked to do. He wanted these distracting thoughts to stop and pulled out his binoculars to scan the area. He repeated this process regularly as he made his way to the Second Division.

He figured that he was halfway to his destination when he heard something. Footsteps. He dove into a bush nearby, but the footsteps continued to approach. He took out his rifle and leapt from his hiding place aiming at the figure not more than ten meters away.

"Stop!" he yelled.

The man instinctively put up his hands.

"Who are you?" Moric asked.

Not a man, by any means, but a boy not much older than him, stood frozen with hands stretched high. His clothing was shabby, and his face was drawn. Dirt and grime creased his cheeks.

"My name is Mehmed and I'm from Druzinovici."

"What are you doing up here, Mehmed?" Moric asked sternly.

"I don't know. I saw you and I thought maybe you could help me. Please don't shoot."

Moric lowered his gun. He could see that Mehmed was shaking and malnourished. He reminded him of himself when he escaped Drvar for the mountains before being found by the Partisans.

"Sit down, please," Moric said, as he reached into his rucksack, beckoned him over, and handed him a piece of cold potato.

The boy devoured it in one bite. "Thank you for that. I haven't eaten much in a couple of days. Grasses mostly. Can I ask you your name?"

"It's Milan."

"Why are you out here, Milan?"

"Let's talk about you first. Why are you here all alone?"

Mehmed appeared to be calmer now. He looked away from Moric before returning his gaze. "It's been hard for me. There are some days that I think, today's the day I'm going to die. But something inside me won't allow that to happen." Mehmed paused.

Moric recognized the familiarity of Mehmed's story. "Go on," he said.

"Several days ago, the Chetniks came to our village like they'd done to many other villages. Druzinovici is small. We have some Croatians, and more Muslims, and we all get along. The Chetniks were bloodthirsty. They killed many villagers. My grandmother, who could barely walk, was burned alive in her house with some others. I saw them burn other houses where old people lived. They pulled my mother and two younger sisters out of our house and... and... I can't describe what they did to them. My father told me not to move as he raced out of our hiding place to stop them, but they shot him in the head. I heard the screams and the bullets that silenced them all. I hid behind thick brush. I ran as they burned my village to the ground. I've been running ever since. I've tried to find my relatives in other villages, but the Chetniks visited every village that didn't have Serbs, and destroyed them."

Moric could see that Mehmed's teeth were chattering, except the three that were missing.

"It's cold. Very cold. I have a rucksack that I dropped over there. It has some warm clothes and a water pouch that my father gave me a while ago. It was his in the last war. I've melted snow for water. But I can't live like this. And when I hear the guns or tanks, I get so scared."

Moric looked away, and stared at a large, ice-covered rock next to him. He couldn't leave Mehmed out in the woods.

"Listen, I need to finish what brought me out this way. I can take you with me, and speak to the Partisans about taking you in, if you want. It may be your only hope of surviving. I'll tell them some of your story, so they understand why you're with me. We're fighting against the Chetniks, too, as you've probably heard. What do you think?"

Without hesitation Mehmed answered, "Yes, please. I don't know how much longer I can last out here."

"Good. Go get your rucksack, and let's finish what I started to do."

Moric found his bearings again as they traversed the next kilometers.

Mostly, Mehmed was quiet; they were both lost in their own thoughts. Moric thought about the upheaval brought by the Nazis to his once beautiful and peaceful country.

When they arrived, Moric first found an aide to the Commander and explained who he was with. The aide said that he would bring Mehmed to one of their soldiers, also a Muslim, to get some food, clothes, and to rest.

Mehmed put his hand on Moric's shoulder and gave it a gentle squeeze. "I'll never forget what you've done for me, Milan. I hope we can see each other in times of peace."

Moric watched Mehmed melt into the fabric of the camp. He was struck by how similar they both were. *Jews, Muslims, Catholics, Orthodox, Communists, Socialists, or nothing in particular, we are all cut from the same cloth. We are all brothers and sisters. Why was that so hard for some human beings to understand?*

23 BATTLE FOR THE WOUNDED

When Moric arrived back at his camp, he went to Juric's tent to give him the Commander's response. Then he found Djuro and told him about Mehmed.

"I'm wondering what our next order is. I know you can't breach the envelope that it's in, but do you have any idea what Tito wants us to do?" Djuro asked.

"No, of course not. We'll know soon enough."

"Are you feeling better now? When you left yesterday, I was worried about you."

"I'm better, I guess. The truth is, sometimes I can't get Mika out of my head. I miss her so much."

"Me too. I know she'd want us to remember that she'd take a bullet before she let the enemy win. We just have to keep that in mind. We do this for liberation, but we'll do this for her, too."

Just then a call to order was made, and all in the camp had to assemble near the fire pit. Once there, Luka Juric gave them their orders. "We're going to have a rendezvous with the Second Division. Then, we're headed for the Jablanica Bridge to cross the Neretva. There will be some fighting beforehand to help push the enemy back and pave the way for our comrades to move across the bridge with the wounded."

With the Germans temporarily in retreat, and Chetnik Divisions on the eastern side of the Neretva, Tito gave the unorthodox order for his engineer corps to blow up all the bridges in the vicinity of Jablanica.

"Why would he do that?" Djuro asked Moric.

"I don't know. We're supposed to cross there. Let me see if Peja knows what's behind this?"

Peja was in a foul mood.

Moric walked over to him, hesitated, and then made a hasty retreat.

Peja yelled for him to come back.

"Comrade, I can see that you're busy. I can come back later," Moric said to the patrol leader.

"I know what you want. It's what everyone wants to know. Are we just fodder for the Germans with nowhere to escape? Well, I don't have an answer. I truly don't. But we've been told to stay put until we receive our next orders. We can use the rest anyway."

Moric returned to Djuro, who was with others.

"Did you learn anything?" Djuro asked.

"Peja said that we need to wait for our next orders. Actually, he was not in a good mood."

There was grumbling around them.

"Listen," Bogdan said. "Tito is our leader. We have to believe he knows what he's doing. We have to continue to believe that we're fighting for change, for the people, and for freedom. Let's be patient. I have some concerns, but let's stay together on this."

The men and women went back to pack up their gear in case they needed to move suddenly. There seemed to be agreement with Bogdan's call for patience.

This was a valuable lesson Moric had been learned during his time with the Partisans – trust and patience.

However, as the hours passed, the restlessness seemed to grow as the soldiers became testier with one another. Small flare-ups erupted, particularly pertaining to Tito's decision to destroy the bridges, their only escape routes. Some of the civilians connected to their brigade were openly challenging the decision. Little was known, or if it was, it was not shared by Juric and his top aides.

The weather continued its mastery over them with frigid temperatures and sporadic snow showers.

There was no mission to distract them from the cold. Doubt about Tito's decision was growing steadily.

German command believed that the destruction of the bridges meant that the Partisans were heading northward on the western side of the valley with no other route to take. The German army repositioned its troops and artillery to intercept them.

This is where Tito's plan showed its brilliance.

Destroying the bridges, which prodded the Germans to move their troops out of position, gave the engineer corps a 19-hour window to build a wooden platform on the Jablanica Bridge just above the river for escape to the eastern side of the valley. A lead unit of Partisans successfully attacked the Chetniks on the other side of the bridge to clear the way.

Orders for the Second Division and First Proletariat Brigade were to cross the bridge, and head through the Prenji Mountains, going northward.

The tactic confused the German command, but they recognized their mistake. However, it was too late to move their troops. Instead, they called for aerial attacks. Partisan tanks and anti-aerial guns were doing their best to take down the planes as columns of Partisan fighters, civilians, and the wounded crossed the river.

Moric and Djuro were among them. The river below them was raging. The sounds of attacking Stuka planes firing their machine guns, and the intense flow of the rapids, made it impossible to hear one another.

As Moric and Djuro crossed, just in front of them, Drago was hit by a torrent of bullets from one of the divebombing planes. He turned to he watched his arm detach from his body, disappearing in the river below. In an instant, Drago fell into the water almost as if he went to retrieve his arm.

Moric watched Drago being swept into strong, swirling currents, quickly disappearing. Moric's eyes bulged, staring back at the empty space Drago had just occupied.

The Stuka planes had always struck fear into him, and seeing his comrade, even one he didn't like, brutally cut down, stopped him from taking another step.

Djuro grabbed him by the arm. "Let's go!" he yelled.

Moric did as Djuro commanded, and continued over the bridge, despite feeling like he was moving through thick mud.

Heading straight to the adjacent forest, the planes were now unable to spot them through the dense trees, and they rose up into the sky to continue their aerial raid elsewhere in the valley.

"Machi, are you alright?" Djuro asked.

"Yes," he said panting heavily, both hands on his knees. "Let's move further into the forest."

They met up with soldiers from the Second Division and their own brigade. Taking stock of the dead and missing had already begun. It was reported that the wounded from the central hospital were on their way to safety in eastern Bosnia.

Moric and Djuro joined their division to head north across the Prenji Mountains, with the goal of reaching the town of Ulog in the upper Neretva.

The thick snow made it difficult to walk. The beauty of the mountains and valleys did not alleviate the strain of their trek.

Moric felt the snow leach into a widening gap of split leather at the tops of his boots. The exhaustion of leaving Kozara, the battles afterwards, and almost losing his life crossing the Neretva, weighed down each step he took. The brightness of the snow made it difficult to see; he just followed anyone who was in front of him, as if he was being pulled by a rope tethered to their waists.

Beginning another ascent, Djuro came up from behind his friend. "Machi, what's going on with you?"

"I don't know. I feel very tired, and my feet are freezing."

"Do you want to stop? We can catch up later."

"No, it seems like this is the last climb we have to make. I'll just take it one step at a time."

"I'll stay with you until we get to the top, to our new camp."

"Thanks. Let's talk so I don't think about how I'm feeling."

"Look at the beauty out here," Djuro said. "Who would have guessed that the planes were shooting at us not too long ago? It's so peaceful here. And the sky is the most perfect blue."

"It's cold, but peaceful. Sometimes I forget what peaceful looks like. When I was younger, we used to visit family in Prijedor in every season. Winter was my favorite season because of this. My cousins and I would head up into the woods and build forts out of sticks and leaves and snow. We'd bring baklava and chocolate to eat inside. It felt good to have such an accomplishment."

"That sounds like fun. I didn't do that with my cousins. Sounds like I missed out."

"When this is over, and my shoes don't leak, maybe you and I can build a fort of our own in the snow. I'll bring the sweets!"

"I'd like that. Look, our comrades are setting up camp just ahead. You made it."

"We made it. Sometimes I don't know what I'd do without you."

The conversations were quiet around the campfires that evening, but talk of Tito's brilliance lifted their spirits.

Moric took off his boots and socks to dry. He observed that his feet and toes were a deep scarlet color, but not black from frostbite. Someone gave him a couple of scarves to wrap around them. Otherwise, he listened to the conversations his comrades were having. He stared at the flames, as feeling returned to his thawing body.

"It gave me a great deal of pleasure to see the Chetniks get wiped out before we crossed the river. They've caused misery for so many people," Peja said.

"I heard that Tito ordered that our comrades throw the tanks and big artillery down into the river from their perch on the ridge. They never would have made it over the bridge and through the forests. We'll capture more weaponry in other battles, I'm sure. Most importantly, our wounded made it out. Tito truly is a master tactician!" responded Milja.

"I guess he is," Bogdan replied.

"I wonder how much closer we are to winning this. The Germans invaded Yugoslavia in April, almost two years ago. How much longer?" Djuro asked.

"I don't know. We have to keep on fighting until whenever 'over' is," Peja replied.

Moric faded out of the rest of the conversation. Looking around the small fire, he noticed how yellow and gaunt everyone's faces looked. It was like looking into a mirror; likely, they saw him through their own mirrors. Little food, always on the move, facing death almost every day; the potential of your own death would waste anyone.

He removed the scarves from his feet, and rubbed them gently. Feeling returned to his toes. He put his dried socks back on along with his boots. The split in the leather was softened by the warmth of the fire, but he hoped new supplies would come in soon. He had asked Peja to see if central supply could bring him replacements.

"Get in line," Peja teased him.

Of course, they were never new, but used ones that were whole would certainly suffice.

For Moric and Djuro the victory was bittersweet. They had lost Mika, as well as many others who had fought alongside them. They yawned in unison, both getting up to find a dry place to sleep. They found a spot with very little snow, having been protected by the cover of evergreens above. Scooping the white powder away, they laid down on blankets, and threw whatever they had on top of themselves.

"Today, when I saw Drago get hit and fall into the river, I froze — you saw that. The screaming of the planes' engines pierce right through me. And then seeing Drago go down... well, it was as if I was next in line to be hit. I wasn't able to think clearly. I just wanted to escape; jumping into the river seemed like it would have been a relief. You yanked me back into reality. I know what going in would have done to me. In that moment, it was more like, I have to leave this place! Thanks for not letting me do that."

"I don't like to swim. Jumping in after you wouldn't have worked out well."

Moric responded with brief smile.

"We have a long trek ahead of us in the coming days, let's try to sleep," Djuro said.

They bid each other goodnight, but despite their bone-deep exhaustion, it would be a long while before either fell asleep.

24 THE NURSE

The brigade marched into Kalinovik with other liberation forces and took control, fighting hard against the Chetniks and Italians. They besieged the small city of Foca and surrounding towns, destroying the Italian presence at Pivka Javorca and the Italian-Chetnik garrison in Kolasin. The various Partisan fighting forces loaded up on the abandoned military supplies, medicines, medical devices, food, and other things critical to their war efforts. Moric and some of his comrades revealed their new Italian-made boots.

"Happy birthday," the recipients yelled at one another as they strung up their laces.

During this phase of fighting, Supreme Headquarters moved onto nearby Mount Durmitor.

Although Moric and his comrades were worn out, their morale was still high. Many were killed or wounded, but they had survived the daring events of Neretva Valley, and gained momentum with their recent victories.

Still, the suddenness of the attacks and counterattacks, bullets, grenades, tank shells, and other artillery fire, always put Moric on edge. One minute it would be quiet, the next, it was as if thunder and lightning were cracking in his ears.

Perched in a new encampment outside Kalinovik, a lull in the fighting took hold.

"Rest is good," Milja said, as he joined the group, which included Moric and Djuro.

"We did well," Bogdan responded.

"We surely did. Hey Bogdan, after the meal, pull out the accordion and let's sing," Milja said.

Mid-May was closing in and the evenings were getting milder. The low-lit fire boiled a soup of onions, carrots, and a few potatoes. The shank bone of a lamb, given to them by a local farmer, was simmering alongside the vegetables, enriching the stock. This was going to be an exquisite meal compared to what they had been eating thus far.

Bogdan started to play *Mitraljeza*, and they all joined in singing. Some of the men and women stood up, locked arms, and danced around the fire. Their voices rose and echoed into the hills. There was a sense of relief, release from the intensity of the recent months.

Moric and Djuro didn't join in the dance, but Djuro sang loudly, staring in the fire. He briefly looked over at Moric and saw his silent friend holding his head with his hands, watching the flames do their own dance. When he attempted to pass the celebratory bottle of rakija to him, Moric just put his hand up gesturing "No." It was unlike Moric to turn down a shot of the potent brandy, it was a ritual when there was cause for celebration.

"Are you alright? You don't seem to be enjoying this. Did you eat some soup?" Djuro asked.

"I had a little. I'm not very hungry."

"Have you been drinking water?"

"Not much. Listen, I can't keep my eyes open. I'm going to sleep. I'll feel better in the morning."

"Right. I'll see you later."

Djuro got back into the upbeat mood of the evening, now with less vigor.

The next day when Djuro woke up, Moric was still sleeping. This was very unusual; Moric was often the first one up. He tried to wake him, but he barely opened his eyes. He just asked for water, which Djuro got him. He was shivering, so Djuro put an extra blanket over him.

Djuro went to look for help. A medic attached to his unit followed him back to examine Moric.

"I believe he has typhus," the medic pronounced.

"Where's the nearest medical bunker?" Djuro asked.

"You'll recall we're never given that information. The enemy would love to know where they could slaughter our wounded."

"Of course. What can we do?" Djuro asked calmly not wanting to betray his worry.

"I'll go over to headquarters. We have wounded in our camp, as well that need more care than I can provide."

The medic found Djuro upon his return. "We're in luck. A patrol unit with a nurse will be here shortly. I'm told that they'll take Machi and the others into the forest to their medical bunker."

"He seems pretty sick. I'm worried about him," Djuro said. He thanked the medic and proceeded to pace nearby his friend. He kept looking for the approaching medical team.

In less than an hour, ten armed soldiers assigned to protect the medical bunker arrived. They were accompanied by a nurse, a medic, and a nurse's assistant, a local villager woman trained by the Partisans.

Ana, the nurse's assistant, was sent by the nurse to see the typhus patient. The disease was rampant in various camps due to substandard sanitary conditions. So far, there was only one patient in this one.

The nurse and medic were led to an area designated for the wounded. Fortunately, five of them could be tended to on-the-spot. Two other men had fractures in their arms requiring more involved care, while another had a shrapnel wound in his hand with only a bandage around it. When it was unwrapped, the yellow blistering showed that an infection was developing. Another man had what appeared to be a break in his left femur, and he couldn't walk, like Moric. Italian-made stretchers were rolled out to carry the two patients. The others, who could move unassisted, joined the rest as they headed back into the forest.

The assistant reported back to the nurse that the boy had a high fever, chills, and couldn't keep his eyes open long enough to talk. It seems likely that it's typhus, she told the nurse.

"He's headed in the wrong direction," she said. "We need to get him back for treatment as soon as we can."

The nurse sent two of her Partisan escorts to bring a stretcher and place a couple of blankets on him.

Djuro was waiting by Moric's side. When the stretcher arrived, he let go of the breath he had been holding in. "You'll be alright, Machi. I know you will. We'll meet up soon."

Moric opened his eyes for a second, and attempted to speak, but nothing came out as he lapsed back into a fevered sleep.

He was brought to the boundary of the camp, where the others were already waiting.

The nurse had been tending to the soldier with the infected hand. She moved away from the man and reported to the medic that it was under control, but required much greater attention.

"Ready?" asked the patrol leader. "Let's move out."

The group was five minutes into its hike to their hidden medical bunker when the nurse dropped back to see the typhus patient. From a distance, he looked familiar. As she neared, she thought her mind was playing tricks. She had treated injured comrades who hallucinated, but she wasn't injured or sick. She was right next to him when an audible gasp erupted. "That's my baby brother!"

The two men carrying Moric's stretcher stopped.

"No. Let's keep moving. We have to get him... to get them, to our facility," exclaimed Judita.

Judita composed herself. She didn't want to cry. She desperately wanted to hug him but knew that it wasn't possible at that moment.

The medic, Marinko, a teenager himself whose compassion outweighed his experience, dropped back to join Judita and Moric.

"I just heard that this young man is your brother. When did you last see him?"

"We were in Prijedor. It's been almost two years; I'd thought we'd lost him. I can't believe he's here. I have to help him. We have to."

"Of course," Marinko said. "We will."

Judita made her rounds to the others in the group, but rushed back to her brother as soon as she could. She was clearly off-kilter. She desperately wanted to help him, but also to speak with him, hear his voice, share stories. More than anything, to say she loved him.

Their bunker was a dugout cut located in a thick, dense, evergreen forest. Inside, the walls were covered with tar paper to keep it dry. Wood planks were used to make bunks for patients, holes were bored into the upper walls for air, and there were metal plates to repel rainwater. There were shelves containing medical supplies, food, medicines, casting material, disinfectants, and simple medical devices.

Moric and the other soldier on a stretcher were lowered down into the bunker through a two-by-three-meter opening after the branches and brush covering were cleared to the side. They were placed on adjacent bunks as typhus was not an airborne disease.

While the medic and nurse's assistant attended to the others, Judita filled a syringe with recently delivered penicillin, and slowly injected it into her brother's right thigh. He didn't react to the needle piercing his skin.

After removing the needle, she placed the syringe into a pan of boiling water that had been prepared by Ana. She removed her rubber gloves, and put them in a separate pan of boiling water. She was meticulous about disinfecting the medical supplies, which was not the case with other medical teams, especially near battlefields.

She looked at her brother, staring at his face. He looked much older than when she had last seen him on the train to Jasenovac. There were dark circles around his eyes, and his skin, which was yellow, lacked elasticity. His cheeks were sallow. His physique, though difficult to truly discern, was more filled out. There was muscle developing in his small frame, despite evidence that he lacked a steady food source, something not uncommon with many of the Partisans.

If only she could tell her parents and sisters that Moric was alive. She wiped the tears from her eyes and swallowed hard, while silently praying that the antibiotic would work.

The next morning, Moric stirred in his bunk. Judita went over to check on him, but he was still asleep. She peered down at his sweet face, touched a finger to her lips, and placed it onto his forehead. *Please come back to me, Moric. Please.*

She stood and turned to climbed out of the bunker to speak to Marinko, who was outside having a cigarette.

Before she could leave, Moric woke up. "Judita. Is that you?" he whispered.

She practically leapt off the top rung of the ladder. "Oh, Moric. Oh, my sweet Moric. Yes, it's me."

"Where are we? Home?"

"No, not home, but we're together." She checked his forehead for fever – it had come down. She brought him a cup of water. "Drink slowly. I don't want you to choke."

Moric did as he was told. "Can I have a little more, please?"

"Of course. But not too much more. Your stomach may not appreciate it just yet."

"I'm not dreaming, am I? It's really you?"

"You're not dreaming. We can talk soon when you're feeling stronger. But I'll take care of you until you do. I can't explain how it's worked out this way, but I'm the nurse who was called to treat the wounded and sick from your unit."

"God works in mysterious ways, like Papa used to tell us," Moric said softly.

Judita smiled. "How's your stomach?"

"A little unsteady. I may vomit, actually."

"I'm going to give you a five percent Dextrose water solution by injection, to help quell the nausea," she said approaching her brother's arm with a needle.

"Go ahead, but I'm not going to look."

"You'll hardly feel a thing."

Moric slept a couple more hours, and woke up hungry.

"Judita," he called, as she cleaned some medical devices on the other side of the bunker. "Can I have something to eat?"

"Sure. I'll ask Ana to bring you over something. No fancy meals here, but plain bread will help. How's your nausea?"

"Like I never had it."

"After you eat, I want to see if you can sit up."

"Sounds good." Moric devoured the bread, and immediately asked Ana for more.

After the assistant left, Judita returned to her brother. "You've been here a few days now. The others have gone to our main hospital for more involved care, so you're the only patient here now."

"Another hospital? How is that possible?"

"We have secret hospitals and bunkers just like this one all over Yugoslavia. Since they're secret, very few know of their locations. Our more severely wounded are taken to the main hospitals by special units that know where they are. I don't know how you, such a young boy, have survived this war."

"One thing Judita, I have a secret, too. My name is Milan Adamovic, but my comrades call me Machi. I don't want anyone to know my real name right now."

"Of course, Machi. I understand. I've told people on my medical team about me, so if they've even thought about it, Ana and Marinko know that you're Jewish. They don't care in the least. Still, I understand."

"Can I go outside for some air?"

"Of course. Just go slowly."

Moric was unsteady at first, but his sister held onto him. Marinko came down into the bunker to guide the boy up. Once outside, sister and brother, arm in arm, slowly made their way down a short path and sat on the ground against a fallen tree.

"It feels good out here. And no sounds of tanks, planes, or cannons. No guns," Moric said.

"Sometimes, when it's quiet, I can almost forget about the war. I imagine our family is together again in Drvar, Mamma stirring a stew over at the stove, and Papa coming home after working at the store. How I long for those days."

"Me too. Do you know what's happened to them? To our sisters?"

"That's a long story that we'll tell for a long time, I'll tell you another time if this bloody war ever ends. They're all alive as of six months ago when I joined the medical team."

"Oh God. They're alive!"

"I hope so. I think so. After you escaped, Mr. Lipovac met the train at the next station, knowing that it was going to stay there for a few hours before leaving again. It was night when he knocked on our wagon door and asked for Mr. and Mrs. Albahari. When Papa answered, he told us to lower ourselves through the same opening in the floor where you escaped. Miraculously, many of us did just that, and ran into the woods. Unfortunately, the older and sick people couldn't come. They told us to save ourselves. I don't know what happened to Mr. Lipovac, but I hope no one discovered what he did."

"Mr. Lipovac was an Ustasha. But I guess he really wasn't. At my music lessons, he always told me how important it was to be kind to people. It must have been very hard for him to be in the Ustasha army."

"I'm guessing he hated what the Ustasha and Nazis were doing to Yugoslavia, too, but he felt he had no choice but to join them or his family might have been put in prison or worse."

Moric's memory of Mr. Lipovac at the train station was vivid. The man was a hero to him. He, too, hoped that no harm had come to him.

"Where did you go?" Moric asked.

"We hid in a few villages that were under Partisan control. It's then that I met a Serbian doctor who told me that the medical teams for the People's Army needed more personnel. I told him that I had to get back to Drvar first with my parents, but that I'd go wherever he suggested for training. Mamma and Papa gathered some belongings and joined the Partisans, too. They were part of a group that was talking to villagers about joining the movement. They would stay in many different towns and villages – that's what they told me they'd be doing. Flora and Rahela joined the Partisans, too, although I'm not sure where they are, what they're doing, and if they're alright. I pray that they are."

"They could all be alive, can't they?"

"Yes, they could be."

Moric told Judita what his jobs were in his unit. He told her about Djuro, Bogdan, Milja, and even little Jakov. He told her about the battles he had been in, but tried not to worry her with too many details. He also told her about Mika, and what a great loss she was to him.

Moric spent two weeks recovering in the bunker. At that point, Judita told him that she needed to move to another place, but she wasn't told the location. It seemed that there was heavy fighting in the Sujeska Valley, and casualties were high. She had also heard that there were many wounded that the Partisans were trying to protect from the German onslaught by breaking through the enemy encirclement tightening around them. There was strong evidence that Tito himself was on the run since he was being hunted down. There were many moving parts at this stage of the war, and she was called on to set up elsewhere.

As he gathered himself to go with a couple of the medical team's soldiers, he and Judita hugged tightly.

"I'm so thankful that you're alive, my little brother. I wish we could stay together, but that's not possible. What is possible is that this war ends in victory, and we're together again — all of us." She sighed before continuing, swallowing hard. "These comrades are taking you to Ribnik, to your brigade's new headquarters. That's the order I received earlier today. It'll be a long ride, but a transport vehicle will be waiting for you about five kilometers from here. It'll take you only through liberated territory. I love you. Be careful."

"I love you too. I know I never said that when we were home, but you never saved my life either."

Judita laughed and mussed his hair as Moric tried to duck away.

She watched him move up the path toward his new destination. Her heart was drenched in all sorts of emotions. As he was about to leave her line of sight, she whispered to herself, "Keep him safe. Please, God, keep him safe."

25 WELCOME TO RIBNIK

Headquarters in Ribnik was a house that had been vacated by a resident of the town. It was there that Commander Slavko Rodic made difficult decisions regarding the newly formed brigade, which included other brigades folded together to create a bigger fighting force.

Unlike Luka Juric, Rodic was more hands-on. He had a larger-than-life physical presence and could bore a hole through anyone with his piercing gaze. It was also said that he had a much better demeanor and sense of humor than Juric.

His exploits were more widely known, both as a commander and a fighter who had participated directly in a number of battles. It was Tito himself who ordered him to remain out of military confrontations.

The Germans had marched into Bosanski Petrovac and Drvar without a fight. They were preparing a more strenuous hunt for Marshal Tito, who they had learned was hiding in a cave in the area. According to intelligence by the British and Americans, who were now allied with Tito, the German military leaders didn't expect the Partisans to fortify other locations in the vicinity in response to their "Seventh Military Offensive." The Germans were fooled.

An important component of winning support and increasing the military might of the Partisans was to routinely send photographs, stories, posters, and other positive images and messages to the local populations. Moric continued to do his part, though lately his courier duties took priority.

He and a new colleague in Ribnik named Ivica, were ordered to transport a printing press used for various liberation documents from Bukovaci to Ribnik for safekeeping.

The two couriers met to solidify logistics and decided to leave before dawn.

An hour before dusk, Moric decided to ride a horse up the road from headquarters and hitch it to a cart in a storage shed hidden about 50 meters from the gate so that the next day they could carry the printing press back to Ribnik without wasting time. He thought Ivica would find this plan brilliant.

As he rode his horse up through the barricade onto the dirt road, he sensed danger. About 75 meters away, he saw a rider on a horse coming toward him. He knew that the enemy could be sending reconnaissance through the area, and an internal alarm signaled that he had just encountered one of their soldiers.

Moric leaped off his horse and into the brush. He pulled out his rifle. At the same moment, the other rider also dove into the brush. Now, they were in a standoff.

Moric was in a panic. He still hadn't shot anyone before, but it was one-on-one now the enemy's life or his. He took in slow, deep breaths to calm himself. In the still air, he listened for the slightest of movements. Suddenly, he heard the clicking sound of the enemy's rifle. Moric quickly engaged his.

In his best attempt at mimicking a threatening voice Moric yelled, "Who goes there?"

The response was an equally fearsome voice in Serbo-Croatian, "What's your password?"

Moric knew that the language the man spoke was the one used by Chetniks, Serb nationalists. So this was who the chess match was to be with, he thought. *He's trying to trick me into thinking we're on the same side. How could he think I'm so dumb?* His mind was swirling with options for his next move, though he was unsure of all of them.

Suddenly, two shots were fired in the air in between Moric and the Chetnik. Moric peered over to where the gun had been fired. He immediately recognized who shot it.

From the Chetnik he heard, "Commander!"

Moric raised his voice too. "Commander!"

Both rose to see Commander Rodic, who was looking in both directions, laughing at his couriers.

"You two idiots can come out now."

Moric and the other man, who turned out to be Ivica, disengaged their rifles, stood up, and sheepishly walked over to Rodic.

"Did you not notice that your horses are calmly grazing over there next to each other? Or that each has the same saddle and markings from our brigade?"

"No, Commander, I guess we didn't. Um... I see that now," Moric said.

"Yes, Commander, I see that we made a big mistake," Ivica confessed.

"If I hadn't come up here, your mistake could have cost you your lives. Did you have fun?" he laughed again.

"Um, no Commander," Moric stammered.

"Well, it will make for a good story anyway. We need some laughs now and again," the Commander said. "Get your horses and get on with whatever it was you two thought you were doing."

Moric and Ivica couldn't look at each other at first. They gathered up the reins of their horses and started walking. Moric was the first to speak, "Look at the rear of our steeds. That's us. A couple of horses' asses."

Both of them broke into nervous laughter, but they knew that this story would haunt them for a long time.

Each had had the same idea of attaching a wagon the night before their mission, but neither bothered to tell the other.

The next day, they retrieved the printing press with no difficulties. They delivered it to the Commander's house, which was in the confines of the barbed wired base. Željko, the Commander's aide, met them and thanked them. As they left, he commented that they looked quite stout for almost shooting each other in the rear end. They could hear his hearty laugh as they disappeared back into the camp, their faces redder than the radishes they'd eaten the evening before.

Two days later, Moric was summoned to speak directly with Commander Rodic at the Fifth Bosnian Corps headquarters.

"Comrade, we're fighting on many fronts in Drvar. Marshal Tito is the enemy's target, and we've dispatched many brigades to defend against his capture, or worse. I'm aware that you know this area quite well. You'll need to find your way to a small enclave outside of Klujc, meet another courier named Nikola, and give him my order. There are many of our fighters in this region, but also many enemy troops. And the Allies are running flying sorties for us, so there will be a lot to be alert for."

"Thank you, Commander. When should I leave?"

"At midnight tonight. Željko will give you a map and my orders and show you the safest route to go. He'll explain all of this to you."

Rodic told him that this delivery was extremely critical. But there was little conversation other than what he was told.

The Commander dismissed him, wishing him a safe journey.

Klujc was about 20 kilometers from Ribnik, but the enclave where he would meet the other courier was a few kilometers further. Moric understood that his journey to meet Nikola was time sensitive, but he always weighed speed against the risk of being caught.

Moric was thankful that Djuro had taken his rucksack with him after he went for treatment in the medical bunker. Returning to where they had both set up to sleep, he found Djuro sitting against a nearby tree reading a *Borba* newspaper.

"Hi, Machi. I'm just catching up on how we're doing in the war. With the Italians switching sides last September and not only sending some of their brigades to fight for us, but also sending a lot of their equipment, the tide has turned greatly in our favor. Maybe this thing will be over soon."

"Maybe. It feels like it's been going on forever. I still have trouble remembering what I was like when I was a boy."

"You're not much older. But both of us are soldiers who've seen more than most our age ever will."

"That's very true. I mean, those damn Germans turned the world upside down. And even if it turns right-side up, how can we ever forget what we've been through?"

"We never will. You look like you wanted to say something to me. What is it?"

"Commander Rodic himself gave me an order to deliver. It must be important for him to do that. I have to leave at midnight. I'll speak with Željko soon to get the details."

"That's something. The Commander telling you directly."

"Yeah. I need to pack my rucksack and prepare to leave."

"I plan on seeing you here when you get back. You make sure that happens."

"Of course. Nothing will stop me. Not even a Luftwaffe aerial bombardment."

They both laughed. Moric packed up and went to Željko's office to retrieve his orders before heading over for dinner.

As they ate their evening meal, Moric said little to Djuro, who unsuccessfully attempted to bring some levity into the conversation.

"Sorry. I'm just focused on what I have to do later. The map Željko gave me includes stops at a couple of villages that our comrades control. Still, I'll have to traverse fields along the way, which will make me a bit more vulnerable to being seen."

"You're Machi. You're the wildcat. Wildcats can be pretty slippery. Just don't eat any mice. I hear they don't taste too good."

"Funny. This will be my longest run. Can you come with me to help take inventory of what I need to bring, just to double-check?"

"Of course. Whenever you'd like."

After dinner, the boys filled Moric's rucksack with necessary supplies.

Midnight had arrived and a dense fog settled in. Moric had to delay his trek. At 2 a.m. the fog lifted and he headed to Klujc. It was a clear, moonlit night, and his shadow joined him.

He could hear some of the artillery echoing off the surrounding mountains, although he was unsure where it was coming from. It was still at a distance, so he wasn't too concerned. But as he knew well, the direction of the artillery, or the incursion of fighter planes could change any moment.

He peered at the map to make sure that he was going in the right direction. German patrols were known to be in some of the areas he would have to pass through. If need be, he thought, he'd take a longer route.

He cautiously strode through the darkness, his eyes constantly scanning, ears listening for sounds to alert him to any danger that might be nearby. He had been out for over two hours, but didn't get as far as he would have liked due to the late departure.

A deviation from the route on his map brought him better cover in the woods, with the sun just beginning to light the dawn sky.

Moric had been thinking a lot about his future lately. He loved and missed his family. But his calling was greater than that. His loyalties had subtly shifted away from his parents and sisters. He was becoming a true Partisan. It's not that he didn't love and miss his family, but the cause of liberation superseded that.

He sat down near low-lying brush to sip some water. Before leaving the spot, caution led him further into the woods. As he rose, he heard a dog barking.

Taking out his binoculars, he could make out a patrol of what appeared to be about 20 Wehrmacht soldiers, one of which had a snarling German police dog that was straining its leash.

Moric slowly retreated back into the bushes. Suddenly, he heard the soldier with the dog yell a command. He looked up to see the dog racing across the field toward him.

His heart pounding, sweat formed on his forehead. He pulled out his rifle and pointed it toward the incoming dog. He was trapped. If the dog came at him, he would have to shoot it. But if he shot it, the patrol would track him down and kill him. He suppressed his panic, knowing he had to act, not think.

He peered around to see if there was an escape route through the woods. He would need to kill the dog and sprint. The dog stopped barking as it sniffed around the bush. Moric held his breath, pointing the barrel of the gun at the dog's heart.

The soldier, who had lost control of the dog, was running toward the bush, ranting about its stupidity. Two members of his patrol followed him. As he got closer, Moric prepared to pull the trigger. But the dog only lifted its leg to pee. It turned around and went back to its handler.

"*Dummkopf! Was zur Hölle machst du?*"

He grabbed the dog by the leash and went back to his patrol. His fellow soldiers were laughing and mocking him and his dog.

Moric nearly followed the dog's example – his bladder at the brink of letting go. He watched the soldiers move off into the distance. When they were out of sight, he ducked into the woods to relieve himself, gather his composure, and continue with his mission.

He looked upward and thanked God with a short prayer he had learned in his religious studies a few years before.

As he took a longer route, he had to decide whether or not to tell Djuro about this. Seeing that his pant leg was wet from the dog, he decided to keep it to himself for now.

With limited food available these days for his brigade, he often performed courier missions while hungry. This mission was no different.

He had to return to the open plains. Scanning the terrain, he spotted something that made his stomach growl. It was a small plot of land growing cucumbers. His eyes lit up. He hadn't had a fresh cucumber in a very long time.

He peered around the periphery with his binoculars, all was quiet. Though the landscape was unremarkable, and like much of what he had seen in the Krajina, this lone garden struck him as odd. But odd or not, he was famished.

He moved quickly, figuring that he would grab a few and continue on with his mission. He leaned over the leafy vines, a slight drool forming around his lower lip from the sweet smell of fresh vegetables. He didn't like the first few he spotted, but five meters away was a plant of English cucumbers, which were the best of all.

He was about to remove them from their vines when he heard planes overhead. Spitfires. The Brits were back to take out some Germans, he thought.

He loved those planes and the fact that Britain was on their side. He lifted his hand to wave at the pilots.

Just then, one plane veered downward toward Moric. The pilot pulled the trigger and unleashed a barrage of bullets at him. *My God. What's he doing? We're on the same side!* Panic.

The pilot must have mistaken him for the enemy. With his heart pounding, Moric crawled through the vines like a jackrabbit, churning dirt into his face. He made it to the perimeter of the garden and tore into the nearby woods. He could hear the plane searching above, divebombing toward the ground and lifting upward.

Entering the cover of the trees, Moric moved several meters further and hid behind a large beech tree. He tried to slow his breathing, taking in long, slow gulps of air.

That pilot thought I was a German soldier. And he almost killed me. All I wanted was a few cucumbers.

Though he was still shaking, Moric waited for the planes to disappear into the distance. He quickly returned to the cucumbers, grabbed a few, and ran back into the woods. *Hunger can make one do some risky things*, he thought.

That's twice I could have been killed in the past hour. No more testing me, please!

He said a prayer one more time, and continued with his mission.

As the small village enclave appeared, Moric breathed a sigh of relief. *Our territory.*

He found the courier, Nikola, and delivered the message. Nikola had arranged for Moric to stay overnight in a nearby village with an aunt and uncle.

It was midday and Moric was hungry. Nikola's relatives were very kind and offered him whatever food they could. His aunt got a couple of eggs from the hens they owned, and some fresh milk. They told him of the upheaval in their lives, of moving from hiding place to hiding place courtesy of their nephew, and how it was currently safe for them to be in their home. Moric thanked the couple, and went outside to walk around the Partisan-controlled village. The late afternoon sun shone its light on the cobblestone streets.

There were liberation fighters sipping coffee in the only local café. Moric checked to make sure his red-starred cap was properly seated on his head. He sat down at a small table in the café and greeted his comrades. They looked no different from his own unit's soldiers. A few of them struck up a conversation with him. "Hello, Comrade. Where are you from?"

"Fifth Corps," he replied. "I brought a message from our post in Ribnik."

"Have you seen much action over in Ribnik?"

"Some, but we all know what's coming. Like you, we're getting ready. If we know that Marshal Tito is in the caves somewhere around Drvar, the Germans do, too."

"My friend is part of the special unit guarding him. I saw him here the other day. They have contingency plans. Of course, he couldn't tell me what they are."

Moric didn't want to say that he knew the caves quite well, having grown up in Drvar. He didn't want questions raised about his family.

"Before the Fifth Corps, I knew one of your comrades. She gave her life for our liberation. Her name was Mika."

Moric nearly spit out his coffee. He had tried to bury her memory somewhere in the far reaches of his mind. Just hearing her name drew an audible sigh from him. "She was a good friend of mine. How did you know her?"

"We went to school together in Bosanski Petrovac. She was a pretty amazing girl. She didn't back down from anyone, especially when some of the boys tried to intimidate her. I respected her for that. And she was very pretty, but there weren't any boys brave enough to approach her. We were young kids, so our bravado was pretty non-existent anyway. She and I would kick a soccer ball around sometimes. She was pretty good for a girl. Actually, she was good for anyone, boy or girl."

"Did you know her family?" Moric asked.

"Sure. They were very nice people. Her brothers were funny little kids, if I recall. They liked to sing as they walked around town. Her parents were respected, too. When the Ustasha came... Well, I'm sure you know the rest."

"She told me. She was very brave. I miss her a lot."

Moric paused for a few seconds and then said, "I need to get on my way back to Ribnik. It was good to speak with someone who knew Mika like you did."

"By the way, what's your name?"

"Milan Adamovic. How about you?"

"Matija Kostic."

Moric stood up and tipped his cap to Matija. As he was about to leave the café, Matija called his name. "Milan, I have a feeling we both thought very highly of Mika. Very highly. She was a good soul. I'm sure that she died a hero. I hope your journey back to Ribnik is a safe one."

Moric waved goodbye and slowly made his way back to Nikola's aunt and uncle's house.

Thoughts of Mika flooded him. Lately, he had managed to keep them at bay. Matija was right, she had died a hero for our liberation. He repeated that to himself a few times. *This is a bigger cause than our individual lives. Our people, our freedom, our flag.*

But he still ached terribly over what he had come to accept as his first love.

After dinner with Nikola's family, Moric told the couple that he would be leaving before dawn. The aunt packed some dried fruit, bread, and refilled Moric's canteen with water for the trek back to Ribnik. Moric thanked them before they went to bed. He also told them that it was important that they have an escape plan because there was a strong likelihood that the German army and their collaborators would be swarming the area. They told him they did have plans, and that they counted on Nikola's help.

Just before dawn, Moric woke up, gathered his rucksack, dressed, and quietly slipped out the door. He had taken out his map the night before to plan his return to headquarters.

A familiar rumbling was heard in the distance – planes. The British and Americans were running flying sorties to counter the German Luftwaffe. In fact, along with the Soviet mission, the three allies set up headquarters on the island of Vis in the Adriatic. They had started conducting flights against the enemy from there, as well as Bari, Italy, in recent months.

Moric wanted to avoid the plains this time, but in some places, the mountains were too rugged to cross.

An hour after he had left, a British Halifax plane came roaring over his head, flames and smoke pouring out from the engines, and crashed into the forest about three kilometers from where he stood. He had been in many battles and seen a lot, but he had never actually seen a huge Halifax before, let alone watched one being blown up.

The sound of the crash, and subsequent fire were monstrous. He thought about the pilots who would have been killed if they hadn't parachuted out of harm's way. He turned back around and saw where the parachuted soldiers hit the ground. *Thank God. I'll see if they need my help.*

Moving toward them, Moric could see they were now standing up and brushing themselves off. As he approached the men, they drew their guns and pointed them at Moric. He stopped abruptly.

"Don't come any closer," one of them said.

Moric didn't speak English, but the guns being leveled at him required no translation. He threw his rucksack on the ground, and put his hands high up in the air.

"*Sprichst du Deutsch?*" Moric asked whether they spoke German

"What's he saying?" one of the men asked.

"*Parlate Italiano?*" He asked whether they knew Italian.

"What does he want?"

"*Habla Español?*"

"*Si, yo hablo Español,*" responded the soldier who said his name was David Garinjo.

"*Gracias Dio. Yo hablo Español.*"

"*Eres Partidista?* [Are you a Partisan?]" Garinjo asked.

"*Estoy con las Partisanas* [I am with the Partisans]," Moric answered.

"He says he's with the Partisans."

"*Como es que hablas Espanol?*"

"*Yo soy* Sephardic."

"I asked how it is he speaks Spanish. He says he's something that I've never heard of, but that's why he speaks Spanish."

"*Puedes llevarnos con tu comandante?* [Can you take us to your commander?]" Garinjo asked.

"*Si. Pero esta 20 kilometros de distancia.*"

"He said yes, but it's 20 kilometers away," he translated. "Let's get going. Lead the way."

Moric picked up the rucksack and told them to follow him. He told the Spanish-speaking soldier to stay near, so that he could provide them with instructions. He beckoned them to head toward the woods.

Moric had never met British or American soldiers before. Upon his precarious encounter a few minutes before, he thought this might be the first and last time. Now, he felt that his mission was made doubly important. He had to get the men to Ribnik safely.

As they made their way into the woods, more sorties were flying overhead, but enemy artillery was also firing. Whatever offensive the Germans had planned, it was now engaged.

The sounds of trees splitting from the explosions caused Moric to move faster and deeper into the woods.

They had gone several kilometers when Garinjo asked Moric to stop, so they could rest and drink water. The sounds of battle lessened the closer they came toward Ribnik.

They sat on downed trees, the allies pulling out food that was unrecognizable to Moric. They offered him some. Moric thanked them, but he pulled out his own food and offered it to them. They politely said no.

"So, you told us your name is Milan, and your Spanish is pretty good. But I don't know what Sephardic is," Garinjo said.

For the first time since he joined the liberation, Moric was ready to acknowledge who he was. He explained the Jewish exodus from Spain hundreds of years before, and how Ladino developed. He spoke about Sarajevo where many Sephardim settled.

Garinjo told this to his fellow pilots who were intently listening, while the sounds of fighter planes passed over them.

"I must ask from you and the others to not say anything about me being a Sephardi when we get to headquarters. I have to protect my identity. I think there are many of us with the Partisans, but we're cautious about revealing our identities," Moric said. "I don't always know how our comrades will react to my being Jewish."

"Of course, Milan. I'll relay this to my friends."

"Thank you, Sir," Moric replied.

"We should get going," Garinjo said. "The bombardment isn't slowing down, and I worry that it may come closer than we care for."

They all stood up and Moric showed them the route on his map.

Within three hours, Moric and the allied soldiers walked into the headquarters in Ribnik. They immediately went to Commander Rodic.

Met by Željko, Moric explained who he was with and how he came across them.

"Excellent work," the aide said. "We'll need you to translate for us."

Moric turned to Garinjo and told him what to expect. Željko told Moric to tell them they can use the facilities in the house and return to get some food. He directed Moric to go back to change his uniform if he needed, and grab something to eat, but that his translation services would begin soon.

Back with Rodic and the soldiers, Moric informed the allies that they would be transported to a secret airfield and then flown to Bari. He continued to provide information to the men until Željko dismissed him.

As they bid each other goodbye, Garinjo thanked Moric for his service and said he had never met anyone like him, and that he'd never forget him. Lastly, Garinjo told him that he and the others thought that Moric was one of the bravest young people they had ever known.

Moric beamed at the compliment. Like Kluz, these men made him want to be a pilot. Unlike Kluz's small, antiquated plane, their plane was the biggest he had ever seen. Although he hated the destructive force of the German Stuka planes, he marveled at their advanced technology. *Someday*, he thought, *I'll get up into the sky and fly my own plane*. He walked back to find Djuro, eager to share his news.

When he got to their site, Djuro's rucksack was gone, as was he.

26 MESSAGES

Moric went to find Peja to see if he knew where Djuro was. Peja told him that his friend was among the first wave of Partisans dispatched to the northwest of Ribnik. With Marshal Tito being hunted by the mass of German, Chetnik, Ustasha, and Croatian forces, the Partisans needed to be nimble and strategic in their efforts to gain control of the area around Drvar.

Reports of heavy aerial and ground attacks by the Germans had Moric very worried about Djuro and his comrades. It was late May 1944, and although the Yugoslav People's Army had grown considerably, there were many key battles taking place throughout Yugoslavia. The allies were significant support, but the bulk of the fighting was left to the Yugoslav People's Army.

Moric was summoned to report to the Commander immediately. Rodic's aide, Željko, was waiting outside the abandoned house-turned-headquarters to give him his orders.

"Machi, you'll be joining a unit moving out tomorrow. Radio contact isn't possible with all of the German troops around Drvar. You'll be needed to bring us reports on their movement. You'll only do this when the Commander believes it's safe for you to return here. You'll be no more than five kilometers away. There, you'll likely see your friend Djuro."

"Thank you, Comrade. When are we moving out?"

"At 6 in the morning."

"I'll be ready."

Moric had an uneasy feeling about this. For the past several days, the Luftwaffe was attacking up and down Drvar and Bosanski Petrovac. There were *panzer* divisions, glider attacks with soldiers parachuting into the territory, and paratroopers. The Partisans were trying to keep the Germans and their axis friends at bay, giving Tito and the attached British and Soviet missions an opportunity to escape.

The next morning, his unit left headquarters. As they closed in on their assigned position, he heard the thunderous booms of artillery, including mortar rounds, which particularly frightened him, reverberating off the mountains. His unit joined the existing line of defense. Their mission was to protect the headquarters in Ribnik, and also prevent the German and axis troops from entering Drvar along the road to Bosanski Petrovac from Ribnik.

Moric reported to his unit leader, Lipovac, who coincidentally had the same last name as his former music teacher, the person who'd saved him in what seemed like another life. Saying his name always jolted him into recalling that time, and thinking about his family that he'd left behind in the cattle car. He reminded himself that he had to focus on the task at hand, not the past, which often made him very sad.

Recently, Moric had gotten to know another comrade, Mujo, who had joined the newly formed Fifth Corps, a part of the expanded Krajina Division.

Both were standing next to Lipovac.

They had instantly bonded. Mujo was lighthearted and quick with a joke, but he also had an intensity that emerged when he spoke about fighting for liberation.

In his early twenties, Mujo had an athletic build that had served him well during the many soccer games he played for his village team, 100 kilometers outside of the Croatian capital, Zagreb.

The two warmly greeted each other, but it was clear that neither was in a chatty mood.

Mujo wished Moric good luck and told him to stay strong, as he took his machine gun down the road to set up in a trench for a presumed enemy attack.

Moric set up his things at the rear, a distance from the front line of his unit.

He stayed near Lipovac, ready to receive any orders or messages that had to be delivered back to Commander Rodic.

On the morning of May 28th, the day after Moric arrived, the Germans unleashed their attack on the units protecting the road to Ribnik. Rumor had it that Tito and his entourage were still in the area. In addition to capturing or killing Tito, the Germans wanted to render the headquarters in Ribnik inoperable. But the Partisans were in key positions on a ridge, peering down at any attacking troops.

The smoke and sounds from the battle unnerved Moric. Once again, he had to remind himself not to think, just do. But knowing what was going on in battle, and the loss of life that always mounted, still challenged his ability to stave off his deep-seated fear. He had convinced himself to stay strong, as Mujo had wished for him. Djuro never hesitated to tell him the same. Still, he heard the screams of men hit by bullets or cannon fire and knew how they suffered.

Lipovac gave Moric a message to run back to headquarters. Gathering his rucksack, he quickly moved into the forest about a kilometer from the road. The gun and mortar fire faded as he dashed up and down the hills in an evasive zigzag.

Overhead, he saw enemy gliders containing single paratroopers heading toward Drvar. The silence of the attackers sent a shiver down his spine. He told himself that he could not waver.

Reaching their base, he nodded at the two guards stationed at the entry as he passed through. When he found Željko, he gave him the message from Lipovac.

Commander Rodic left the house and took the message given to him by the aide. He read it as though he was playing the card game, Žandari; there was hardly an expression on his face.

"Thank you, Comrade," he said to Moric.

He went back into the house without dismissing the courier, meaning that a response was forthcoming. In 20 minutes, Rodic came back outside. "Please take this to Comrade Lipovac."

Moric returned past the guard post and barbed wire. He darted into the hills again, scrambling over rocks a bit higher than his previous route to make sure he changed things up. In less than an hour, he was with Lipovac.

"Thank you, Machi. What's going on at headquarters?"

"It's pretty quiet right now, not like over here."

Moric noted that many soldiers were no longer in the immediate vicinity. There was only a small ring of Partisans on the perimeter of where he was standing – machine guns poised and ready.

"Our comrades are engaged in battle. I've gotten reports that we're holding the line," he told Moric.

The explosions and gunfire signified that a battle was, indeed, raging. The thought of trees being destroyed in battles also disturbed Moric. He loved nature and was taught to respect it; war had no such respect. He walked toward the perimeter gunners to see if he could get a different vantage point of the firefight, but he couldn't.

"Machi," Lipovac said, "Commander Rodic has an order for you, too. You need to go up the road about two kilometers and take this message to all the gunners in the trenches on the northeast side of our line: They're to stay in their positions and defend the road along that corridor. They need to hold that line. No advance, no retreat."

"Yes, Comrade Lipovac. I'll head out now."

Moric had delivered messages to his comrades in trenches before, but rarely during fierce firefights. Often, after these excursions, when things calmed down and the surviving fighters returned to the camp, they mussed up his hair or patted him on the back.

"This is why you're the wildcat," they'd say.

Moric wondered when his luck as a wildcat would run out. He was acquainted with death, of course, but couldn't fathom what his own would feel like. Sometimes, while sleeping, the nightmares visited him. In them, the unit leaders called out, "Move forward," or "Charge," and he pulled himself out of a trench, only to be met by a barrage of bullets, or worse yet, a mortar. He often woke up covered in sweat, though for a brief moment he believed it to be his own blood.

As he neared the rim of the northeast quadrant that protected headquarters, he could feel the intensity of the battle. The ground shook and bullets whizzed through the trees. He waited for the right time to leap into action. He looked left to right and jumped into a trench where two soldiers were reloading their ZB 30J machine gun.

"Machi, to what do we owe this pleasure?"

"Mujo! A message from Commander Rodic who says to hold the line. Intelligence finds that the Germans and Chetniks are losing their momentum."

"Thank you, Machi. We've noticed they're not coming in waves like before, but they're still coming."

As soon as Mujo, who was the gunner, said that, an advance by several Germans headed toward them. Mujo fired and most of the enemy went down. The surviving soldiers continued to shoot their submachine guns. One pulled out a grenade, but Mujo killed him. The two remaining Germans retreated.

"You alright, Machi?" Mujo's partner Stefan asked.

"Yes, Comrade. I can't say I enjoyed that though." Moric tried to steady his trembling hands.

Mujo and Stefan laughed. It always amazed Moric how his comrades could find some levity during the heat of battle.

"Keep up the good fight, Comrades," Moric said as he got ready to leave their trench.

He waited for a pause before scrambling out and traversing the woods to the next machine gun nest about ten meters away.

He repeated the same message in the next several trenches he jumped into. He successfully managed to make it to the very furthest one. When he jumped in, there was only the gunner and no other soldier to feed the ammunition.

"Relja, I'm here to give you a message from Commander Rodic."

Moric proceeded to relay Rodic's order.

"Where's your help?"

Relja fed the gun with ammunition as he spoke. "Dragan was killed in our other trench over there," he said, while pointing his head westward.

"I'm sorry, Comrade."

"Me too. He was my friend."

Relja loaded his gun with another round of bullets, but three Wehrmacht soldiers appeared out of nowhere. They weren't more than 20 meters away when they unleashed a barrage of bullets at Moric and Relja. Moric burrowed as deeply into the trench as he could. He looked over at Relja, horrified. Blood leaked out of his left shoulder and forearm.

"Machi, quick, come here, squeeze the trigger, and fire at them. If you don't, we'll both die."

Moric had seen how the gun was fired, but never used it himself. He abandoned all thought and did what Relja told him to do. He fired at the advancing soldiers, hitting two of them. The remaining soldier grabbed a grenade from his belt and swiftly moved his hand toward the pin. Without hesitation, Moric gunned him down before he could activate the grenade.

"You did it! You did it!"

Moric released his fingers from the trigger and watched his hand shake as he moved it away from the gun. His mind was blank as he gazed at his hands.

"Machi, what is it?" Relja said, wincing in pain.

"Nothing. I'll find something in my rucksack to wrap around your arm to slow the bleeding," Moric said, with little affect.

He pulled out his scarf, which he had left there to keep a part of Mika with him. As he retrieved it, his thoughts wandered back to when Mika had covered his eyes to give him the present for his birthday. He hesitated just for a moment, but Relja was now moaning quietly. He used it as a tourniquet to stem the bleeding.

He remained in the trench keeping an eye on Relja's wound. If Relja was speaking with him, he couldn't tell. What he had just done, killing those soldiers, began to come into focus. He heard Stefan yell to his comrades that the enemy had retreated, and for all the wounded or their comrades to call out for help.

Moric said nothing as he lifted himself out of the trench. He turned his head toward Stefan, pointing at Relja.

He then walked forward to see the dead German soldiers. Nearer now, he saw them sprawled in contorted angles, all facing the sky. Two of them still had their eyes open.

Moric moved next to them and stared. They were only boys, he thought, not much older than him. He had killed boys.

He took three steps to his right and leaned his hand against a large oak tree, roots exposed, and vomited.

I killed three boys. I know they were our enemy and would have killed us. I don't care. I murdered three young boys.

Mujo had joined Stefan to aid in carrying the wounded or dead back to a truck that had just arrived. He saw Moric next to the dead soldiers, trails of phlegm still dangling from his mouth.

"Machi, what's wrong? Did you get hit?"

Moric wiped his mouth with his sleeve, and looked up at Mujo. "No, I didn't. I must have a stomach bug or something. Maybe it's what I ate at breakfast."

"Are you sure? Walk with me to the truck. Let's get you some water."

They walked back in silence, Mujo periodically looking over at Moric. When they reached their destination, he told Moric that he had to help Stefan. Moric thanked him and told Lipovac that he was feeling better after the water, and that he had to walk back to headquarters.

After reassuring the squad leader that he was better, he slowly headed back through the forest.

The air felt good, as did the pause in fighting. He didn't know if he could emotionally absorb one more sound from battle. He needed to think.

The image of the dead German boys was hard to shake. *Their families will never see them again, never see them growing up, or have their own families.*

On the other hand, they were the enemy, the Nazis. They would just as easily have killed him and Relja. What would they have done if they knew he was Jewish?

Lost in thought, and with no sense of time, Moric walked through the gate into headquarters. He wasn't ready to report to the Commander.

He walked to the furthest corner of the camp where visitors were scarce. He sat down on a soft grassy patch and stared at the trees only meters away. It calmed him to be alone and hear nothing but birds chirping, bees buzzing, and the gentle rush of water from a nearby stream.

Moric stopped thinking about the German soldiers and the heated battle he had just survived. He pushed aside memories of Tito, Rodic, Relja, and his fallen comrades. He didn't dwell on thoughts about his family and Drvar. He longed for some rest.

In accordance with protocol, Moric knew it was his duty to report to the Commander, despite his inner turmoil. He adjusted his Partisan cap, stood up, looked into the forest one last time, and then made his way to headquarters.

Željko welcomed him back and got Commander Rodic.

"Sir, my mission was accomplished. I left when the wounded were being brought to a truck for transport back here."

"Thank you, Machi. Excellent work. Stefan just told me what you did for Relja, and I guess for yourself."

"Yes, Commander."

"Go get cleaned up and grab some food. You deserve it."

"Yes, Commander. Thank you."

Moric returned to his rucksack. He was neither hungry nor in the mood to change his clothes. As he came closer to his belongings, he noticed Djuro, seated nearby, casting a glance in his direction.

"Djuro!"

"Yes, it's me despite how I look right now covered in gunpowder, dirt, and grime."

"I was worried about you," Moric said.

"No need. I'm safe now. I heard what you did back there. That's something."

"I guess. I was told that you were in the northwest quadrant."

"That's true. The fighting was heavy, but they retreated. We lost a few comrades, though."

"I've heard about that. I was scared that you'd be one of them."

"You know that I'm damn good at feeding the machine gun, right?"

Moric nodded.

"What's wrong? You look upset."

"I'm fine. It was very tense back there. But I'm fine."

Djuro intently looked at his friend. He wasn't sure what to make of Moric just then, but he would keep an eye on him.

"I'm going to clean up. We'll talk later," Djuro said.

Moric laid down hoping to sleep, even for a few minutes, but it was obvious that rest wouldn't come. Haunting memories returned. He couldn't shake the images of the faces and bloodied corpses of Wehrmacht soldiers. Although he implored them to leave, they wouldn't listen.

He turned on his side and began to cry. Not wanting anyone to hear, he buried his face into his jacket. When his cries became sobs, he pressed his face further into the balled-up coat. Wiping his cheeks, he reached inside his pocket. It only took two gulps of rakija to settle him down. He relished the numbness that the brandy brought him. Exhaustion and the alcohol finally led to sleep.

The next morning, he woke up with Djuro sitting nearby. "Good morning. You were moaning and shouting in your sleep. I've never heard you that distressed."

"I don't know. I'm still groggy." Moric wasn't ready to talk.

Perhaps some cold water on his face and a bit of food was the answer. It helped, and his fog lifted.

Željko found him and said that the Commander wanted to see him.

Though he was feeling better, he didn't want any more messages to deliver at that moment. It had not been easy since coming to Ribnik. Not at all.

"Machi, please come inside to my office."

"Yes, Commander."

"I know that you aren't quite 15 years old yet. Of course, we have other young fighters, young comrades who do so much for our liberation, and so many of them are brave like you. But what you did for us was a wonderful example of the courage that we must always honor. Relja had no words to describe your deeds; perhaps this will serve as a good enough substitute."

He handed Moric a pistol. Moric held it limply in his hand.

"This is — or I should say, was — my M1934 Beretta. It was something I picked up when I was in Italy before the war. It's a beautiful gun, perhaps more of a showpiece than anything, although you never know if you'll actually have to use it someday. It's yours as a thank you for your bravery."

He was overwhelmed by the Commander's words. To be given this gift from one of the great heroes of the liberation, left him speechless.

Moric gripped the gun firmly, looking at it more intently.

"Thank you, Commander Rodic. I'm truly honored by this."

"You deserve it. Thank you for what you do for our cause. Now, you may go back to whatever it is you were doing. And Machi, be proud of yourself."

A mixture of emotions swept over Moric. He was overwhelmed by what had just transpired, but killing the soldiers didn't seem to warrant such an honor. He told himself to just accept what had happened, on all accounts. Yet, accomplishing that would prove to be the biggest challenge of the entire war, thus far.

Commander Rodic summoned the entire Fifth Corps to a meeting. Clearly, he was in a triumphant mood. Moric, Djuro, and Mujo sat near the front of the group.

"Welcome Comrades. We are here today to honor one of the many victories we've had and will continue to have for the liberation of our nation. The occupiers attempted to capture or kill our leader, Marshal Tito, and they failed. Tito managed to evade them nearby in Drvar. He, along with his aides, our special unit assigned to protect him, and the British and Soviet missions, made their way to the Island of Vis. This island now serves as our new national headquarters where we anticipate launching our final push to liberate our people. You're to be commended for your bravery and commitment in helping make this happen. We'll have more battles ahead, and more comrades who will sacrifice their lives in the name of freedom. But we know now that the enemy is not having their way. All across Europe, the fight is being won. Here in Yugoslavia, we have made a name for ourselves. With the free world recognizing our cause, I know that we can be proud of our part in eliminating oppressors wherever they show up. Today, let's celebrate our accomplishment and honor those we've lost along the way. Here's to the liberation of the people, by the people!"

Cheers and song rang out. The Partisans knew that the fight would continue, yet, they also grasped the significance of their achievement in dealing a decisive blow to their adversaries.

As the celebration ended, Moric was approached by Željko. "Machi, Machi, over here!"

"Yes, Comrade, what is it?"

"This just came from the second division. Their courier brought this message for you."

Moric had never received a message specifically for him. He excused himself from his friends and stepped over to the side. His eyes widened as he read: *"My beautiful son, Papa and I are alive. So are your sisters. We have all been a part of the great liberation. We have been searching for you for the past two years. We never gave up hope. We saw Judita only days ago for the first time, and she told us about you. Papa will be there tomorrow to hug and kiss you. With all my love, Mamma."*

Moric reread the note three times before he believed it. *My family is alive. Papa will be here tomorrow.*

He folded up the note and put it in his shirt pocket. He went back to find Djuro, who was cleaning out his rifle, and said, "My parents and sisters are alive!"

Djuro stopped what he was doing and looked up at his friend. "That's wonderful! How do you know?"

Moric handed Djuro the note.

"This is amazing news."

"I know. I'm in disbelief. I had to read it three times to let it sink in. My father and I will see each other tomorrow."

"I'm happy for you. Very happy."

Moric had trouble settling down for the rest of the day. Fortunately, headquarters housed an enlarger, allowing him to develop his negatives into proofs and ultimately into photographs. The process of developing photographs provided cathartic relief from whatever troubled him.

He mechanically developed a roll of film, lacking his usual immersion in the process. Then he organized supplies in his unit's storage and tidied up.

Yet another sleepless night ensued, with many thoughts racing through his mind. Foremost among them was the anticipation of seeing his father. Since joining the Partisans, he had changed and the prospect of facing his father filled him with anxiety. He was uncertain of how to behave. He would show his father the new version of himself, he concluded. He would be proud of his son.

Moric woke up with a start before dawn. Not knowing exactly when his father would arrive, he got some food and brought it over to the trees and stream which provided him with requisite calm.

He then made his way to a spot just outside the Commander's house, where he waited anxiously for word of his father's arrival.

The sun was bright now, and the air was filled with the sweet smell of summer grasses. Željko, noticing Moric's restless pacing a few meters away, called out to him, announcing that his father had arrived.

As they walked to the rear of Rodic's house, Moric could see his father's back. He was staring off into a distant field and appeared to be lost in his thoughts. David turned around, sensing that his son was nearby. "Son, my son, you're here!"

They embraced, but Moric quickly disengaged. He wanted to show his father how grown up he had become. He felt an odd numbness in his father's presence. "Hello, Papa, it's good to see you."

David wiped away the tears that had formed around his eyes. He stepped back to look at his teenage son.

Moric noted that his father looked thinner and older since they had last been together. Wisps of his prematurely graying hair fluttered in the breeze. His green eyes lacked their sparkle and were more muted. Since Moric had gotten a bit taller, he was looking at him almost at eye level.

"My God, look at you. You're practically a man now. How old are you? Almost 15?"

"Yes. Papa, can we walk?"

"Of course."

They walked onto a dirt road on the outskirts of Ribnik.

Puffy clouds punctuated an otherwise bright, blue sky. Moric remembered that in Drvar, when he was younger, he used to lie on the grass just outside of town and identify all the animals he could see in the form of clouds. He didn't like to see them dissipate, but would invariably move on to another and create a new animal. Today, he saw nothing but the clouds themselves.

"I can't stay long, Moric, but I needed to see you. Mamma sends her love, and she can't wait to see you either. We've been on the move, going from village to village to recruit people for the Partisans. We were in Petrovac when I heard you were here. When Judita told us about your typhus, and the miracle of her being the one to find and cure you, our spirits were lifted so high. Now, to be with you is beyond our hopes."

"I wasn't sure any of us would be alive to be together again. Judita told me that you escaped thanks to Mr. Lipovac."

"It's true. After escaping from the train, we've been going to many places seeking safety. The villagers are very kind and take care of us. We heard from a few sources that Flora and Rahela are fighting for freedom, too."

"It's good that our family is part of the liberation. It's going to happen soon. I just wish it was now. I wish Mamma was with you. I do miss her, and I want her to be proud of what I'm doing for Yugoslavia and for Tito."

"I know she will be. When this is over, we'll meet at your uncle's house in Sarajevo and fix up our place to move back in. We don't know when that will be exactly, but we all want it to be soon – for this to be over."

"Do you know about grandma and grandpa, and the rest of our family?"

"I'm afraid I don't. But I'm very worried that they were taken to Jasenovac or Auschwitz."

Moric sighed deeply.

"I need to get back on the road now. Željko has arranged for a ride to where your mother and I are staying. I don't want to tell you where that is just now, because I don't want you to try to find us. You have an important part to play in this. Željko briefly told me what an amazing person you are. I have no doubt."

"I wonder how Željko knew that I was Moric? I guess you asked for me by that name?"

"Actually, Judita told us that you've been going by Milan Adamovic. Very clever using your best friend's first name and the butcher's last. Mamma and I had to laugh about that one."

Moric grinned. He wondered if he had impressed his father. He thought about meeting up in Sarajevo after the war. He wasn't sure about that. He had a job to do in the liberation of his country and his father acknowledged that. Even if he knew where his parents were staying now, he could never leave the Partisans. After a brief hug, he waved goodbye. He suppressed the urge to run after his father. The loyalty he felt for his father was now replaced by a loyalty for Tito and his Communist Party.

In his notebook that night, Moric returned to a theme that had been making its way into his writing for the past several months. His confusion about who he was never left him, but on this day, he vowed that even though he loved his family, he could never live with them again. He was a Partisan, and if Marshal Tito needed him to continue to defend the cause of liberation, that would be his priority.

Curiously, he left that part out of his journal.

27 PLIVA LAKE

Ten days had passed since the calendar turned over to October, and Moric was soon to turn 15. He was no longer the same child that was forced to live like a wolf. Nothing from back then resembled him today.

The past years had changed him immeasurably. The fight for liberation had impacted him deeply. The war continued, but the feeling among his comrades was that the tide had turned.

His brigade had just set up headquarters not too far from Travnik, where plans were being made to take control of the city.

At times, he could fall into a sadness that tore at his heart. The loss of comrades, the remorse that still weighed heavily over killing the German boys, and the anxiety he felt about reuniting with his family were just some of what tied him down.

Sitting alone next to his rucksack, he reached inside to pull out his notebook. When the mood struck, high or low, he would scribble his thoughts into it. Today, melancholy had gripped him quite profoundly.

I'm about to die
because there is evil everywhere in the world
where I will dream an eternal dream
no one will know
no one will go around my grave
Only the nightingale will sing

my song of the dead.

*Our fathers fell as did our
mothers and we don't know
the street that raised us,
was home to us.*

He paused to look out over the mountains, the fir and beech trees. The fading yellow and orange leaves of the beech were readying themselves for their renewal in the spring, while the evergreen fir stood firm. *When will I be renewed?* This thought didn't make it onto the page.

He turned back a page to see what he had written a few days before, on his birthday: *Soon, I will have passed 15 summers, I continue to step toward 16 summers, in which I hope that the day of freedom will come, which the suffering people of Yugoslavia eagerly await. On my birthday, I got boots from Comrade Štrbac. I was more positive a few days ago. Stay hopeful. You're better off that way. All of this brutality is so that free people can live good lives.*

Moric closed the notebook and placed it into the secret lining of his rucksack, along with the self-doubt he wished to quash.

He felt something familiar in his pack that he hadn't noticed a few minutes before. He pulled it out slowly. It was the scarf that Mika made for him and that he used to slow the bleeding from Relja's arm.

As he was staring at it with unblinking eyes, Mujo walked toward him. "Hello, Machi. So you found the scarf. I know it's a little late, but happy birthday!"

"What? How?"

"Before Relja left for his new assignment, he told me to give this to you. He even washed it several times to remove the blood from the bullet wounds that your heroics may have saved his life. His transfer happened rather abruptly."

"I'm overwhelmed," he said as he leaped up to give Mujo a huge hug. He wrapped it around his neck and smiled.

"I have another belated present for you. Yesterday you said you wanted to take a ride on a motorbike to Pliva Lake over in Jalce. I found two of them just waiting for us, ready to go. How about it?"

In an instant, Moric was uplifted by the wonderful gestures of Relja and Mujo.

"Why not? I could use an outing. And, as you said, it'll be a birthday celebration."

"Great. Let's go get the bikes."

Mujo had detached the sidecars, making it easier to maneuver the large Ural motorbikes. He had also ensured that the gas tanks were full. They hopped on, revved the engines, and took off down the main road from Travnik to Jalce.

Heading west to Donji Vakuf and then turning north to Jalce, Moric reveled at the wind pushing back his hair and the sounds of the engine pulling him further away from headquarters, and the funereal gloom that had found him that morning.

Getting back Mika's scarf and the gratitude he felt for Relja and Mujo pulled him away from the gloominess that had found him that morning. About midway to their destination, Moric signaled for Mujo to pull over. "I just want to take in the silence for a minute, to breathe in the fresh air." Moric felt the sun on his cheeks, and the warmth penetrated his soul. A moment of respite during the war was a rarity. He told himself to just enjoy this brief moment with his friend, on a beautiful day, freed from the shackles of war's battles.

Moric turned to Mujo. "I can't wait to get to the lake. I'll race you!"

He jumped on his bike and sped off. Mujo did the same. They tore through the countryside, passing burned out fields and farmhouses. They flew by abandoned, destroyed tanks and trucks, lifeless within the thick brush, tall trees, and occasional waterfalls.

They pulled into a dirt lot near the lake, and walked to the lake's edge, peering at the gentle ripples that reflected the sun's brilliant rays. Moric took off his rucksack and handed Mujo an apple.

"Thanks. Where'd you get that? I haven't seen one in a while."

"There's more where that came from. I found a basket with a bunch of them outside the supply room near the mess tent. No one seemed to mind that I took a few. Well, actually, no one saw me."

"Now that's the Machi I know. They'll never know they're missing. And we deserve some treats, don't you think?"

Moric laughed for the first time in a while. "Let's go sit by the lake before we head back."

The two munched on another apple and Mujo produced his own surprise – a chocolate bar.

"Happy birthday! Don't ask, just enjoy it. I love German chocolate, don't you?"

Moric gave Mujo a crooked smile, opting not to inquire further about its source.

As they lounged on the grass, Mujo pulled out a pack of cigarettes and offered one to his friend.

"Why not? It's about time I tried one, huh?" Moric replied, as Mujo lit the end of it while he took in a drag. He coughed a few times while his friend laughed at him.

"You'll get used to it."

"Maybe," Moric replied.

"I heard from Djuro about your friend Mika. I'm sorry that I never met her. She sounds like a wonderful person, and a great hero."

Moric took in a deep drag of the cigarette and didn't cough this time. "She was."

Despite his yearning to escape from thoughts of war, Moric found himself prepared to discuss her.

He told Mujo about Mika while lying on his back, looking at the bright blue sky. When he finished, he turned toward Mujo and propped himself up on an elbow. It empowered him to reminisce, as opposed to how it used to drag him down.

"She sounds a lot like a woman in the Tenth with me. You may have even heard of her: Marija Bursac. She's the first woman to be named as a 'People's Hero of Yugoslavia.'"

"I read about her in the bulletin that Supreme Headquarters sends to us. In fact, she was from Kamenica, near where I'm from in Drvar."

"She was something. We became friends when she joined our brigade. That woman had so much energy and strength. She used to tell me how she collected clothing, food, and supplies for us Partisans. She'd get sick, but nothing could keep her down. She'd bounce back in a day or so and be right back at it. The stories she told me! She was a political commissar, too. But I knew her when we fought together last year until the fall when she died."

Mujo paused, dragging deeply on his third cigarette. He sat up and wrapped his arms around his knees, peering at the shimmering lake.

"She was a nurse. When I had a slight leg wound, she took care of it in no time. She wasn't afraid to fight either. Sometimes when she was sick, she'd tell our commander that she'd rather die than just watch the battle from afar. He couldn't stop her. But then..."

Moric thought again about Mika. He pictured her in heaven with Marija, telling stories about the war.

"It was September and the brigade had fought many tough battles against the Croatians and Germans. We attacked the German base at Prkosi. She threw grenades with tremendous accuracy at their machine gun nests. Sadly, bullets found her leg. After the battle, we retreated. I was one of those who carried her on a stretcher to a field hospital at Vidovo Selo, which one of my comrades fortunately had heard about. Our mood was lifted by the idea of the hospital. She sang our victory songs much of the way, I think to distract us from her wounds and the battles we just fought. Anyway, it took three days to get her there. She sang less and less as she got weaker. Sometimes she'd call out to her mother in her fevered dreams. I knew we were losing her, but I wanted to have hope that the hospital could help. When we finally got there, the leg had developed gangrene and her body was burning up. The hospital didn't have much to treat her with. Not long after we arrived, she died."

"I'm so sorry."

"Me too. But she taught us all about real courage. I'll always carry that with me. I'll never forget her."

Mujo laid back down and both of them gazed upward. They remained quiet for a few minutes.

Then Mujo told Moric that he wanted to take a brief nap before heading out. In fact, they both dozed off, relishing the time to do so.

When they woke up, Moric accepted another cigarette. This time, he smoked as if he had been doing so his whole life.

It was mid-afternoon and time to get back to their base. They peeled themselves off the grass, promising each other they would do this again soon. The sadness Moric had felt earlier was gone. They hopped on their motorbikes, revved up the engines, and returned to the main road toward Donji Vakuf.

Moric noticed smoke and sputtering coming from Mujo's bike, and he signaled for him to pull over to inspect it.

"It looks like your bike is dead."

Mujo tried starting the engine, but it regurgitated black smoke.

"I think the carburetor is the problem," Moric said. "If I only had some tools, I could fix it."

"Hmmm... Good thing we're not too far from headquarters. I think it's about six kilometers. Time to push."

They disengaged the brakes and began to push the heavy bikes toward Travnik.

"After such a pleasant day, you had to sabotage your bike to get out of work, didn't you?" Moric teased.

"Of course. That was my plan all along."

The motorbikes were heavy and unwieldly. Pushing them uphill and keeping them from rolling downhill was cumbersome.

"Let's stop for a minute. This thing is tiring me out," Moric said.

They moved the bikes over to the side of the road and leaned them against the rutted pavement. With the sun steadily setting, they realized they were still roughly three kilometers away from headquarters.

"Shhh," Mujo said. "I hear something."

"Voices. Over there about 100 meters."

Mujo had packed his short rifle in his rucksack, he retrieved it. They then moved into the brush within sight of their motorbikes, remaining silent.

The voices drew closer. Ustasha had been spotted in the area a few days earlier, but no recent reports had surfaced since then.

As the two figures came into view, it was evident that they were armed with rifles. Moric and Mujo were close enough to hear their conversation.

"Look Anto, two motorbikes. Let's go see. The engines are cold. They must be abandoned."

Each Ustasha soldier held their guns ready, scanning the perimeter, prepared to shoot at any moment.

"All clear. Let me try this bike."

Anto tried to start Mujo's, but of course the engine didn't turn over.

"That's why they're abandoned. They're no good."

"I don't like it here, Marko. I think we better leave."

"What's the problem?"

No sooner had the Ustasha soldiers began to debate whether to stay or leave, when Mujo emerged from the bush, his rifle pointing straight at them.

"Don't move or I'll blow both your heads off. Drop your rifles, and put your ammo belts and rucksacks on the ground. Then lay face down on the dirt over here."

The militiamen did as they were told. Moric grabbed their guns and ammo, and opened their rucksacks to see if there were any other weapons or ammunition inside. Nothing. Only a canteen and some chewing tobacco. He took the tobacco, and threw the rucksacks far into the brush.

"Should we kill them, Comrade?" Mujo asked.

The Ustasha let out a muted shriek.

"Let's think about this," Moric said. "If we do, we'll have to drag their bodies into the woods so they're disappearance isn't discovered too soon. I'm pretty sure, after pushing our heavy bikes, moving them will be easy."

"Good point. I have an idea of how you two can remain alive. Anto, get up on all fours now. Good. Crawl. Stay along the roadside, so we can see you. Keep heading away from Travnik. But don't get up. Don't look back at us. If you do, we'll have to shoot you. We're not in the mood for any of this right now. Our broken-down bike has already ruined a lovely day. So do as your told."

As Anto crawled, Mujo waited until he was a good 20 meters away.

"Now, Marko. It is Marko, right?"

The man nodded.

"Get up on all fours. Crawl across the road. When I give you the signal, start crawling in the direction of your friend. Remember, looking back toward us might be met with a bullet to the head."

As Marko began to crawl down the road, Mujo fired a bullet into the air.

Both Ustasha stopped.

"Remember what I said. If you get up, or look back, it's going to be the last thing you do, so think about the chance at life we just gave you."

"Yes, yes. We know. We promise that we'll crawl for a long time," Marko said loud enough for Anto to hear.

"You make sure you do," Mujo said.

A couple of times, Mujo yelled out that he was still watching them.

Mujo and Moric waited until the Ustasha soldiers were sufficiently far away ensuring they couldn't hear them before resuming their journey, pushing the motorbikes down the road.

They took turns looking back, eventually losing sight of the Ustasha.

They pushed their motorbikes until, exhausted, they made it through the barricade in front of their camp. Heaving from exertion, Mujo took in one more deep breath and burst out laughing. "That was an adventure!" he said.

"You were something. I wasn't sure what we were going to do, but you took care of it without shooting them. That was brilliant," Moric said.

"I guess I can be clever at times. I really didn't want to kill them. I'm sure they wouldn't have done the same for us, but I've shot enough of the enemy, and didn't want to ruin our day even if it ended with a broken carburetor. And besides, we got some weapons and chewing tobacco."

They returned their motorbikes to the shed. The next morning, Moric's innate technical skills went to work, repairing the motorbike as if it had never broken down.

Moric decided to write about this in his notebook, but he would leave the incident with the Ustasha out. He only wanted to be reminded of their pleasant trip.

As he walked to find Djuro, he peered into his rucksack, gently touching the scarf.

28 TRAVNIK

The fall of 1944 saw the Ustasha Militia putting up a fierce battle for the control of Travnik. The small city was located in central Bosnia, in the valley of the Lasva River, between the Vlasic Mountains to the north and the Vilenica Mountains to the south. Getting in and out of Travnik was a challenge for any military engaged in a land battle.

Moric's brigade had been moved there earlier to support the push to take control of the city. Two heroes of the Partisan military struggle, Petar Mećava and Josip Mazar Sosa, had moved their units to join the fight.

Moric was in awe of their exploits.

The two went to the new headquarters, which sat a few kilometers outside of Travnik, to finalize attack plans with Commander Rodic. The Commander asked Moric to bring his camera to commemorate the visit.

Feeling the weight of responsibility as he prepared to photograph the men, Moric rose from his chair in the front waiting area of the Commander's house-turned-headquarters. Mećava and Sosa greeted him respectfully and inquired about where they should position themselves for the photographs. "It's an honor to meet you both. I know of your heroism, and what you've meant to our liberation. Please come outside. There's a tank nearby that I believe is a good backdrop for the photos."

Rodic joined them outside.

Moric first asked for individual shots. He had taken a number of pictures of the Commander, so it was understood that Rodic's participation in the photo-shoot would come later.

Moric directed his subjects to position themselves in poses that showed their strength and commitment to the liberation, which flowed naturally from each of them. They stood in front of the tank peering at his camera, he also had them stand to its side and gaze outward to the mountains surrounding Travnik. He then asked Commander Rodic to join them.

He had been snapping pictures for about 15 minutes when Rodic put up his hand.

"Thank you. That's enough for now."

"Yes, Commander. Thank you for letting me take these photographs. I'm honored."

Mećava and Sosa tipped their hats to Moric, and then turned to Rodic, who was leading them back into the house.

Moric marveled at his own composure in the presence of such renowned fighters. It underscored his ability to focus when tasked with his duties.

Returning with the film to where he and Djuro had set up their tarp and sleeping gear, Moric recalled Commander Rodic's request to wait before developing them. He deduced that an imminent attack on Travnik was likely, and he might soon be called upon to deliver supplies or messages to the soldiers. Djuro was sitting under the tarp when he arrived. "What was that like?" he asked.

"Special is a word I can use to describe it. To be in the presence of these war heroes is something I'll never forget as long as I live."

"Good work. I'd love to see the photos when they're developed."

"Commander Rodic didn't want me to develop the film yet. I'm guessing that the battle for control of Travnik will be very soon."

"Yes, I know. Peja told us we're moving out early tomorrow morning."

"I figured that. The Commander said that I should be ready in case called upon to deliver messages."

"The Ustasha have barracks in town with several hundred soldiers and lots of weapons. This will be a tough fight."

"We'd better eat, get some rest, and be ready to take Travnik."

Mobilization of all the fighting units began the following morning. Moric reported to the Commander's house, and was told to stand by for an assignment.

The tank unit of the brigade was getting ready for an initial assault, the soldiers would attack next.

The powerful rumble of the engines startled the birds, sending them into flight. The roaring echoes reverberated off the surrounding mountains. Surely, the Ustasha heard this, too, and they would be getting their own units ready for battle.

As Moric awaited his orders, he found himself reflecting on the legendary heroics attributed to Mećava and Sosa. Seated in the chair where he had waited to photograph the three men the day before, he could vividly envision Mećava and Sosa standing proudly by the tanks in his mind's eye. In May 1942, Mećava and his unit fought inside the city of Prijedor. He found the lieutenant colonel of the Ustasha militia inside the city's secondary school, and killed him. He then climbed up into a church bell tower, ringing the bell to announce the liberation of the city. During the Battle of Kozara, his unit broke through the encirclement of the German army from outside the ring and cleared the way for other liberators. Only the previous month, his company fought to liberate Banja Luka. There were too many stories for Moric to recall, but the man was among the bravest.

Sosa, too, was a larger-than-life figure. He led his company through the Battle of Kozara, and his courage in many battles was known to be legendary.

Moric was still feeling honored that he had been asked to photograph them. Now they were about to join the fight with the recently named Fifth Bosnia Corps.

The fighting began within an hour of Moric's arrival at Commander Rodic's house. Djuro was part of the second wave to slog its way through the city.

Tanks were unleashing their shells upon Travnik, yet they were met with retaliatory fire from the Ustasha, who also launched their own barrage in response. Smoke and fire licked the sky while earsplitting explosions rocked the ground.

Milja led a third wave of fighters, who were getting ready to join the battle. Moric was told to join them and then return to headquarters with reports from the battlefield leaders.

"Move forward!" yelled Milja to his unit.

Moric stayed behind the last line, but was as vulnerable as anyone.

"Machi!" yelled Milja. "Mujo's up ahead. Get to him, and have him lead you to the perimeter of the city. He's expecting you. You'll head up into the hills to scan the action below. Then, report back to me. Hurry!"

Moric found Mujo a few hundred meters ahead. Mujo greeted him with a stiff smile.

"Machi, take out your rifle."

Taking out his gun brought back the killing of the Wehrmacht soldiers outside of Ribnik. But he knew he had no choice – just in case.

The two scrambled up a hill, settling behind any protection they could find along the way. The firefight was becoming more intense as they got closer to Travnik. They remained at a distance from the fighting, though close enough to clearly observe the action. Mujo used his binoculars to scan below.

"Peja is down there. We have to get to him for a report."

"It looks like he's waiting until the first unit is fully engaged. Let's go."

They scampered down the hill and jumped into the trench dug by Peja's group. He was with several others from his unit, including Djuro.

"Peja, Commander Rodic wants your update on the fighting."

"Good. Tell him that we're about to enter the city. Inform him that Comrades Mećava and Sosa's units are inside and we'll be joining them soon. Add that we're already gaining an upper hand."

Moric and Mujo scrambled back up the hill. They skirted around to the farthest edge where there was no active fighting. Mujo told Moric that he would accompany him close to headquarters, and then return to the fight.

As he turned to leave Moric, Mujo quickly said, "Be well, Machi. Live to take another motorbike ride with me someday."

"That goes for you, too."

Moric reported to the Commander, who seemed satisfied with their attack plan.

"I believe we'll take it, Machi. For now, stay close enough for Željko to find you, and await any further assignment. You've done well."

Moric thanked him and walked through the mostly deserted camp. He took a sip of water from his canteen, and rested his rifle against his rucksack, grateful that he didn't have to use it.

That evening, another courier returned to give the Commander bad news. Josip Mazar Sosa was dead.

Moric took the news of Sosa's death hard. The man had led so many important victories and was one of the key people that brought the liberation to the brink of total victory. Having recently photographed Sosa made this news even more disturbing. As the battle for the city continued, most of the Partisans either remained on the front lines or rotated in for brief respites at the camp. Djuro was among those temporarily relieved from duty.

"I heard," Djuro said. "We got the news after it happened. I also heard that Commander Mećava was very angry. It's said that he's regrouping to make one final attack to completely take over the last of the Ustasha barracks."

"Sosa died a hero," Moric said with a crack in his voice.

"I go back into battle in a few hours. I'll fight hard for him. We're winning, you know. It's only a matter of time before Travnik is in our control. Do you know what Commander Rodic wants you to do next?"

"I have to report to him soon to find out."

"Keep your head low. Even though we're winning, strays often get through without any warning."

"I will. We have to make it to the end of this war. We have to be free."

Moric left Djuro to see the Commander. It was October 22nd and the attack on Travnik had been ongoing for a few days. The Commander conveyed his assurance that they were nearing the end of the fight. However, he emphasized the importance of Moric joining Mujo before entering the city. He instructed Moric to gather reports from unit leaders to "provide us with an assessment of our proximity to victory."

"This will be more dangerous, but I trust you'll be cautious. Mujo arrived earlier to accompany you."

"Yes, Commander."

As he said this, Mujo came from around the other side of the building. "Let's go, Comrade. It's time to complete the mission."

Moric and Mujo took a circuitous route to Travnik. They entered the city behind a row of smoldering apartment buildings. The sounds of shelling and bullets punctuated the air.

The two moved closer to the center of the battle. This time, Moric took out his binoculars while Mujo had his gun, just in case. Moric peered at the Ustasha barracks as it went up in flames. He could see the remaining soldiers fleeing the building as they were gunned down by the Partisans.

He watched as some of them ran, screaming, while their bodies burned. He stared at the scene and for a moment couldn't move. Human flesh was being seared in the name of freedom. Yet, he felt little remorse for what he was witnessing. He lowered the binoculars, handing them to Mujo.

"I guess we have our report," he said to Moric.

The two stayed for a few more minutes and observed the carnage. Moving again, they found a safe path toward headquarters. Pausing behind a large fallen oak tree, they turned around for one more view of the fiery city below.

Moric practically hissed as he spoke, "I hate them. I don't feel sorry that they're dead. I hate them. They've destroyed our country. All of our lives."

"We all hate them, and I'm guessing none of us feel the least bit sorry when they're killed."

"I know. But that's not me. I don't want to be so hardened. Yet, my blood boils for all they've done."

"Maybe someday we'll find some way to forgive them, but I doubt it. I'm sure not all are bad, like your Mr. Lipovac."

"True, Mr. Lipovac was a kind man who got caught up in the fascist frenzy. Maybe he never wanted to be an Ustasha but he had no choice."

"There's got to be others like him. But believe me, when I see dead Ustasha, or Chetniks, or Germans, I'm very happy. I feel no remorse for them. My father was usually pretty quiet until he got much older. I guess he wanted to let me know about war in case I had to be in one. He once told me that World War I was terrible, and some of things he did were terrible, too. But eventually, he learned to live with whatever he did. After all, he would tell me, it was kill or be killed."

"My father told me the same. He hated war and told me about the pain it brings to so many people."

As they stood up to leave, Moric turned back one last time to see the smoldering buildings, burning tanks, and dead soldiers, both his comrades and enemies.

They hustled back through the woods and over to headquarters, where they found Commander Rodic sitting outside on the front porch. It was unusual for him to do so. Željko was sitting by his side.

"Commander, we've come to report the good news that we've broken through. The Ustasha barracks have been breached."

"Thank you. That's good. Tomorrow, we'll all gather to go over plans for those of us moving into Travnik. Our fighters are combing the city for any Ustasha that may be hiding. You can leave now."

As they walked away from headquarters, Moric spoke first, "That was strange. The Commander didn't seem very happy."

"I know. I wonder what's going on?"

"I guess we'll find out tomorrow."

The next day, at 6:00 a.m. a somber Commander Rodic called all to a meeting. "I'm proud of you. We continue to show that our movement, our revolution, is getting closer to ousting the fascists and bring peace, freedom, and stability to our land. Yet, we see our brothers and sisters lose their lives in battle, not in vain, but in triumph. We mourn those who've left us, of course. I've heard that there are rumors about Commander Mećava. I need to report to you that he was killed in battle. He and Commander Sosa died as righteous heroes of our revolution. Commander Mećava drove a tank toward enemy barracks, and yelled, 'For Sosa, Travnik must fall tonight!' And it did. Last night, we took control of the city. It's ours, and its citizens will be free. We'll be organizing a full takeover in the coming days. Thank you for the magnificent and courageous fight."

A mournful silence followed. What should have been revelry and celebration, was silenced by the loss of two great men. Fallen comrades. Fallen heroes.

Moric walked over to sit under his tarp. Djuro was not back yet. He pulled out his notebook and recorded what pierced so deeply through his heart:

The whole day passed watching the quiet autumn rain that fell and saddened the heroic deaths of Šoša, Mećava and young Morin. Now in the evening, the moon has already broken through the clouds and shines a light on the newly liberated city of Travnik, I look at that scene and sing slowly, it's a sad Sunday.

He laid his head on his rolled-up blanket and reflected, unprepared to face the day. Having just celebrated his birthday, he found himself caught in the swirling thoughts of a boy-turned-man, whose upbringing as a Partisan instilled in him the duty to honor the sacrifices of his fallen comrades.

29 PICTURES

With much of the People's Army fiercely battling the Germans and their collaborators around the country, his own Fifth Bosnia Corps was scattered throughout the Krajina.

Many of Moric's comrades were gone for days before returning to rest and regroup. He was ordered to focus on developing film from his cache, and other photographers' rolls. This meant that his courier job was curtailed for the moment, a respite he desperately needed.

He set up a developing room in a house adjacent to Commander Rodic's. Rodic was able to procure proper darkroom equipment so the room in Travnik was similar to a professional studio.

Moric had glimpsed the photos showcased in Tanjug, the Yugoslav News Agency established the previous fall, and he harbored a quiet hope that someday his own photographs would find their place among them. He remained indifferent to whether his name, or those of any other Partisan photographers, were acknowledged. What mattered to him was the opportunity to contribute to the end of the war by showing the bravery of its heroes and the resilience of ordinary citizens. He enjoyed the process of creating images out of cellulose acetate reels. In darkrooms, particularly in this one away from the sounds of war, he felt insulated within the red safelights.

Moric received a delivery of several rolls of film to develop. The envelope was marked "Critical." He pulled the descriptions out of a separate envelope that was attached to the box of film reels. Then he opened the photographic manual given to him by his mentor, Ivan, who was killed during the battle for Travnik. Moric vowed to carry on Ivan's mission of preserving the spirit of liberation within the photographs. Ivan's recent death would not be in vain.

He reread the techniques and revolutionary topics as laid out by Milan Stok, the famous Slovene Partisan photographer. He then looked over the names and instructions for the following:

- *Mihajlo Škundrić 2 films 6x9*
- *Dušan Čopić 8 films 6x9 - 4(1/2)-6*
- *Comrade Mijuška 1-6x9*
- *10 'increase' of Marshal Tito*
- *30 copies of 69 for teachers' school*
- *10 copies of the late Šoša and Mećava*

He put on an apron to shield his clothing from chemicals, dusted the room's surfaces and shut the door of the darkroom.

Mihajlo Škundric was a photographer from another brigade; he didn't bother to see which one. That wasn't important to him – bringing the pictures to life was. Moving from processing to the enlarger machine, he watched as the photograph appeared, almost like a magician pulling a rabbit out of a hat. A close-up of a nurse in her Partisan uniform slowly became visible. She was peering into the distance, head slightly turned, eyes sparkling in the midday sun, with a slight smile that expressed the joy associated with the revolution. He thought of Judita but had to set aside the longing that it brought him. He developed two copies per the instructions.

Next, with no photographer's name, he developed the pictures of the famous journalist and writer, *Dušan Čopić*. Moric developed pictures of *Čopić* with Marshal Tito, other military figures, and with ordinary Partisans. He had read some of *Čopić*'s articles in *Borba*, but never paid much attention to his appearance. Now, seeing that the man had a mystique about him, he joked with himself that he could still never pick him out of a crowd.

Comrade *Mijuška* was a fighter killed in the operations in Banja Luka. A slight man with piercing dark eyes, he was the epitome of determination and willingness to sacrifice for the good of the cause.

The photographs of Marshal Tito were grand. Although Zivko Gattin, a well-known photographer, took these pictures while Tito was in Drvar, this wasn't written on the envelope. It was the greatness of the man that mattered. These were going to be delivered to gymnasiums, the Partisan schools, and all-around Yugoslavia when victory was achieved.

Lastly, he came to his own reels of film. *Šoša* and *Mećava*, along with Commander Rodic, were the most special to him. As the images began to appear, so did a feeling of emptiness, of being alone. He found that the intimacy of developing photographs brought up a mixture of emotions from deep within. He was the one to see and experience his subjects coming to life, so to speak, before anyone else.

When they involved those who had passed, those who he was privileged to memorialize, it often hit him hard. While viewing Mećava and *Šoša*, his thoughts swung to Mika. He hadn't thought about her much lately, but he considered her just as much of a hero as the two famous Partisans. Unzipping the hidden pocket in his rucksack, he pulled out the individual photograph of her and the one with her and Djuro, taken when he did his first solo shoot. Staring at Mika for a minute, he placed it back in the unmarked envelope and into the hidden compartment of his rucksack. These were his forever, never to be archived.

He returned to processing whatever film he still had and hung the photographs to dry.

As he was about to leave, he saw a photograph of a man he not only recognized, but revered, hanging in another corner of the darkroom. A note below read: "Franjo Kluz, beloved pilot of the Yugoslav Air Force, member of the command, Bosanski Krajina region, died in battle over Split, Croatia on September 14, 1944, a true hero of the Partisans."

Moric stared at the picture. *My God, Comrade Kluz... Did Ivan develop this before he died?*

He recalled the great impact the man had in such a short period of time. Seeing Kluz brought him to double down on his commitment to becoming a pilot one day. He would fly planes to honor this great man.

He hadn't noticed how much time he had spent in the darkroom; it had been several hours and the fading daylight had surrendered to evening darkness. He shut the door and headed over to the mess tent. Although he felt a powerful sense of satisfaction, deep down he still wrestled with the ghosts of war.

30 WHAT DJURO SAID

On April 6, 1945, the operation to liberate Sarajevo was partially successful. The Fifth Bosnia Corps fought north of the city, but the Germans managed to escape to the northwest, destroying anything and anyone in their path. Still, the Fifth joined the Second and Third to take control of the capital of Bosnia and Herzegovina.

The city was in chaos. The shelling of buildings and streets had damaged a considerable swath of it, and the Partisans saw evidence of the Ustasha's massive and brutal killings almost immediately.

Moric, Djuro, and their comrades maneuvered around Sarajevo as Moric captured photos and the others took out any enemy that posed a threat. People slowly left their apartments, but a sense of despair hovered.

While his unit traversed the city, it stopped at the "Alley of Chestnuts." Entering the narrow road, they saw 55 Sarajevan Partisans hanging from chestnut trees. The putrid smell of decaying flesh filled the nostrils of Moric and his comrades. A hush fell over the unit.

"My God, is this what the fascists decided to leave as their farewell present? They're animals," Moric said to Djuro.

One of the patrol leaders ordered the unit to take out their knives, climb the trees, and release the dead. He instructed them to cover the bodies with blankets and put them onto trucks he had called for so that they could be buried in a mass grave in the nearby municipal cemetery. He also ordered that a temporary sign be put up honoring the fallen heroes, until a permanent one could be installed.

Later that day, the name Maks Luburic could be frequently heard among the Partisans throughout all brigades. It was Colonel Luburic, the city's Ustasha Commander, responsible for the Chestnut hangings and hundreds of murders through a hastily assembled kangaroo court that issued death sentences by hanging, blunt force, and other brutal forms of torture and killings. Shallow mass graves were discovered throughout Sarajevo and its outskirts revealing what was called, "Luburic's Bloody Tyranny."

There were still Ustasha militia and Ustasha sympathizers that needed to be weeded out. Patrols of Partisans rounded up those believed to be the enemy to be brought to various locations for execution or imprisonment for their war crimes.

Gunfire was regularly heard around Sarajevo, while barracks taken over from the fleeing Germans became housing for the Partisans.

Moric was assigned to accompany one of the patrols in the outskirts of the city to produce one of his photo documentaries.

He anxiously waited for the war to end. His family had an apartment in the city that hadn't been used since he was a child. It was there that his father had told him they would all come together when the war was over. As he thought about this, doubt began to resurface within him – did he really want to be there?

Right now, there was still work to be done. The Ustasha Militia, under the command of the cruel and feared Petar Rajkovacic, had left Sarajevo close behind the Germans. However, they retreated only to Odzac, Rajkovacic's hometown, to fight one final battle against the Partisans. The Croatian Home Guard and Chetniks had been neutralized. The Germans were on the run and the end of the war was near. Victory was imminent.

In early May, Moric and Djuro were dispatched to join a small patrol unit on the eastern side of Sarajevo. The patrol's mission was to ensure that no fascists were hiding in homes or other buildings, including damaged ones.

Moric had photographed numerous scenes since they arrived. In the main Partisan Headquarters, he had a fully equipped darkroom to develop his photographs. He put all his film cannisters into a pouch, anticipating the opportunity to have time to develop them. He loved this work more than anything. The days of lamenting that he couldn't keep his photos were long gone. In Sarajevo, when he was finished developing the pictures, he would bring them directly to an archivist in the basement of the building. Where they went from there, he was not sure. He assumed that they were still used to show the people that the liberation was near. He knew that there was much work to be done to bring Yugoslavia back to life under the great Marshal Tito.

Moric asked Djuro to accompany him to see what the situation was just outside the city. When it was deemed safe for the two of them to go, they hopped into a jeep driven by a comrade.

They drove to a small town, established hundreds of years before, situated between lush hills with lovely views into the distance. They walked around the uninhabited streets, peering inside the buildings that were in less danger of collapse.

"Some nice old buildings here. Sad to see so many of them destroyed," commented Djuro.

But Moric – embodying his role as a photographer – was lost in capturing pictures of the now familiar damage. He had learned to see things that others didn't, like fissures in monuments or chards of glass that tell a story.

"It's getting dark. I'm glad we brought our sleeping gear to stay the night. It looks like it's going to be a mild one. When have we ever gotten to just gaze at the stars without worrying about being killed?" Moric said.

"1935?" Djuro said, and they both laughed loudly.

"Up that hill," Djuro pointed.

As they looked for a place to sleep, they noticed the human remains of enemies and Partisans. Although a rather familiar sight, they still took off their caps out of respect for their fallen comrades.

The gentle, mild breeze made it unnecessary to light a fire. It was silent, and it felt safe.

They ate the potatoes and dried beef they had brought with them. Moric was in a good mood, and was thinking about the future. "The war is just about over. The Germans are about to surrender and we can go home. I can't remember what that actually feels like – home. Right now, I just want to lie here in the grass and not think about any of it."

"That sounds good to me. When the war is truly over, we'll all be creating our new homes as free people," Djuro replied.

"That dream is almost here. I've heard rumors that some of us are going to the Soviet Union to get more military training, including aviation. I heard that they have pilot school for those who want to fly. You know that's what I've wanted to do for a long time. Maybe that's where I'll be living for a while."

"So you're going to leave me?" Djuro said, poking fun at his friend.

"You can always apply to become a pilot."

"No thank you. I'll leave that to you and the birds. First, I need to see if my family is alive. I'll start by our home near the Danube to see if they're there, or any of my relatives; just to know," Djuro said.

"I believe my family might be in Sarajevo. When I saw my father in Ribnik, he and my mother intended to go back to the apartment he bought for our summers in the city. It's strange though, I want to see my family, but on the other hand, I don't. We're part of a bigger movement now, one that we fought hard for. I feel like we have a commitment to making sure Yugoslavia becomes whole again."

"I agree with you that we fought too hard, lost too many, and learned so much that the most important thing for us is to build our future. Hey, can we just look up at the night sky now?"

"Oh yeah, we're supposed to be doing that, aren't we?" Moric said.

Before they fell asleep, Moric added one more thing, "You've been my big brother and a great friend. Sometimes I still think about Mika. If not for her and you, I don't know that I would've made it. We must make sure we always keep in touch."

"Of course little brother, I promise. No matter where we go after the war, we'll always be the best of friends."

Djuro stretched his arms high above his head and yawned loudly. "I'm having trouble keeping my eyes open. Tomorrow morning, let's walk around the hills and then head back to base."

"Sounds good. Sleep well, Djuro."

"You too, Machi. And thanks for being my best friend, or should I say, my best little brother."

A slight breeze blew in the hills of Vogosca. Moric stretched, yawned, and stood up. He didn't want to wake Djuro. They were going to walk through the hills later and meet their friend, who was driving them back to the city in his jeep.

He found a spot to relieve himself, rotating his arms to get the blood flowing. He took in a deep breath of fresh air and smiled, relishing the peace and quiet.

To the sounds of bird songs, he peered up at the cloudless, blue sky and his mind wandered to what it would be like after the war.

I just want to be of service to Yugoslavia. No more fascism. No more death and destruction. No more bullets and bombs... You still live like a wolf, even though you're with your comrades. Time to move forward now.

His thoughts were suddenly interrupted by an explosion that knocked Moric off his feet. He instinctively covered his head and turned to see where the blast took place. No! It was just a couple of meters away from where they had slept.

He scrambled to his feet and raced over to see if Djuro was alright. He halted at the spot where the earth had been churned up, a chaotic mixture of dirt and rock amidst clouds of swirling dust and smoke, greatly obscuring his vision. As the dust settled, he saw that Djuro was lying on his side bleeding badly. His breathing was heavy and stilted.

"Djuro!"

"Machi," Djuro coughed out blood as he spoke softly, "I think it was a landmine. I was coming over to you."

"Save your strength. I'm going to try to stop the bleeding."

"I thought we'd made it..."

"No, don't say that. Please."

Djuro opened his mouth, struggling to get his words out. "Machi," he whispered, "I'm a Jew, like you. My name is Djuro Stern." Djuro made one last gasp, and then he was gone.

Moric pulled his friend into his lap and rocked him. Tears welled up and dripped onto Djuro's lifeless body.

"Djuro, no, don't leave me. Djuro..."

Moric rocked his friend for several minutes before lowering him onto the ground. He staggered over to the spot where he and Djuro had slept, tears streaming down his cheeks. He found his friend's rucksack. He removed a few items and placed them into his own pack, including Djuro's rifle. He looked under Djuro's collar for a chain but there was none.

With his hands, Moric slowly cleared the hole created by the blast. He looked over at Djuro, hoping that he would wake up, praying that this was not real. He hovered over his friend, who had a peaceful expression, and carefully picked him up. He then lowered the body into the makeshift grave.

Moric stood up and noticed that the birds that had been singing only moments ago were gone; the explosion had frightened them away. *I'm awake, this is not a nightmare*, he found himself thinking. *My friend, my brother, is dead.*

He wanted to ask Djuro how he knew that he was Jewish. He wondered if others knew, too. It truly didn't matter anymore.

Moric reached into his rucksack and felt around for Mika's scarf. He had kept it in his pack ever since Mujo gave it to him. In Jewish tradition, men wear a tallis, a prayer shawl, during prayer to bring them closer to God. If there's one thing he had learned in the war, it was how to adapt to whatever circumstances he found himself in. He brought the scarf behind his neck and around his shoulders as a makeshift prayer shawl. He found his army cap to use as a head-covering, a show of respect for God.

Standing beside Djuro's body, he quietly recited the Mourner's Kaddish, rhythmically bowing at the knees and straightening. This was the ancient prayer for the dead repeated by all Jews mourning the loss of someone; a prayer as old as the Jewish people; a prayer that honored the life of the deceased and marked their passing from Earth to Heaven.

He removed the scarf, carefully folded it and placed it next to Djuro. Kneeling by the grave's side, he clawed at the piles of dirt that had been scattered by the blast and watched as Djuro disappeared. Tears rolled down his cheeks as he stared at the pile of dirt covering his friend, his brother. He then pulled himself upright. Once again, the pain of deep sadness burned in the pit of his stomach.

31 ALONE

Sitting in an International Red Cross office in Zagreb with a few dozen other Partisan youth under the age of 18, Moric munched on the sandwich that a kindly volunteer had given him. The lump in his throat was from the dry offering, he assured himself. He sipped on a cup of water and swallowed hard.

By orders from Marshal Tito himself, each young person was given their next assignment, which either amounted to further communist education in the schools (known as gymnasiums) in Sarajevo, Subotica, or Osijek, or attending military high school in Suvorov in the Soviet Union.

Moric was assigned to the latter.

He said little to the others, but none of them gave any indication that they wished to talk. In fact, he noted that all of them, including himself, seemed a bit shell-shocked.

The Red Cross volunteer brought out a platter with an ample supply of baklava. Moric hadn't had his favorite dessert since well before the German invasion. He was the first one over to the table, and proceeded to eat one, two, three, and when all was said and done, nine pieces of the scrumptious pastry.

"You enjoy those, Comrade. You deserve them," said the volunteer.

"They were delicious. It's been a long time," Moric replied.

He and the others waited in the Red Cross office for their transports to the next phase of their training. Though apprehensive, Moric welcomed his assignment. The opportunities offered by the military school in the Soviet Union were given to very few. It gave him a sense of pride, despite the distance it would create between him and his family, assuming they were still alive.

It was his obligation to the revolution-turned-liberation to defend Yugoslavia. If this is what Tito wanted, he was ready to serve.

That evening, awaiting transportation out of the country, Moric began to feel sick. The cramps in his stomach quickly increased from slight to intolerable. He doubled over in pain and moaned out loud. The others turned their heads to look at him. One of the youths went into a small office adjacent to their room and got a volunteer.

"My stomach. It's killing me. I don't know what's going on."

"We'll need to get you to the hospital. It's just a few blocks away."

The woman called her colleague over radio relay, who brought a jeep to their office.

Moric crawled into the vehicle and lay down on the back seat. When they arrived at the hospital, a wheelchair awaited him, and he was taken into a room for evaluation.

A doctor examined him and asked several questions. Moric could barely answer.

"So you ate a cheese sandwich, had some water, and ate nine pastries?"

"Yes," he said between moans.

"Hmmm... I'm going to give you this which should temporarily stop the pain. From my exam, I'm guessing you ate something which had salmonella. We'll get you a bed on a medical floor and start giving you liquids. Lots of water. You're going to have to go to the bathroom a lot, but you should be fine in a couple of days."

Moved to a room on an upper floor, Moric felt more comfortable lying down. The nurse gave him a big cup of water, and then another after he finished each cup.

He lay there with a few other patients nearby. Late that night, when the hospital was very quiet, his eyes opened. The pain he had experienced earlier had exhausted him, but his racing thoughts did not allow him to sleep. Loneliness gripped him like a vise.

Tears streamed down his face. He suppressed his sobs as best he could to prevent a nurse or orderly from asking him what was wrong.

He only slept for a couple of hours. When he awoke, he cried once again. A nurse came to ask him what troubled him. He was unable to speak. She handed him tissues and coaxed him to drink more water.

Where is my family? My friends and comrades are gone. I'm all alone now in a city that is foreign to me. I don't know a soul. I'm lost. I'm sick.

That afternoon, he got out of his bed to walk the halls, but he didn't speak with anyone other than his short, stunted answers to the nurse's questions. It took him three days to recover. However, Moric's melancholy didn't subside. Before he was discharged, someone from "the Party" visited him.

A short, bald man with wire-rimmed glasses in a dull, gray suit and bow-tie, pulled up a chair next to Moric's bed. He introduced himself as Comrade Markovic. "Milan, unfortunately, you're not going to be able to go to Suvorov. The transport left two days ago. Instead, you'll be going to one of our Partisan gymnasiums, but it's one of the finest schools in Sarajevo. The nursing staff told me that you're ready to be discharged. In about two hours, the bus to take you and the others to Sarajevo will be parked across the street. We had more comrades of your age join us. They're at the Red Cross office as we speak."

"Not going to Suvorov? Are you sure? Isn't there a way to get me there later? I'm counting on this. I want to be a pilot."

"I'm sorry, but you'll have to find a way to be a pilot some other way in the future."

Moric closed his eyes tightly and turned his head away from Comrade Markovic. He squeezed his fists into a ball and berated himself for eating so many baklavas. What was he thinking? Of course, he got sick. Wasn't this a fitting way to end his military service? He hated himself.

"Let me inform you of one more thing. I went through your rucksack to see about any items that belong to the party. I took an envelope with photographs inside. As with all of your photographs, it's important that we keep them as part of our historical record of victory over fascism. It is property of the State. Yours and all the other photographers work will be archived."

"My photographs? I can't keep them?" *Mika and Djuro.* He didn't know what more to say. He was a member of the Party now, and if this is what it wanted then he would have to shut up.

"I understand. If my work aids our cause then please, do what you need to do."

Inside Moric was screaming. He understood what the man was saying. He even agreed with him. This was the commitment he had made when Ivan first taught him how to take pictures. But couldn't he just keep these?

He stared at the man. Without forethought, he spoke up in a louder voice than he had intended, "Comrade, one thing though. My name is Moris Albahari. I'm a Sephardic Jew from Drvar. My ancestors travelled to Bosnia to escape hatred. In this war, I fought for our liberation no different than any of our comrades. Please make sure that the gymnasium has my real identity." He had been waiting to say this for a long time, on his own terms.

"Of course, Moris. I'll do that. I'll even let the hospital know to change their records. Thank you for telling me."

Comrade Markovic left and Moris packed up his few belongings. He reflected on what led to his outburst. He was tired of hiding his identity. After Djuro died, he promised himself to no longer pretend.

And then the man took his precious photographs, carrying away the only physical memories he had of the two most important people in his life.

Moris repeated to himself, *I'm Moris Albahari, a Sephardic Jew from Drvar.* He had to climb out of his depression. He had to take control of his life. He felt like he had just taken his first steps up what would be a tall ladder.

Moric took a deep look inward. He wasn't going to the Soviet Union, but maybe this change of plan was for the best. He would embrace his impending Partisan education and he would be part of the new Yugoslavia. If he wanted to be a pilot, he would get there. It might just require a bit more patience than he had planned.

32 PARTISAN EDUCATION

Moris and the other students were housed in a dorm near the school in the heart of Sarajevo. There were several rooms with four to eight people, segregated by gender. His room had six boys. All of them attended school from morning until evening. They were taught about the core of communism, along with civics classes on how their government functioned. In the classrooms, a big poster of Marshal Tito showed the man in a suit, displaying the powerful leader who was now recognized on the world stage.

In addition to their studies, the students were tasked with cleaning up the bombed city. They relished being a part of Sarajevo's revival. Many of the children, like Moris, were from villages. Although Moris had spent summers there with his family and their relatives, rarely had any of them been to Sarajevo. Being there gave them a sense of pride and purpose. They saw themselves, and were seen by others, as good, loyal communists helping to rebuild their great nation. This reinforced their sense of importance in shaping the ideological superiority over that of the former king, and the conquered fascist occupiers. It was more than just a victory for the people. It was a victory that brought about great change.

The people of Sarajevo called them "Little Heroes." They carried flags and sang Partisan songs as they hauled away debris, or cleaned streets of the rubble, dust, and dirt of wartime.

They nicknamed their school, "Gun Powder" because all the students brought weapons to class. Moris was proud of the beretta Commander Rodic had given him, and showed it off to his classmates.

At night in their beds, when there were no public accolades, the stress from the war surfaced. Moris had regular nightmares, and was told by one of his roommates that he was often yelling "Move forward," or "Charge" in his sleep.

One day, one of the students threw himself on the classroom floor arms flailing, kicking, and screaming. His eyes were closed as he yelled, "Assault! Ahead, proletarians, brothers, fighters, Comrades!" With raised fists, he hit himself in the chest and banged his head on the floor. The teacher called in a colleague to help calm the boy down. When he awoke from his tantrum, he didn't remember a thing.

As a matter of fact, all students suffered from some kind of stress-induced episodes. The children called it "nervous disease."

Dr. Nedo Zec joined in a class discussion about their time fighting in the war. He wanted to observe the behavior of the students. Dr. Zec provided the school with a supply of pills to settle these episodes. He referred to it as "Partisan Hysteria."

Moris had become friends with a Croatian student who sat next to him in his classes. As they were leaving school one day, Moris approached him. "Luka, why are you always looking down?"

The boy hesitated to answer, or even look at Moris. His pale skin seemed to take on an even lighter shade.

"I'm ashamed of what my father did as an Ustasha soldier. I think he sent lots of people to the concentration camps."

"None of us had a choice in what our fathers did. You didn't hurt anyone. In fact, you're here now, right? You lived in the mountains like me. You joined your uncle with the Partisans, didn't you? Don't feel ashamed. You did nothing wrong." Moris hugged his friend.

"Thank you, Moris. I hope that I can heed your words. What the Ustasha did was cruel. I don't want to be associated with them in any way."

A few days later, Luka brought Moris three boxes of food: fruit, cakes, and vegetables, food items that were in short supply at school and in the city.

33 FAMILY REUNION

One morning when he was free from school, Moris walked to the apartment his father had purchased a few years before the war the place where his family had planned to reunite. He sat on the steps of the building across the street; he needed a moment to gather himself. In fact, he wasn't ready to interact with them.

Wearing borrowed sunglasses, an old fedora he found in his dorm, and a shirt too big for his small but muscular frame, he waited to see if any of his relatives would appear.

After an hour of waiting, David and Luna stepped out onto the street arm in arm.

Moris's initial reaction was to run up behind them and yell, "Surprise!" But that was what the young Moric would have done. Instead, he sat for a few more minutes before walking in the opposite direction of his parents.

At least they're alive. Thank God. He was lost in several conflicting thoughts. Though he wanted to see them, he didn't want them to know that his loyalty was with the State, not with them. His family had been Partisans, and his parents, especially his father, understood the toll war took on soldiers. However, they had held onto hope that their family would reunite something Moris no longer wished for. Yet, how could he tell them this? It would break their hearts. On the other hand, he was almost 18 years old, no longer the child they knew before the war. He was practically a man, and a man makes his own decisions.

When he arrived at the dorm, he flopped onto his bed. He needed to think about what to do. For now, he had to stay focused on what Tito wanted the young Partisans to do: rebuild for what would be the most glorious time in Yugoslavia's history.

It was a Saturday when one of the dorm's supervisors came to Moris's room. He was doing homework when there was a knock at the door. "Moris, I have a message for you. A man says that he's been looking for you for a while. He's outside now."

"Thank you. I'll come to see who it is."

As he stepped outside, Moris recognized his father. Up close, he seemed a lot older than when they'd last seen each other in Ribnik. His hair was almost all gray, he was quite thin, and his shoulders stooped forward slightly.

Moris didn't rush to hug him. He felt very unsure of how to greet his father. He no longer felt obliged to his family, though he still loved them. He was a young communist who fought for liberation and would have died for it, just like Mika, Djuro, and so many others. He had been indoctrinated into believing in the collective good at all costs.

Moris extended his hand to his father. "Hello, Comrade."

David grabbed his son's ear as he had done when Moris had badly misbehaved as a child.

"Ouch. Why'd you do that?"

"I'm not your Comrade, not your friend, I'm your father."

Rubbing his sore ear, Moris composed himself. "How's Mamma?"

"She's fine. She misses you, as do we all."

"All?"

"Yes. Your sisters survived. They all played a role in our liberation, as you know. I hope that you can come see us. We're living in the apartment here in Sarajevo. It needs some fixing up, but we're working on it. We all survived and that's the most important thing. I fear that we lost many of our relatives though. And there aren't many Jews that have returned. The

Ustasha and Nazis took away so many of us. I'm hoping that some are alive and we'll see them soon."

Moris felt almost numb towards the man standing before him. His feelings confused him, but he had much to do to ensure that the Party was served, and the city was rebuilt. "I want to see Mamma and my sisters but I'm not sure when I can come over. Where's Mamma now?"

"She's at home cooking, Moric or should I say Moris? That's what the dorm supervisor said your name is now. She was expecting that you'd be able to come over today."

"Unfortunately, with my studies and work fixing up the destroyed library, I won't be able to this time. Can I come over next Sunday?"

"Yes, you can," David said.

Moris could sense his disappointment. "I'll do that. Tell Mamma that I look forward to seeing her and eating her delicious food."

After thanking his father for coming to visit, Moris walked back to his room, rubbing his ear.

He got ready to return to the library with his assigned work group. He put on his Yugoslav People's Army uniform, including the red-starred cap, and looked into the small mirror over the desk. He stared at his reflection, noting that he was beginning to look like a young adult.

Why did I act like that towards Papa? He wasn't able to answer this question, but he had to go to work. He was part of the collective now, superseding his family, or so he had been taught. He wasn't ready to delve into this any further. He would visit his family's apartment the following week, and this was how it would be from now on. He stepped out of the door and made his way to his assigned task.

Sunday arrived. Moris woke up and put on his clean uniform. He fiddled with the collar and adjusted his cap several times to make sure it looked perfect. One last look in the mirror, and out the door he went.

His family's apartment was a couple of kilometers away. The walk and fresh air did him good, and besides, compared to all the walking, running, and climbing he did during the war, this was nothing. He missed his family, especially his mother's hugs, and hoped they would understand that he couldn't live with them anymore.

He rang the bell outside the door of their second-floor apartment. He heard footsteps clicking down the staircase, and then the door unlocked and opened.

Luna didn't wait for an exchange of words. She put her arms around her son and hugged him for a very long time.

"Let me see you," she said, as she took a step back. "My son. My sweet boy. You look like a young man." She sighed. "I missed seeing you grow up."

"Mamma, I'm here. We're together. That's all that matters."

"Come in. Come in."

She put her arm through Moris's and they walked up the stairs together. His sisters were standing at the top of the stairs, waiting for their brother. They gave him long hugs, accompanied by almost girlish giggles.

David stood in the apartment and patiently waited until they were done. "No handshake this time. Here we hug."

Moris felt his father's thin frame next to his.

Though he was thin himself, Moris had grown muscle, and made sure not to squeeze his father too tightly.

"No typhus, I see," said a smiling Judita.

"That's because I had a wonderful nurse."

They all laughed.

The siblings chatted about safe topics, speaking about their war experiences only in passing. David and Luna spoke of their part, recruiting peasants. Judita and Rahela lived in collectives and worked for the Party. They all agreed that Josip Broz Tito was a savior. David also spoke of his cousin, Nissam Albahari, who was instrumental in the movement. They talked about people praised for their heroism. Moris even mentioned his connection to Mećava and Sosa, and the sadness he had felt at their loss. Flora happened to be visiting from Italy, where she had moved with her new husband.

The home smelled of steaming broth. Moris's mouth watered. He hadn't realized how much he missed his mother's cooking. The poverty of those who moved back to Sarajevo was evident. For the Albaharis, the Joint

Distribution Committee of the US provided food and other necessary supplies. Tonight's meal couldn't have been made without their support.

"That smells delicious. Are we going to eat soon?"

"Yes, Moris," said Luna. She made sure to call him by his new name.

The meal was good, though not as abundant as before the war.

"It hasn't been easy," David said. "Children, do not worry. As long as your head is on your shoulders, you can start over and then there will be more. We'll be alright, I promise."

It was getting late, and Moris needed to return to the dorm. Flora was staying with her parents, but Rahela and Judita had to return to their dorms as well. Moris was the last to leave.

As they both tamped down their tears, Flora and Luna gave Moris big, long hugs before David walked his son down the stairs. "I know what wars do to people. I'm sorry I reprimanded you last week. I should've been more understanding. It may take a while for you to feel like you're safe again, and your mother and I know that you have a lot to do for our new country. You're welcome here anytime, and you can stay with us, of course. You don't need an invitation. You're our son, you're my son, and I'm proud of you."

Moris hugged his father at the threshold of the doorway. As he walked down the boulevard, he turned around to see his father watching him. They waved and smiled.

Moris put his hands in his pockets and slowed his pace, reflecting on the evening. Although it felt good to be with his family, he was not ready to move in with them, not even close. In a way, he was a stranger. *War changes people. I love them, but not like I did before. They'll have to understand that I'm not the Moric they knew; I've changed. I have a different purpose. They'll see.*

He walked past intact buildings that stood next to those in shambles. Moris looked up to see a full moon. It was a new Yugoslavia, and he would be a part of bringing it to life.

34 MOVING FORWARD

One year after Moris returned to Sarajevo, an elder in the Sephardic community visited the gymnasium. He was asked to give a talk in a Civic Projects class that Moris attended.

"My name is Jacob Tolentino. My family came here hundreds of years ago escaping the Spanish Inquisition. Though many of my people did not return here after the war, I didn't want to lose this city that means so much to me and the surviving Sephardim.

"Your teacher kindly invited me to come here to speak about a project. You've done a marvelous job cleaning up our city. It's beginning to look like its old self."

Jacob surveyed the room, squinting his eyes to see his audience more clearly. "Somehow, I made it through the war. Many of us Sephardim did not. The old synagogue has been destroyed in some parts, but we aren't ready to repair it yet. There's another new temple, which can be used by Jews who survived the war. In this temple, the main floor was desecrated by the Nazis. They used the sanctuary as horse stables. A few of us have decided that we must erase the memory of hate that still lingers. According to our laws, the first floor can never again be used as a place of worship. But it can be used in some other positive way, like as a social hall for our celebrations. We aren't sure of where, but we'd like to find a place for our small community to gather, pray, and celebrate our long history. The second floor has not been defiled like the first and could therefore serve as our new sanctuary once the place is brought back to life."

The man gently pulled and twisted the frizzled hair of his gray beard. His bony hands gestured broadly when he raised his singsong voice, which wasn't particularly loud. His eyes expressed how harsh the war had been for him.

Moris knew the synagogue; he had celebrated holidays there, and had prayed there with his family and relatives. *How could the Nazis desecrate such a beautiful holy place?*

"We'd like to get some volunteers to help restore it."

Moris's hand shot up before the man had finished his sentence. Others followed suit and a group of volunteers was cemented.

"Thank you so much. However, I need to add one more thing. I don't know how this will affect your kind offers. We've asked for help from a man who currently sits in one of our prisons for fascist soldiers. He's German. His name is Hans Meier, and he was conscripted out of architect school. He said that he was in an office shuffling paper when he worked for the Nazis. Although many fascists have acted as if they had nothing to do with killing Jews, Hans's story checks out. He hated Hitler. Now he just wants to help rebuild the synagogue. Please raise your hand if you'd rather not volunteer."

No one did.

Moris hadn't been in the synagogue since his summers in Sarajevo. This was going to be special, he thought. As for the former Nazi, that didn't bother him. If the man wished to pay back whatever debt he felt he owed for his country's crimes, then that was alright with him.

The following week the volunteer group met with Jacob, who introduced them to Hans Meier. The man was prematurely bald with a boyish face and slight build. Meier explained his passion for architecture, and his love for the synagogues in his city. He had studied Judaic architecture and art while in school. It was an honor for him to be able to work on this important project.

Moris looked around the first floor and imagined horses living in the sanctuary. The idea of it hurt him. He recalled being there during services. Now, the walls were peeling and the artwork was gone. The floors were rutted, and the strong odor of the horses was still present.

The group walked up the limestone staircase to the second floor. This had been where the Orthodox Sephardim designated the place of worship for women, who, according to their customs were separated from the men. It would become the main sanctuary for everyone.

Hans had requested tools, brooms, trash bins, painting materials, and cleaning supplies. The volunteers were divided into two groups. Moris's group was assigned to cleaning the second floor, while the other group cleaned the first. After a few weeks, the sanctuary was ready for its facelift.

Hans had created simple, readable blueprints, and the groups were separated into smaller teams. The architect scurried up and down the staircase to discuss the plans and their execution.

Moris was one of the painters; he took care of one corner of the walls. His corner was rather large, and painting it properly required climbing the scaffolding to scrape, prepare, and paint the high wall. He was meticulous in his work.

Going back to the dorm in the evenings, he felt lighthearted. He was part of the team transforming the main religious site of the city's Sephardic Jews, which had been reclaimed by survivors, the majority of whom were Sephardic themselves. Ashkenazim from other parts of Europe had fled to Sarajevo, so they were also going to be part of the new, smaller, inclusive Jewish community.

Moris's joy was often muted. He usually wandered around the Jewish section of the city before visiting his parents, who lived nearby. Cleaning up the neighborhoods didn't help alleviate the misery that so many had suffered during the war. Places where his friends had lived were gutted, and most of them hadn't returned. Presumably, they were murdered in the camps.

In his old neighborhood, Alifakovac, he passed a chocolate factory with its boarded-up windows, previously owned by a Jewish family. He remembered that he and his friends played near the factory during warm summer days, the sweet smell of chocolate filling the air. They would sing their afternoon request in Ladino. "Please put out a bonbon for me, a bonbon please." And every morning someone did just that. He remembered children of other religions had often played in his neighborhood. Those times would never return.

It had been almost two years since Moris had returned from war, and school was ending soon. He was formulating a plan for his future, envisioning training as a pilot. He had kept up his routine of school, helping to rebuild the city, and had recently finished the synagogue project.

On a stifling hot summer evening, his restlessness was particularly acute. The heat of the dorm room he shared with other students was closing in on him. There was no air circulating, and he needed a cigarette.

Outside, the city was quiet. The oppressive heat was unbearable for its residents. Very few people stayed indoors, and he noticed a number of them fanning themselves on their balconies. Moris felt alone, a feeling that was not foreign to him. His tee-shirt dripped with sweat and his trousers were stained with it.

He stood near a streetlamp, catching the occasional breeze. It did little to cool him off, so he lit a second cigarette. Putting the cigarette out underneath his shoe, Moris slowly walked further away from the dorm. He wasn't sure of his destination, but that didn't matter to him. He just needed to walk and think.

It was getting late, when he came upon an open café. He stopped and peered inside. A large fan was attempting to cool the place, but he figured that it was only moving the hot, stale air around. Still, he walked in. One shot of rakija might help to shake the loneliness and misery of the heat.

There were only five patrons inside. Cigarette smoke swirled with the fan's assistance. Moris asked the bartender for a shot of his favorite plum brandy, while he lit another cigarette.

"Hot as hell again tonight," the bartender said.

Moris nodded and thanked the man for the drink.

"I've seen you around here before. You've been helping to clean up our city," the man said.

"Yes, I've been going to the gymnasium not too far here, and I'm just about finished. Maybe I'll learn to fly and join the air force. I'm not sure just yet."

"Did you fly during the war?"

"No, but I met some very important people who did. It's one of the reasons why I want to join. They inspired me."

"Very good. I'm sure you'll make a damn good pilot. I'd never get up in one of those planes. Flying is for birds, not humans."

"I'm ready to be a bird then," Moris said, sporting a wide grin.

"There was a guy in here a couple of nights ago who also wants to be a pilot. I don't know his name and hadn't seen him in here before. But I was a little worried about him, actually. He didn't seem happy, even though he told me about his plans.

"My father was in World War I. I was only three years old when he was deployed. When he came back, he was very quiet. Honestly, when I talk about him with my sisters, we don't remember much. My mother was more at the center of our lives. Even as I got older he didn't talk about the war, but I'm sure it was hard for him. It never seemed right for me to ask him. He lived his life, went to work, raised us children, and then died early."

"Wars take a toll on those who are in them, and those who live through them. I lost many comrades, and I lost a lot of family members."

"Sorry to hear that. Were they Jewish?"

"Why do you ask?"

"I had a good friend here in the city who was Jewish. We grew up together. We went to school together, played on the same soccer squad, and spent a lot of time together. He always made me laugh. I miss him. He was taken to Jasenovac with his parents and brother. They never returned. This is why I'm grateful for the Partisans. We lost so many people, but if not for them, the Germans would have taken over, and then what?"

"You're right. It wasn't easy out there, but we had to defend freedom. Say, can I have another shot?"

The bartender picked up the bottle, which was resting on the bar in front of Moris, and poured him another.

"You know, lately I've realized that what we did was to change the course of history for the Yugoslav people. Some of us are lucky that our families are still here – that they survived when so many didn't. I need to remind myself of this. And, yes, I'm Jewish."

The bartender stared wistfully at Moris for a brief second, and continued, "Hmmm, it's funny, but I've become a good communist, and I'm grateful beyond words for what you and your comrades did for us. But I lost a few family members myself. I couldn't go to war because of this foot of mine. It hasn't worked so well since I was about 16. I hid with my mother and sisters, and we scrambled for food, but we made it. So yeah, I'm grateful. I'm relieved that we are where we are now. And Tito isn't letting the fascists get away with anything. My family comes first. I'll follow what Tito wants because I believe it's best for Yugoslavia, and so will my family. We've got to stay close to those who we truly care for and who truly care for us."

Moris nodded but didn't respond. The rakija comforted him a bit, but he wanted to go back to his room. He didn't want to hear any more, though he appreciated what the man had said. He thanked the bartender and pulled out some money to pay for his drinks.

"No, the drinks are on the house. Come back again. What'd you say your name is?"

"I didn't. It's Moris. Moris Albahari."

The air was still, that hadn't changed. Moris took the long way back, pondering what the bartender had said. These same sentiments had been simmering below the surface for him.

He would soon turn 18. Moris realized that he had been given a gift by being reunited with his parents and sisters. There were too many families that were not so fortunate.

He came to some important realizations that had eluded him thus far. The war had left its mark on him, and the transition to civilian life was difficult. The indoctrination of valuing the collective over everything else was faltering. He wasn't going to live in a collective forever. His family, his flesh and blood, was alive. The war had taken 37 members of his kin in the slaughter at Jasenovac, other Croatian death camps, and in Auschwitz. He could feel himself regaining his balance. He loved his parents, and they needed to know it and to feel it. He vowed that they would.

He loved Yugoslavia. He was going to leave Sarajevo for a while to learn to fly, but he would return. He was still ready to fight and die for his country, if it came to that.

His life had taken many twists and turns and coming to this café, speaking with the bartender on this hot night, was part of God's plan for him.

There was no replacing his family, as much as Tito wanted the Party to be Yugoslav's new family, most people would likely not accept that. They'd do their part for the good of Yugoslavia, but family was family.

He couldn't wait to wake up the next morning and ring the doorbell of his parents' apartment. He looked forward to sharing a cup of coffee with them and indulging in their favorite raspberry pastries, which he would buy at the bakery along the way.

EPILOGUE
MY FATHER

By Dado Albahari

Probably like every son or daughter after the passing of a parent I often wonder whether my father and I could have had many more gatherings, chats, discussions, or hugs.

Before I share the somewhat complicated relationship I had with him, it's important to highlight a few events that made my father so unique and special to me, to my mother, and to so many.

My father fulfilled his dream of being a pilot, and training others in the commercial and military arenas. His love for flying rubbed off on me as well, long before I learned to fly. It took a while for him to support this.

He was part of a team that planned and designed the Sarajevo International Airport. As director of the airport, he often met with officials from around the world. He primarily collaborated with experts and technical professionals from airports in France, and enhanced the airport's operations, which fascinated him.

Sometimes I was allowed to be there with him, learning as much as I could understand. As a matter of fact, as a child, I remember big and very dangerous construction machines scattered all around the runways. I would endlessly fantasize how I might plan the airport, while playing in the sand.

My father was well known internationally for his staunch human rights efforts.

Among his encounters with international statesmen, a particularly memorable one occurred in 1977 with King Juan Carlos in Madrid. He was mesmerized by his appearance, firm attitude, and his kind and friendly words. At the king's invitation, a gathering of former Spanish Civil War fighters from Yugoslavia was organized. These individuals participated in the first battles against Spanish and German fascism. My father was invited by these former resistance fighters to join them.

He and the King struck up a friendship. Though he didn't tell me directly, I learned that during the Siege of Sarajevo in the early 1990s, my father sent a letter to the King requesting that the Sephardim of Bosnia be granted the right to Spanish citizenship in order to escape the violence. From what I gather, the King granted the request.

In another significant meeting before the end of the Siege, my father was one of the representatives of the Interreligious Council of our country. Through this, he met with Pope John Paul II when he visited Sarajevo and the Jewish community. When I asked my father what he talked about during his audience with the Pope, his response was: "Nothing in particular. We told each other jokes."

For some reason, my life separated me from my parents and extended family after the last war, which ended in early 1996. It was the same for most of our generation, who left their families and hometowns for a long time, that is, if they ever returned at all.

If I think about it now, in our reunions during my arrivals and departures, the same questions would always remain: whether my father and I had finally put all the things in life in their right place, or if there was still too much unfinished business between us undefined and unexplored.

Yes, it is likely that this is so. Since his death in October 2022, I often feel a need to call him for help and advice. I would have liked him to reach out again as a father to his son, especially because I was his only child.

Today, when I think about some of our moments full of turbulence, competition, outsmarting, proving who's right, they were almost always accompanied by a smile on his face. I remember various situations where he consistently tried to distract me from my childhood dreams or sports games, and redirect me toward his dream of me jumping immediately into adulthood, perhaps as he was forced to do at such a young age. Fortunately, he did not completely succeed. For all of my team sports, I somehow managed to sneak out of the house to play with my friends on our street. I wanted my upbringing to be like that of my peers. He wanted to live his whole life modestly and unobtrusively, inconspicuous while at home.

I remember...

My friends and I followed our favorite sports teams throughout our childhood. It was unimaginable to my father that his son was "wasting time" spending his days with his friends running after balls on the playgrounds. He preferred me to be on the school's gymnastic equipment, especially the pommel horse, believing that soccer, basketball, and tennis were not for me.

While growing up, one needed sports equipment. I couldn't afford skating with my friends, so I built my own skateboard of course with help from my dad, which I appreciated.

I wanted to join the sailing nautical club, but I needed his approval. He told me that it was unacceptable for me to purchase even a small boat. During the whole year, the sea felt so far away from me. I could join, my father said, but we had to build my boat. It took a long time to accomplish this. For me, it felt like an eternity to build a sailboat in the backyard of our house. Day and night, all the tools he had, and those we needed to buy, were constantly being taken out and put away again. Of course, it had to be made of waterproof plywood with sewn sails. It looked like a massive vessel in our yard, but like a mere walnut shell in the middle of the bay. At the time, I found this task incredibly frustrating. Yet, upon reflection, those are the moments I realize he helped me hone my technical skills and maybe even find a little patience, too.

I finally started to feel his wings growing out of my shoulders; the pull of flying was quite strong. I had to hide my air club membership from my parents as best I could. To hide my flight training, one of my trainers and I tried to ensure that our experimental plane would not appear at the airfield when dad and I visited. I manage to keep this secret of mine until the end of my lessons. Before my first solo flight, I was given high praise by my trainers, one of whom told my father, his good friend. He wasn't very happy that I'd taken lessons without telling him.

On one occasion, at a big family anniversary, Dad came to the celebration in a formal suit, which to my mother's and my astonishment was smeared with grease and dark oil.

He always carried basic car repair tools in his trunk, and he couldn't hold back from suddenly repairing his friend's car that had broken down.

I remember him being in charge and responsible for all the snow maintenance equipment around Sarajevo before the 1984 Winter Olympics in Sarajevo. His morning briefings tended to be extremely authoritative, full of issues and orders to workers, mechanics, drivers, and to me, who he allowed to sit in and perform some tasks. I ambitiously wanted to do more than he gave me. I didn't have the right training to maintain the snow machines though I wanted to anyway. I remember him very clearly telling me with pride, "When you finish your mechanical engineering studies, you will find your own machine for maintenance."

Sometimes, when I wanted to borrow my father's modest car and go on a long trip with friends, he didn't allow it. But he had a plan. One summer, he arranged for three wrecked Citroens, known as Charltons, to be delivered to our home, intending to refurbish one for me. The cars arrived in various colors and took up a significant portion of the street. The local kids were not happy as it disrupted their street soccer games.

While my friends were off to Trieste in Italy, or to the beach with girls, enjoying themselves, I spent my entire summer vacation in a garage, dismantling old cars to create a new one. We managed to assemble a bronze-colored car, complete with seat covers displaying newspaper articles. Looking back, it was rather hideous.

Unfortunately, the car could barely get me to the university, losing power along the way.

My father was not materialistic, in fact he was quite the opposite. He often said, "I hate gold and trinkets; it did us so much harm in World War II."

He reminded my mother and me many times that the war criminals robbed Jews for their money and other valuables. Indeed, one of his uncles was targeted and killed shortly before the war after being robbed while riding his horse home from the bank. This certainly reinforced his belief that money was not the path to happiness for anyone.

I enrolled in the University of Architecture and Urbanism and was fully convinced that I had lost my father's trust. In my free time, I didn't engage in any of the sports my father would have liked, nor did I fulfill his dreams of my studying mechanical engineering or working in the automotive robotics industry.

During my studies, I began working as a volunteer at the City Institute for Urban Planning, where I joined a team of experts as a young urban planner enthusiast. Cities were increasingly left without clear guidelines for preserving their cultural identity. Suburbs had to be developed with new production capacities. Villages had to be equipped with modern agricultural technology and infrastructure. With the support of my mentor from the university, and through my father's business acquaintances, I was quite involved in projects and feasibility studies for the development of the entire region. For certain tasks we got some small pay. We were proud to be part of professional teams with clear objectives for the humane development of Sarajevo and the surrounding area.

Through my deep interest in comprehensive digital development (Geographic Information Systems), I wanted to include my father as a negotiator and organizer of the presentations and workshops.

We were never more connected or happier than during that time, full of optimism and trust for each other, just before the outbreak of what many in the West referred to as a civil war (1992). But there was nothing civil about it. It was more about one group targeting another in acts of hate and violence, not unlike most wars, which ultimately tore Bosnia apart.

Any further dreams remained unfulfilled. That was the worst time in my life, and in certain ways maybe even for my father. The war separated many of us, while it crippled and destroyed human life, and everything related to human rights. Fear, tyranny, and hunger reigned. Hunger for freedom of movement, communications, and peace hung over us all. All humane standards of development were annulled during the war and postwar period, and the destruction of the state continued to spread.

I did not want to leave Sarajevo during the war, but I did at the insistence of my parents. Apart from my internal struggle, I was able to provide better help to them outside the war zone.

This war continues to reverberate, and keeps Bosnians of different ethnicities and religions apart. Despite the destruction of my dreams of joint business and family plans from my previous life, today I must be happy that my parents survived all that; four years of life, death, and suffering horrors under siege.

During the "Siege of Sarajevo," my parents were already active in civil protection organizations despite their advanced age. They remained under the auspices and protection of the Jewish Community and the humanitarian association La Benevolencja.

Following the war, I reunited with my parents, but my hopes for a life together were destroyed. I never went back to live in Sarajevo.

Having seen all the injustice, and the causes of the war in Bosnia and Herzegovina, my father was increasingly recognized as a humanist until the end of his life. He dedicated himself to working for the reconciliation of different religious understandings beyond their parochial interests, and for the preservation of old Jewish and other religious traditions as cultural legacies. He remained determined in his values, and his belief that people are good.

In the end, after the shared suffering and hardship of two wars my father remained one of the most respected and cherished citizens in Sarajevo's tumultuous history.

I began this reflection wishing he and I had more time. I can't complain, of course, because he lived to the age of 93. And my mother, whom I am very close with, is still alive.

My father's life was shaped by war trauma from an early age. It took me a while to recognize that. We didn't always see eye-to-eye, but that's part of growing up. It's the resolution of those differences that defines us. And as for my father and me, I know we had a deep love and respect for one another. He truly was a great man.

ACKNOWLEDGMENTS

The process of writing a book has been one of deep immersion into the subject.

I first learned of his fascinating story from Moris himself in the excellent documentary, *Saved by Language*, in which he reveals some of his experiences in World War II as a speaker of the Ladino language. I was immediately drawn into his story.

While writing about his early life, I could feel Moris's presence. He reminded me of my older eastern European relatives who had emigrated to the US from the late 1800s through the early 1900s. As with Moris, their grace and humility filled the space they entered, and those same characteristics linger on in memoriam.

I know very little about my relatives from Europe, but I do know that they faced antisemitism and persecution before deciding to uproot and flee to a place they perceived would offer more opportunities and freedom to practice their faith. Certainly, the idealistic notion of finding perfection in their new land was dispelled by the challenges they encountered. Nevertheless, their spirit helped them persevere most of them, anyway.

Moris, who never left his beloved Bosnia, didn't share the same journey as my ancestors, but his core desire for equality among people reflected what many in my extended family brought with them. It is a value that Moris epitomized, shared, and left as a legacy. In that alone, I connected with the man. But there was more an intangible sense that Moris could have been a great-uncle of mine. Perhaps someone who could have helped me understand how he took his most difficult experiences and used them to shine a light on what makes people good, and what we all can achieve if we only move towards the good. He was called "Uncle Moco" by many who knew him.

I am grateful to Moris's son, Dado (David). When we would have Skype calls, I felt like I was looking at Moris in a younger form. Dado has his father's spirit and values. He also had the desire to learn more about Moris, which was evident each time we spoke. As I suppose could be expected, this was a personal journey for Dado. He wanted to fill in the gaps that might never be fully known. After all, his father had died only a few months before our first call, and he was still processing his grief.

Although she doesn't speak English Moris's widow, Ela, also shared what she knew from the few stories he wished to tell her. The war was a traumatic time for him, and disclosing the stories behind this was difficult for him. I believe for her, understandably, she was anxious and hopeful that her husband's story be told with fidelity and honesty, or as close as we could come based on the sparse information we could find. Ela and Dado had numerous conversations, motivated by their wish to understand more about what made Moris who he was. I believe that, at first, Dado and Ela were taken aback that I wanted to write a book based on Moris's early life. But as I started to gather information about him and share it, their enthusiasm for the project grew. Perhaps more importantly, they were beginning to learn things about Moris that they hadn't known. Soon, they began embarking upon their own journey to discover more.

Early on in our discussions, they found some pages of Moris's war diary hidden on a bookshelf. Most of it had been lost in a bombing of their apartment during the Siege of Sarajevo, but this added to the many revelations they encountered along our joint mission to learn about Moris. Of course, they shared his stories as best they could. But no one knew exactly what life was like for Moris as a Partisan. I am sure that this was a time of great reflection for them, too. After all, Moris died in October 2022. It was only a few months later that I heard some of Moris's story and felt drawn to it. I hope I remained sensitive to the recency of their loss, while wanting to honor his great life.

I asked some people to read the manuscript to provide me with feedback. I am ever grateful to Dr. Glenn Cantor for his astute eye, and his knowledge of both history and photography. As a scientist, one is trained to see beneath the surface, and Glenn did exactly that. Sadly, Glenn died suddenly in February, 2024. My brother, Ken, also read with gusto and from the perspective of one who didn't know the history particularly well, but whose insight was relished to shape the stories more clearly. I appreciated the constructive feedback given to me by my friend, Akram Abdelmessih, someone who's immersed himself in reading about the Holocaust. My wife of 43 years, Dr. Pina Cardarelli, deserves extra credit. She, too, found time from her important work leading a small biotech company doing cancer research, to read, reflect, edit and share with me very necessary guidance to ensure that readers who are not as familiar with the Holocaust in Yugoslavia, would be clear about it through my writing. Her brother, John, likewise provided me with valuable guidance.

I'd also like to thank the Shoah Foundation of University of Southern California, for providing me with interviews of Moris from 1997. Since they were in Serbo-Croatian, and I don't speak a word of it, I needed translation. For that, I thank Amir Grabovica, who used his technical wizardry to put English subtitles into the videotapes for me. This was critical to understand more about Moris's life as a young man, something that was not easy to find.

It was friend and author, Dina Greenberg, who read most of the manuscript, and made critical suggestions that led me to finding an editor. I can't thank her enough for her forthright critique, for her wisdom and superb writing talent that pushed me to go deeper in exploring the characters than I believed I could.

I am very grateful to my editor Eva Barrows, who provided me with her expertise, insight, and guidance, all with a dose of warmth, to bring the book home.

Very special thankyou to Liesbeth Heenk, founder of Amsterdam Publishers, and her astute editor. Amsterdam Publishers only publishes Holocaust memoirs, true Holocaust stories and some fiction. Liesbeth's mission is to ensure that this horrific chapter in human history is never forgotten. I am honored to be a part of the company's esteemed catalogue.

Lastly, having the support of my family, wife Pina, and children Aaron and Rebecca, always provides me with encouragement to continue to bring my very best into my craft.

PRONUNCIATION OF NAMES AND PLACES

1. Ustasha (Oostasha)
2. Krajina (Kra-ee-nah)
3. Drvar (Dervar)
4. Moric (Moritch)
5. Judita (Yudita)
6. Adamovic (Adamovitch)
7. Banja Luka (Banya Luka)
8. Kladanj (Kladanya)
9. Virovitica (Veer-o-teet-sa)
10. Bosanski Petrovac (Bosanski Petrovahts)
11. Bihac (Beehahtch)
12. Jasenovac (Yahsenovahts)
13. Adamec (Adamets)
14. Prijedor (Pree-ae-dor)
15. Vojovic (Voyovitch)
16. Juric (Yuritch)

17. Milja (Meelyah)
18. Mika (Meekah)
19. Peja (Pay-yah)
20. Djuro (Dooroh)
21. Stjepan (Styepan)
22. Glamoc (Glamoch)
23. Franjo Kluz (Franyo Klooszh)
24. Saric (Saritch)
25. Rakija (rah-ee-yah)
26. Gornji Vakur (Gornyee Vakoof)
27. Donji Vakuf (Donyee Vakoof)
28. Jablanica (Yah-bla-neets-ah)
29. Druzinovici (Drooschinoveetchee)
30. Rodic (Roditch)
31. Zeljko (Zhelj-ko)
32. Klujc (Klyooch)
33. Mujo (Moohoe)
34. Relja (Relyah)
35. Mecava (Meh-cha-vah)
36. Sarajevo (Sahr-a-yeh-vo)
37. Alifakovac (Alleefahkovahts)

ABOUT THE AUTHOR

A former social worker and teacher, Jordan Steven Sher's work reflects the core values developed in those professions, but also those that underscore his desire to depict the challenges that humanity continues to face, and has yet to reconcile.

He lives in Northern California with his wife, Pina. They have two adult children who continue to pursue their life's journeys in their own wonderful ways.

Website: jordanstevensher.com

Previous Books:

- *Surviving the War in Bosnia: Stories from the Diaspora in the United States and Reflections from the Next Generation*
- *And Still We Rise: A Novel about the Genocide in Bosnia*
- *Our Neighbors, Their Voices: True Stories of Immigrant Exodus*

PHOTOS

Moris, photographer with the Partisans, 1943, central or western Bosnia.

Moris and comrades on an Italian Topolino, 1943.

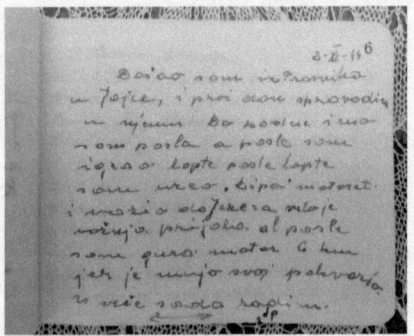

Original diary page written while a Partisan after the Italian capitulation, 1943.

In a truck with comrades at the end of the war, late spring 1945

Moris leaning on motorcycle-photo from his early adulthood finding new adventures. Circa 1955.

One of the first to train pilots in Bosnia, 1960

One of the first pictures in 1960, after meeting his future wife Ela, with whom he spent his whole life.

Moris and future wife, Ela, 1960

Moris and, Ela, married 35 years, in the Jewish Community Center in Sarajevo, helping to preserve their customs and practices amidst a diminished Jewish population after World War II.

During the 1990s war in Bosnia, Moris meets Pope John Paul as part of Interreligious Council of Sarajevo, 1995

Moris and son, Dado, 2014

AMSTERDAM PUBLISHERS
HOLOCAUST LIBRARY

The series **Holocaust Survivor Memoirs World War II** consists of the following autobiographies of survivors:

Outcry. Holocaust Memoirs, by Manny Steinberg

Hank Brodt Holocaust Memoirs. A Candle and a Promise, by Deborah Donnelly

The Dead Years. Holocaust Memoirs, by Joseph Schupack

Rescued from the Ashes. The Diary of Leokadia Schmidt, Survivor of the Warsaw Ghetto, by Leokadia Schmidt

My Lvov. Holocaust Memoir of a twelve-year-old Girl, by Janina Hescheles

Remembering Ravensbrück. From Holocaust to Healing, by Natalie Hess

Wolf. A Story of Hate, by Zeev Scheinwald with Ella Scheinwald

Save my Children. An Astonishing Tale of Survival and its Unlikely Hero, by Leon Kleiner with Edwin Stepp

Holocaust Memoirs of a Bergen-Belsen Survivor & Classmate of Anne Frank, by Nanette Blitz Konig

Defiant German - Defiant Jew. A Holocaust Memoir from inside the Third Reich, by Walter Leopold with Les Leopold

In a Land of Forest and Darkness. The Holocaust Story of two Jewish Partisans, by Sara Lustigman Omelinski

Holocaust Memories. Annihilation and Survival in Slovakia, by Paul Davidovits

From Auschwitz with Love. The Inspiring Memoir of Two Sisters' Survival, Devotion and Triumph Told by Manci Grunberger Beran & Ruth Grunberger Mermelstein, by Daniel Seymour

Remetz. Resistance Fighter and Survivor of the Warsaw Ghetto, by Jan Yohay Remetz

My March Through Hell. A Young Girl's Terrifying Journey to Survival, by Halina Kleiner with Edwin Stepp

Roman's Journey, by Roman Halter

Beyond Borders. Escaping the Holocaust and Fighting the Nazis. 1938-1948, by Rudi Haymann

The Engineers. A memoir of survival through World War II in Poland and Hungary, by Henry Reiss

Spark of Hope. An Autobiography, by Luba Wrobel Goldberg

Footnote to History. From Hungary to America. The Memoir of a Holocaust Survivor, by Andrew Laszlo

The Courtyard. A memoir, by Ben Parket and Alexa Morris

Run, Mendel Run, by Milton H. Schwartz

The series **Holocaust Survivor True Stories**
consists of the following biographies:

Among the Reeds. The true story of how a family survived the Holocaust, by Tammy Bottner

A Holocaust Memoir of Love & Resilience. Mama's Survival from Lithuania to America, by Ettie Zilber

Living among the Dead. My Grandmother's Holocaust Survival Story of Love and Strength, by Adena Bernstein Astrowsky

Heart Songs. A Holocaust Memoir, by Barbara Gilford

Shoes of the Shoah. The Tomorrow of Yesterday, by Dorothy Pierce

Hidden in Berlin. A Holocaust Memoir, by Evelyn Joseph Grossman

Separated Together. The Incredible True WWII Story of Soulmates Stranded an Ocean Apart, by Kenneth P. Price, Ph.D.

The Man Across the River. The incredible story of one man's will to survive the Holocaust, by Zvi Wiesenfeld

If Anyone Calls, Tell Them I Died. A Memoir, by Emanuel (Manu) Rosen

The House on Thrömerstrasse. A Story of Rebirth and Renewal in the Wake of the Holocaust, by Ron Vincent

Dancing with my Father. His hidden past. Her quest for truth. How Nazi Vienna shaped a family's identity, by Jo Sorochinsky

The Story Keeper. Weaving the Threads of Time and Memory - A Memoir, by Fred Feldman

Krisia's Silence. The Girl who was not on Schindler's List, by Ronny Hein

Defying Death on the Danube. A Holocaust Survival Story, by Debbie J. Callahan with Henry Stern

A Doorway to Heroism. A decorated German-Jewish Soldier who became an American Hero, by W. Jack Romberg

The Shoemaker's Son. The Life of a Holocaust Resister, by Laura Beth Bakst

The Redhead of Auschwitz. A True Story, by Nechama Birnbaum

Land of Many Bridges. My Father's Story, by Bela Ruth Samuel Tenenholtz

Creating Beauty from the Abyss. The Amazing Story of Sam Herciger, Auschwitz Survivor and Artist, by Lesley Ann Richardson

On Sunny Days We Sang. A Holocaust Story of Survival and Resilience, by Jeannette Grunhaus de Gelman

Painful Joy. A Holocaust Family Memoir, by Max J. Friedman

I Give You My Heart. A True Story of Courage and Survival, by Wendy Holden

In the Time of Madmen, by Mark A. Prelas

Monsters and Miracles. Horror, Heroes and the Holocaust, by Ira Wesley Kitmacher

Flower of Vlora. Growing up Jewish in Communist Albania, by Anna Kohen

Aftermath: Coming of Age on Three Continents. A Memoir, by Annette Libeskind Berkovits

Not a real Enemy. The True Story of a Hungarian Jewish Man's Fight for Freedom, by Robert Wolf

Zaidy's War. Four Armies, Three Continents, Two Brothers. One Man's Impossible Story of Endurance, by Martin Bodek

The Glassmaker's Son. Looking for the World my Father left behind in Nazi Germany, by Peter Kupfer

The Apprentice of Buchenwald. The True Story of the Teenage Boy Who Sabotaged Hitler's War Machine, by Oren Schneider

Good for a Single Journey, by Helen Joyce

Burying the Ghosts. She escaped Nazi Germany only to have her life torn apart by the woman she saved from the camps: her mother, by Sonia Case

American Wolf. From Nazi Refugee to American Spy. A True Story, by Audrey Birnbaum

Bipolar Refugee. A Saga of Survival and Resilience, by Peter Wiesner

In the Wake of Madness. My Family's Escape from the Nazis, by Bettie Lennett Denny

Before the Beginning and After the End, by Hymie Anisman

I Will Give Them an Everlasting Name. Jacksonville's Stories of the Holocaust, by Samuel Cox

Hiding in Holland. A Resistance Memoir, by Shulamit Reinharz

The Ghosts on the Wall. A Grandson's Memoir of the Holocaust, by Kenneth D. Wald

The series **Jewish Children in the Holocaust** consists of the following autobiographies of Jewish children hidden during WWII in the Netherlands:

Searching for Home. The Impact of WWII on a Hidden Child, by Joseph Gosler

Sounds from Silence. Reflections of a Child Holocaust Survivor, Psychiatrist and Teacher, by Robert Krell

Sabine's Odyssey. A Hidden Child and her Dutch Rescuers, by Agnes Schipper

The Journey of a Hidden Child, by Harry Pila and Robin Black

The series **New Jewish Fiction** consists of the following novels, written by Jewish authors. All novels are set in the time during or after the Holocaust.

The Corset Maker. A Novel, by Annette Libeskind Berkovits

Escaping the Whale. The Holocaust is over. But is it ever over for the next generation? by Ruth Rotkowitz

When the Music Stopped. Willy Rosen's Holocaust, by Casey Hayes

Hands of Gold. One Man's Quest to Find the Silver Lining in Misfortune, by Roni Robbins

The Girl Who Counted Numbers. A Novel, by Roslyn Bernstein

There was a garden in Nuremberg. A Novel, by Navina Michal Clemerson

The Butterfly and the Axe, by Omer Bartov

To Live Another Day. A Novel, by Elizabeth Rosenberg

A Worthy Life. Based on a True Story, by Dahlia Moore

The Right to Happiness. After all they went through. Stories, by Helen Schary Motro

To Love Another Day. A Novel, by Elizabeth Rosenberg

The series **Holocaust Heritage** consists of the following memoirs by 2G:

The Cello Still Sings. A Generational Story of the Holocaust and of the Transformative Power of Music, by Janet Horvath

The Fire and the Bonfire. A Journey into Memory, by Ardyn Halter

The Silk Factory: Finding Threads of My Family's True Holocaust Story, by Michael Hickins

Winter Light. The Memoir of a Child of Holocaust Survivors, by Grace Feuerverger

Out from the Shadows. Growing up with Holocaust Survivor Parents, by Willie Handler

Hidden in Plain Sight. A Family Memoir and the Untold Story of the Holocaust in Serbia, by Julie Brill

The Unspeakable. Breaking decades of family silence surrounding the Holocaust, by Nicola Hanefeld

Better to Light a Candle than Curse the Darkness. A Novel about Loss and Recovery, by Joanna Rosenthall

Austrian Again. Reclaiming a Lost Legacy, by Anne Hand

The series **Holocaust Books for Young Adults** consists of the following novels, based on true stories:

The Boy behind the Door. How Salomon Kool Escaped the Nazis. Inspired by a True Story, by David Tabatsky

Running for Shelter. A True Story, by Suzette Sheft

The Precious Few. An Inspirational Saga of Courage based on True Stories, by David Twain with Art Twain

Dark Shadows Hover, by Jordan Steven Sher

The Sun will Shine on You again one Day, by Cynthia Monsour

The series **WWII Historical Fiction** consists of the following novels, some of which are based on true stories:

Mendelevski's Box. A Heartwarming and Heartbreaking Jewish Survivor's Story, by Roger Swindells

A Quiet Genocide. The Untold Holocaust of Disabled Children in WWII Germany, by Glenn Bryant

The Knife-Edge Path, by Patrick T. Leahy

Brave Face. The Inspiring WWII Memoir of a Dutch/German Child, by I. Caroline Crocker and Meta A. Evenbly

When We Had Wings. The Gripping Story of an Orphan in Janusz Korczak's Orphanage. A Historical Novel, by Tami Shem-Tov

Jacob's Courage. Romance and Survival amidst the Horrors of War, by Charles S. Weinblatt

A Semblance of Justice. Based on true Holocaust experiences, by Wolf Holles

Under the Pink Triangle, by Katie Moore

Amsterdam Publishers Newsletter

Subscribe to our Newsletter by selecting the menu at the top (right) of **amsterdampublishers.com** or scan the QR-code below.

www.ingramcontent.com/pod-product-compliance
Lightning Source LLC
LaVergne TN
LVHW041907070526
838199LV00051BA/2530